Two Times a Traitor

Two Times a Traitor

Karen Bass

pajamapress

www.pajamapress.ca info@pajamapress.ca

 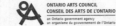 

The publisher gratefully acknowledges the support of the Canada Council for the Arts and the Ontario Arts Council for its publishing program. We acknowledge the financial support of the Government of Canada through the Canada Book Fund (CBF) for our publishing activities.

Library and Archives Canada Cataloguing in Publication

Bass, Karen, 1962-, author
     Two times a traitor / Karen Bass.

ISBN 978-1-77278-024-6 (softcover).--ISBN 978-1-77278-031-4 (hardcover)

     1. Louisbourg (N.S.)--History--Siege, 1745--Juvenile fiction.
I. Title.

PS8603.A795T86 2017   jC813'.6   C2016-907802-7

Publisher Cataloging-in-Publication Data (U.S.)

Names: Bass, Karen, 1962-, author.
Title: Two Times a Traitor / Karen Bass.
Description: Toronto, Ontario Canada : Pajama Press, 2017. | Summary: "Reluctantly touring Halifax with his family, twelve-year-old Laz Berenger accidentally stumbles through a time tunnel to a 1745 war zone. Caught by English sailors from the American colonies, his only hope for freedom is to spy for them in the French fortification at Louisbourg. But he finds himself torn in three directions when the commander at Louisbourg becomes closer to him than his own father"— Provided by publisher.
Identifiers: ISBN 978-1-77278-024-6 (paperback) | 978-1-77278-031-4 (hardcover)
Subjects: LCSH: Time travel – Juvenile fiction. | Louisbourg (N.S.) –History -- Siege, 1745 -- Juvenile fiction. | BISAC: JUVENILE FICTION / Historical / Canada / Pre-Confederation (to 1867). | JUVENILE FICTION / Action & Adventure / General.
Classification: LCC PZ7.B377Two |DDC [F] – dc23

Cover design: Rebecca Buchanan
Cover images: © milyana, © Swill Klitch/Shutterstock
Interior design and typesetting: Rebecca Buchanan, and Martin Gould / martingould.com

Manufactured by Friesens
Printed in Canada

Pajama Press Inc.
181 Carlaw Avenue, Suite 207, Toronto, Ontario Canada, M4M 2S1
www.pajamapress.ca

Distributed in Canada by UTP Distribution
5201 Dufferin Street Toronto, Ontario Canada, M3H 5T8

Distributed in the U.S. by Ingram Publisher Services
1 Ingram Blvd. La Vergne, TN 37086, USA

For Nikki
History connects us all

CHAPTER ONE

Laz had forgotten what it was like to not be angry. For the last seven months he'd lived every day inside a personal storm cloud, ever since his father had moved them to Boston without any warning. So when he stepped out of the restaurant, he felt the electric prickle of a coming storm that had been brewing through lunch. But so far the only sign was the thunder of his father's booming voice.

Electricity crawled over Laz's arms and neck like a hundred centipedes. He shivered and stopped under a blue awning to button up his wool coat. It was spring break, but in this cold Canadian city of Halifax, winter still floated in the air and made the salty tang of the nearby ocean sting inside his nose. Wanting to be anywhere else, he shoved his hands into his pockets.

Emeline nudged his elbow. The gloomier Laz was, the more Emeline shone. She always pushed away his sadness. Now she beamed at him, dark curls framing her face like a halo and brown eyes seeming to sparkle with flecks of sunshine. "Halifax is a like a small Boston, don't you think?"

Laz shrugged. "My best friend is in Boston, not here, Bébé."

"Don't call me a baby anymore. I'm nine." Emeline crossed her arms.

"You're still a shrimp." Laz smiled when she faked a pout.

Their mom made her usual comment about them both being her babies. Laz rolled his eyes and Emeline giggled. At twelve years old he was the same height as Mom, but that never stopped her from embarrassing him with mushy stuff.

Voices light and breezy, they tried to blow away the ugly remains of the argument over lunch when Laz had said he'd rather be called Berenger than Lazare and his dad had flipped out over the idea of calling Laz by his last name. Now Dad cut through the chatter with an icy blast. "Form up. We're heading up Duke Street." He pointed at the intersection a few feet away.

Laz did not want to march around the city like an army troop. "Couldn't I go back to the hotel and swim, maybe watch a movie? I know where it is." He peered down Hollis Street.

His dad's eyebrows slanted inward as he glared down his straight nose at Laz. "You're too young to spend the afternoon alone."

"I am not. I'm almost thirteen." Laz knew Dad didn't like him talking back, but he couldn't help himself. Or maybe he hadn't been trying to help himself. In a way, it felt fair for his dad to be as angry as Laz felt. He had learned about the family's move while he had been at Grandmère's farm. It had happened so fast he hadn't been able to say goodbye to his old friends.

"You're twelve, Lazare, and you're spending the afternoon with your family. That's what you do on a family vacation." Dad pointed, the way he did when he was done talking.

Laz bit back the urge to restart the argument about being called by his full name. It was old-fashioned, and kids at school made fun of it. They called him Bizarre Lazare. Instead he muttered, "Not that the family got to choose. Ryder and I had plans, you know."

He and his friend had saved up to attend an introductory parkour camp. It looked incredible on videos. Parkour was like running an obstacle course, but through the city, over walls and roofs and whatever got in the way. Laz knew he'd be good at it because everyone always said how fearless he was, and he was great at gymnastics. But when Dad used the Look like he was doing now, it was time to give in. The Look could peel skin.

Being fond of his skin, Laz turned away; satisfied he had scored a point. He'd gotten Dad angry, but not angry enough to blow up.

Duke Street climbed a steep hill. Laz pumped along and imagined being old enough to do anything he wanted. His parents let him stay home alone for short periods while they ran to the store or took Emeline to skating. So the problem must be Halifax.

A small hand grabbed his and Emeline gushed, "Dad said we're going to a fort where people dress up in old-time costumes. It's called the Citadel. Mom's ancestor was a soldier who moved from New England to help guard the fort during the American Revolution. His name was Ebenezer Wright."

That explained why they were in Halifax. Martin Berenger was super interested in family history, on both sides. "You're a great parrot," Laz said. "You repeat whatever you hear."

"Squawk!" Emeline laughed then said, "Look at those lion statues."

Laz glanced back. Their parents were half a block behind. "Let's check them out." He looked for traffic and pulled Emeline across the road to where two lions holding shields perched on chest-high pedestals.

He pulled out his cell phone. "Take my picture."

"You were supposed to leave that in the hotel room."

Laz shrugged. "It's my phone." He gripped the edge of the shield and swung himself up onto the ledge of the base. Holding onto the shield with one hand, he waved and grinned while Emeline took his picture.

When he jumped down he took a selfie of them and one lion's head. The picture showed how much they looked alike, except Emeline's nose was turned up and his was straight like Dad's. Her hair was a little longer. His touched his collar now, and he liked the way that bugged his dad.

Emeline tugged him and they continued up the hill. She bounced as she walked, and she talked and laughed like a ringing bell. People smiled at them, which made Laz duck his head and try to pull away. Emeline hung on.

At the next intersection they waited for a red light. That same electric frizzle made Laz shiver. He looked up, in case there was a real cloud ready to zap him with lightning. The sky was blue.

Something swished across his black sneakers and the person next to him sobbed. It was a woman in a long dress with a white apron. She spun around, one hand on her frilled white cap and one on her mouth. Her eyes were wide and scared. A car zipped around the corner. She gasped, jumped back, and bumped against a garbage can attached to the light pole.

Laz reached out to stop her from falling. "Are you okay, lady?" He smelled something tangy and familiar, but couldn't place it.

The woman turned toward Laz, gray eyes so wide they were round. She was barely taller than Emeline. Tiny and terrified, Laz thought. Moaning leaked from behind her hand. She lifted her skirt and pelted down the hill.

"Did you see that, Bébé?"

"The lady in the dress? She must be from the Citadel."

"I guess. She seemed upset." Emeline tried to swing their hands as they started out again, but Laz resisted. He didn't pay any attention to her chatter until she sighed dramatically. He offered a half smile. "What's wrong, Bébé?"

"I don't like that nickname."

"You'll always be my baby sister, so too bad. What's wrong?"

"You and Dad. When you talk it sounds like you're both growling. And I know what the problem is—you don't have any filters."

They reached a stone wall beside a grassy slope below the fort. Their parents were a full block behind now, but Mom waved for them to go left, so they headed toward a white building that looked like a fancy three-tiered cake topped by a green roof.

"Filters?" Laz asked. "What does that mean?"

"You say whatever comes to mind, no matter how much it bugs Dad. Maybe *because* it bugs Dad. You've started your rebellious stage early, and I hope you grow out of it soon."

"You're being a parrot again. Who were you listening to?"

She gave an exaggerated huff. "Mom. I heard her talking on the phone to Aunt Marie."

"Mom doesn't like us eavesdropping, Bébé."

Her brown eyes were shiny with a film of water. "But it's true, isn't it? You're rebelling. You want to upset Dad with everything you say or do."

Laz shoved his hands in his pockets. "He's always upset with me anyway. Nothing I do is good enough."

"But when Dad gets angry with you, it's scary. Both of you become...like tomcats hissing before they attack each other. What if you guys do that some day instead of just arguing?"

"We won't. I know what I'm doing." Laz ruffled her hair because he knew she hated it.

He ran down the sidewalk with her chasing him. At the white building, a wooden staircase climbed the hill. He raced up the stairs, laughing at Emeline's calls for him to slow down. Laz rested on a bench at the top until she arrived, puffing hard, and fell against him. While they sat, warmth uncurled in Laz's chest, and he wished he could sit like this for the rest of the day. He was about to tell Emeline she was the best of the family but didn't get the chance before their parents arrived, panting worse than his sister had been.

Emeline immediately herded them toward the entrance where a sentry in a tall, furry hat, red coat, kilt, and white covers on his boots stood very still. A tourist beside the guard was getting her picture taken. Laz thought that guard might have the most boring job in the world.

A tunnel cut through earthen walls Laz thought were called

ramparts. A bridge stretched over an empty grass moat, where another tunnel with "Citadel" carved into the stone above it, opened into a huge inner yard. Some men, dressed in navy uniforms with red trim and round hats, were doing marching drills. Emeline bounced with excitement.

Laz paced into the middle of the huge yard and turned slowly. There was a long building with slanted roof and red chimneys, a few lower stone buildings, stairs, ramps, cannons on the walls, mounded earthworks. He imagined doing a parkour run here. There were gaps to jump, poles to swing from, walls and cannons to vault over. He knew it would be awesome.

"Lazare," Dad called, "come on."

He squinted at his dad. "Come where?"

Dad worked his jaw side to side then said, "We're going through the timeline exhibits."

Behind Dad, Emeline nodded. Laz almost felt the click in his head, the one that let the storm loose and made him argue. "No thanks. I'd rather look around on my own."

"You can help us look for any references to your mom's ancestor."

Another click. "That sounds boring."

Without warning, the argument began. Anger crackled between them, and when his dad shouted, Laz shouted back. Gravity took over and words spilled out, like water gushing from a downspout in a rainstorm. Laz didn't know what he was saying; he just yelled every angry thing he'd ever thought. His body quivered.

He spun away. Dad spun him back.

"Your behavior is unacceptable." He spat out each word like a marble.

Laz wrenched free. "Don't touch me." He backed away. "Send Emeline to find me when you're done." He trotted backward, away from his father.

"Where do you think you're going, Lazare? Get back here."

"No. If *here* is near you, then I want to be anywhere but here." Laz raced across the yard.

CHAPTER TWO

His heart was pounding so loud Laz didn't hear if his father called after him or followed. Laz knew he'd be put through the grinder later. During summers spent with Grandmère he'd helped her grind meat; he shuddered at the picture in his mind.

Laz shot toward a painted blue door that was propped open. When he saw it led to a staircase, he stomped down the steps. Rectangular gray stones were streaked with red, green, and charcoal. An arch of cobblestone-sized stones formed the ceiling. Near the bottom, a sign in the ceiling read, "Caution. Low overhead."

Black double doors opened to a wide ditch between the inner and outer walls. Laz stood in the space he thought of as the moat and peered at the bridge he'd crossed to enter the fort. Sounds of people on the bridge seemed muffled, as if the U-shaped ditch and walls absorbed it like a sponge.

Laz sat on cool grass, leaned against the rough wall by the staircase, and tilted his head to stare at the cloudless sky. He was shaking. He and Dad had never had a fight that big. He couldn't remember what he'd said, only that he'd felt like a volcano exploding and spewing words like flaming rocks.

He had been out of control, and it wasn't a feeling he liked. He rubbed his itching neck and his fingers rolled over the chain hidden there. He pulled it out and brushed his thumb over his ancient St. Christopher medal. Mom's mom—Nan to Emeline and Laz—had given it to him before she died. "He's the patron saint of travelers," she had said. "I feel like I need to give it to you. This has been in the family over 200 years." "I don't get it, Nan," Laz had replied as she'd draped it over his head. She'd patted his chest. "I don't, either, Laz. Let's call it an old woman's whim. So you humor me, hear?"

Nan had sworn him to secrecy, which he still thought weird, but he had promised. So even though Dad loved family history, Laz was the one wearing a piece of it.

He kept rubbing the medal and tried to recall what had set him off. Dad had shouted something about selfish. To Laz, it didn't feel selfish. It felt like treading water, like fighting with his dad was how to survive the stormy waves washing over him.

When calm returned, Laz tucked the medal back under his shirt and pulled out his phone. He tapped out a message to Ryder: *"messed up 2day"*

The response came in seconds: *"y?"*

"blowout with DM" That's what Ryder and Laz called Dad: Dungeon Master (DM).

"worse than usual?"

"way" When no reply came after thirty seconds, Laz added, *"total explosion"*

"u ok?"

"hanging in"

"learn to shut yr mouth" Ryder knew that was what got Laz into trouble.

Laz knew it too, but it didn't stop him from talking back. He felt better after telling Ryder, even if it only blew off steam. He tapped, *"tbl"* Text back later.

"ok"

No one else was in the trench. Laz walked to the middle and opened his phone's video then turned in a full circle. He recorded the greening grass, the stone walls that reached at least twenty feet up, the grassy mounds on top of the walls. He faced a door in the outer wall directly across from the stairs he had descended. He squinted at the phone's screen as the camera recorded the plain door with big iron hinges. He whispered, "There must be a tunnel under the outer wall. Got to see this." He ended the recording and climbed the two wooden steps.

The door creaked as he pushed it open, and a mix of smells hit him. The strongest was musty dirt, like the cellar where Grandmère kept her potatoes and carrots. The stone in the chamber also seemed to give off a smell, sharper than the dirt. Another unidentified scent teased Laz, but he couldn't place it.

He turned on the video recorder again and began to narrate. "I'm under the outer wall, the rampart, and this tunnel is a series of rooms with doorways but no doors. This room is smaller than my bedroom. Big stones make up the walls." He tilted the phone up. "Small stones make an arched ceiling." He angled right. "This window has wire mesh, probably to keep birds out, and really old iron bars. See that horizontal slit in the bars? I bet that was for firing on the enemy if they got into that grassy moat."

He walked into the next chamber, still talking. "This room is the same size but darker. It just has a slit in the wall. I read about fortresses. It's called a loophole, and it's for firing rifles, but back then it was muskets. The slit protects you more than that window in the other room."

The smell was getting stronger. Laz stopped recording and inhaled deeply then closed his eyes and smelled again, trying to place the familiar scent. It took him a moment to realize it smelled like a hockey rink when the Zamboni was cleaning the ice. That was so weird. There wouldn't be a Zamboni in an old fort like this. His feet scraped across the dirt floor as he backed away from the window. The silence was as thick as the walls. No sound of any kind got inside, not traffic noise or people's voices. Laz had the feeling that if he yelled, no one outside would hear that either. He shivered, glad for the wool jacket his mom had made him wear, even if the collar made his neck itch.

Laz pressed the phone's record button again. "It's cold in here. Smells funny too." He did another turn, recording the way he'd come, the loophole, then the way ahead. His voice dropped to a whisper. "It's kind of creepy. Too quiet. See how dark it is this way? Except for those two little circles of light farther ahead. Maybe from another loophole. I'll check it out."

Talking felt out of place in the murky silence. Laz kept the video on. The next two chambers were nearly midnight dark so he wasn't sure the video would be anything except a blank screen, shuffling noises, and his breathing. He wasn't even looking at the screen as he tried to figure out where the Zamboni smell was coming from.

He paused in the doorway between the two darkest chambers. Behind him, the air looked a bit misty, as if the walls were leaking some kind of gas. The source of the smell, he thought. He could have sworn the tunnel was becoming mistier. The tangy smell grew stronger. His neck hairs prickled and a shiver of electricity ran across his shoulders.

The air seemed to push against Laz, as if it didn't want him to return down the tunnel. Something strange was happening, but he didn't know if it was this chamber, the whole tunnel, or if he'd had too much bacon for lunch. He took a deep breath and his lungs refused to fill. The only time he'd felt that before was when Dad took them hiking in the Rocky Mountains, so high the air was thin, and wooziness had almost made him lose his balance. Heights had never bothered him before or since.

"This is stupid," Laz said, hoping to break the eerie silence. He decided to leave. As he turned, his heel caught on something. He flung his arms out. The phone sailed away. His fingertips brushed stone as he fell. His head cracked against something, and everything went black.

CHAPTER THREE

A rumbling, thundering headache woke up Laz. He tried to think past the pain that rippled out from the pounding, but couldn't. He remembered a cave. Not a cave: a tunnel, a chain of rooms, and mist.

And he remembered falling. Had he hit his head? If he had, the memory was a webpage that wouldn't load. A vague memory surfaced, of something like sliding. There hadn't been any slide's hard plastic surface under him. It had felt like sliding through a big black nothing, where the only sense was his smell and it had been clogged with weird Zamboni fumes.

When Laz groaned and rolled onto his side, his cheek pressed against something cool and earthy smelling. He dragged one finger along the floor and stirred up the smell of dirt.

"Am I still in the tunnel?" he whispered. That floor had been dirt. But this blackness was so thick that he couldn't see his hand, never mind anything beyond it. He eased onto all fours, which sped up the pounding in his head. He rested until it slowed then pushed up. His shoulders hit a knotted, hard surface.

Laz curled into a tight ball to ward off the cold, and hoped he was still dreaming. Sometimes when he was close to waking, he'd think he was already awake. Those times came with the sense of being not right. This qualified. He decided to focus on the weirdness to see if he would wake up faster.

His St. Christopher medal felt like a dime-sized tattoo needle burning his skin. That rated at least six on the weird scale. He wrapped his fingers around its heat, hoping it would drive away the cold. The Citadel's tunnel was stone and dirt, and he guessed it would get cold at night. But its ceilings were smooth, not bumpy.

Maybe he'd fallen under a table with a rough underside. Laz released the medal and got onto his hands and knees again. This time his headache kept to a dull throb. If he was awake, he'd crawl out from under the table. If not, something weird would happen.

He felt around for table legs. Instead he found rising ground peppered with fist-sized rocks and sticks and lumps of dirt. He crept up an incline that felt maybe three steps high. Air lightened around him, and he realized he'd crawled out of a small space. A breeze touched his face, bringing a salty smell that proved he was still near ocean.

Laz decided he'd fallen down an escape hole and was outside the Citadel. He felt around; slapped a hard, mounded root snaking out of the ground; ran his hand up a broad trunk. He had climbed out of a hole beneath a tree. Relief felt as fresh as the breeze. He only had to find someone and ask for directions back to the hotel on Hollis Street.

The relief disappeared when he caught a sniff of that bitter smell on his clothes. Where was the city? If he'd discovered a secret way out of the Citadel, and it was now night, there would be lights and cars and people.

"Now would be a good time to wake up." His voice seemed to make the night rustle. Somewhere, an owl hooted.

Laz felt his way over the massive root to sit between it and another. He leaned against the trunk and rested his arms on the roots like it was an armchair. Dreaming about being in a forest rated maybe a weirdness level of two. He had spent a lot of time outside at Grandmère's farm in New Brunswick. Since his father had moved the family to Boston while he was at Grandmère's, he hardly even texted with most of his Ottawa friends. Ryder had befriended him on the first day of school, which had made Boston bearable. (*Text to Ryder: send search party*) But Laz had never forgiven his father.

Laz checked his pockets for his cell phone then remembered falling and the phone flying from his hand. "This is stupid. Give me my phone back, dream." A second check of his pockets only turned up a marble of lint.

Light flickered near the horizon, silhouetting trees and ground that sloped downward. Laz drew his legs up to his chest as the air chilled him again. When lost, don't move. That's what adults taught. It was a good thing he wasn't afraid of the dark.

The sky lit with several bursts in a row. Lightning. A huge sheet of light rippled across a chunk of the sky. Laz saw the hole he'd crawled out of, the forested hillside, and between the trees, reflected light that could be water at the bottom of the hill. There was no thunder, just the silent light show. The whole hilltop seemed to hold its breath.

A distant sound whispered in Laz's ears. It was rhythmic, a lilt that held his attention. A man-made sound.

Laz jumped up and braced one hand on the tree as he strained to listen. His headache faded and the faint rhythm sifting through the night seemed a little louder. Someone was out there.

He took a few steps and turned back, as if a cord tied him to the tree. He knew he shouldn't wander off. But if there were people in this dark, lonely place, he wanted to find them. He felt around the den's entrance and ripped off some bark then scraped an arrow in the ground, pointing to the hole so he could find it again.

With sporadic flashes of far-off lightning helping, Laz inched down the hill, arms outstretched. Any tree he touched, he broke limbs to mark his path. Shivers kept rippling across his arms and chest, but it wasn't from the cold. Nothing was making sense. Laz would rather have his dad bellowing at him than this weird aloneness. An aching need to be with people drew him forward.

Laz stumbled a few times then realized he was moving a bit faster. Some light source beyond the trees lit his way. The sound he'd heard gathered into definite strains of music from a fiddle and some kind of drum. He walked faster, jerking to a halt when the music stopped. His lungs stalled, only restarting when another song began, and with it, men singing.

Laz hurried forward, pushed through bushes, and halted on a small, bare rise. He sucked in air, clamped his mouth shut, and stared, eyes like Frisbees.

Bonfires lined the shore, each surrounded by men who looked straight off a movie set: *Pirates of the Caribbean, the*

Halifax Edition. More sheet lightning rolled across the sky, a glowing white wave. The silhouettes of at least a dozen ships—old-time sailing ships—stood out against the mirrored water of a giant bay.

The weirdness scale jumped to eight.

"What is this?" Laz asked the night.

"Nay, the better question, lad, is what kind of scab are ye?"

Laz spun around. Lightly brushed by firelight, a pirate pointed a sword at his throat.

CHAPTER FOUR

A flash of lightning streaked white along the silver blade of the sword. Shock kept Laz from moving. The man holding the weapon made him think of Ben Franklin. He wore a pirate shirt, white and loose, with a long, sleeveless coat, knee-length pants, stockings, and buckle shoes. Darkness returned, leaving the negative of the man's image imprinted in Laz's brain.

Firelight pushed back the darkness. Laz gasped. "I *am* awake. My dad set this up." The man tilted his head in a puzzled way. Laz continued, "My father drugged me or something, and shipped me off to a camp for troubled kids, but with this weird American Revolution theme." Having the strange situation explained didn't make Laz feel better.

The man replied, "Cease speaking gibberish. Your father did not arrange this expedition unless his name is William Shirley or mayhap William Pepperrell."

"You're good. So are you a guard or something?" Laz kept his voice calm, but inside he was seething that his dad would do something like this. Had the smell in the tunnel been some kind of knockout drug? And where was this place? It was colder than Halifax had been. Laz decided it was some remote part of Newfoundland. He stared at the man as he imagined sending a message on his phone. (*Text to Ryder: DM a jerk. Put me in prison. Send cake with file.*)

"I was standing sentry duty," the man said. "So now I shall escort you to our captain."

"Great. Take me to your leader. I really want to let him know how fake this setup is."

The man waved his sword toward the beach but didn't lower it.

Laz started down the steep incline, sliding sideways with a steadying hand skimming the ground behind him. "What year is this supposed to be?"

When the sentry reached level ground, he replied, "Are you a simpleton that you don't even know it is the year of our Lord, seventeen hundred and forty-five?"

"Yeah, whatever. Don't expect me to play along with this."

The man followed Laz and poked him a few times as they approached the bonfires, but his wool coat protected him. A man crouched near the middle fire spotted them and leaped up with a shout. "Cringle, what have you there?"

"An interloper. Ready a skiff so we can deliver him to Captain Hawkins." He herded Laz to the edge of the shore.

At first Laz faced the water, taking in the smells and nighttime view of the bay. Then he spun around and scowled at anyone who looked his way. Those who did only glanced at him with quick, puzzled looks, as if they couldn't figure out why he was here. They were all dressed similar to the sentry. A number of them looked young enough to also be inmates, or students, or whatever they called the kids unlucky enough to have super-controlling parents who would send their kids to a prison school.

One of the boys from the closest fire shouted, "Which ship will host the scab, Cringle?"

"Shut your gob, Ben. Our captain gets the honor."

The boy jumped up. "Let me go back to the *Constance* with you. It's going to rain again, and I'd rather sleep under cover."

"If you'll pull an oar, you can go."

With a shout, the boy raced down the beach toward a boat that two men were rowing parallel to the shore, ten feet out. He splashed into the water, hoisted himself over the edge of the rowboat, and fell in.

Laz was usually good at staying calm, but inside he felt a jumble of confusion and worry. *Dad didn't even give me the chance to say goodbye to Emeline or Ryder,* he thought. It felt like leaving Ottawa, only worse. He didn't understand why parents felt they could ruin your life without even trying to talk to you.

The rowers backed the boat toward shore, stopping three feet short of the beach. Cringle, the sword-wielder, ordered Laz to get in. He shook his head. "I'm not getting my feet wet."

Strong fingers captured the back of Laz's neck and shoved him toward the boat. He stumbled and fell to his knees, getting soaked from mid-thigh down. But he grabbed the back of the boat to keep from going completely under. He sloshed to his feet and Cringle swatted the back of his head. "Get in."

Cold clung to Laz's wet legs and feet like iron filings to a magnet. He swung his leg over the side, making sure to splash the rowers. The men swore. The boy laughed. Cringle got in and another man pushed off. They made Laz sit in the nose of the boat. One rower handed Cringle an old-styled flintlock pistol, and he kept it aimed in Laz's direction.

"Are you kidding?" Laz gave his best imitation of the Look. This playacting was way too serious.

Cringle squinted and said nothing. The other three men and the boy began rowing.

As the boat moved away from the shore, someone called to the fiddler and he started playing. It reminded Laz of the Acadian fiddlers who played at events in Grandmère's community. His legs shook from the cold. He hunched over with eyes closed, listened to the music, and imagined being at a gathering with Grandmère, everyone speaking French and laughing. The old people would shove food at him and tease him about girls. He was bilingual because Grandmère insisted everyone speak French in her house, even though she could speak English. The fiddler changed tunes, and French lyrics ran through Laz's mind. He lifted his head. The bonfires had shrunk, but the music carried across the water. He wished he were at Grandmère's— anywhere but here.

The four oars dipped and splashed almost in time to the music. They passed a ship, then another. Oversized lanterns on the stern of each ship lit their way. They drew up beside the third ship, bigger than the first two, and bumped against its side. The nearest rower grabbed a rope net strung along the side. The other rower on the same side also held the ropes, holding the boat snug against the ship's side.

Cringle scrambled up the netting, the boy followed, disappeared, then reappeared to dangle a smaller lantern over the side. Cringle aimed the pistol at Laz. "Climb up, boy."

Laz balanced one foot on the wall of the skiff and rocked it hard as he started climbing. Muttered oaths followed him up the net. Cringle backed up, looking surprised at how fast Laz was able to reach the deck. More proof he'd be great at parkour.

Another man climbed onto the ship, and the other two began rowing for shore. Laz leaned over the rail, watching their lantern-lit path, then straightened. "Well. That was fun. Except for you slapping me, Cringle. You're not a good welcoming committee."

In reply, Cringle handed the pistol to the silent man and drew his sword. "Follow Ben."

"Who?"

"Me," piped the boy. He scuttled across the deck to a low door below the raised area at the back of the ship, and knocked. A muffled voice responded, and Ben said, "We have a prisoner, Cap'n."

The door swung open and a middle-aged man scowled past Ben to skewer Laz with a look that made his dad's seem mild. He stepped back. "Get inside then. Not you, Ben."

The boy's shoulders sagged and everyone else entered, Laz in the middle. The captain slammed the door behind them and Laz flinched. He hoped now they'd tell him what kind of school this was.

The ceiling was a little over six feet with wooden beams hanging lower. Laz had grown a lot but he was still two inches shorter than the evenly spaced beams. The captain directed Laz away from a sleeping area, to the right where maps covered a big table. He plopped down on the nearest chair. The captain came up behind him and whipped the chair to the side.

Laz thudded to the wooden floor. "Hey!"

"You will not sit unless I give you permission to sit."

Angry now, Laz stood and tugged at the hem of his coat. "Look. I don't know what's going on, but I don't deserve this prisoner playact garbage. I shouldn't even be here. You can call Dad and cancel the contract, or at least let me talk to him."

The captain stood, fists planted on hips. He wore a flowing white shirt with a vest that was nearly down to his knees made of fancy, flowery material. Instead of buckle shoes, he had on boots that almost reached his knees, showing two inches of stockings. His broad shoulders suggested he could easily knock down a bigger man. In the lantern light, his gaze was beady. His lips pressed together the way Laz's dad's did when he wasn't happy.

Cringle said, "Since I caught him on the ridge, he has spouted nonsense from time to time, Captain Hawkins. I think the lad's simple."

"Lad, you say? He's nearly as tall as me, but his face certainly has a youthful look." Captain Hawkins took one step forward. "Who is this "Dad" of whom you speak?"

Like Cringle, this captain had a mild English accent. Laz guessed that his stuffy way of speaking was part of the act too. He rolled his eyes. "Martin Berenger. He'll be in your records. And I'm already sick of this. I'm hungry and tired. Just point me to my bunk."

"You are not on my ship's rolls. Are you claiming to be part of this expedition?" His expression was doubtful as he studied Laz from top to bottom. "Your attire is highly unusual."

"Not as much as yours." Cringle boxed Laz's ear. He cried, "Stop that! This setup can't be legal. I'm going to sue you when I get out of here."

"Cringle, Joseph, leave us." The captain rolled up the maps. The top one looked like a map of Nova Scotia, but there weren't any markings showing cities or roads.

"But, sir—" Cringle stiffened.

"Do it. Fetch my sword belt if you're worried about my safety."

While Captain Hawkins slid the map into a leather cylinder and fastened the lid with an attached clasp, Cringle scooped a belt off a knob beside the door. A sword in its sheath hung from the belt. The captain buckled it on and waved toward the door. The two men left, but not before Cringle said they'd wait outside the door should there be need.

Captain Hawkins perched on the edge of the table and crossed his arms. "Who are you?"

"Isn't that in your records?"

"I will not tolerate insolence. I have no records that include one such as you."

Laz shoved his hands into his jacket pockets. "What's that supposed to mean?

"Who are you?" He glared until Laz finally replied.

"Laz Berenger." Laz exhaled loudly. "Lazare."

"Lazare Berenger." He said it slowly, stressing the French pronunciation of Berenger: *Ber-ehn-jhay*.

"So?"

"You're French."

"Not—"

"Not French? Then Acadian."

"My grandmother is—"

"Which means *you* are Acadian. I heard a strangeness in your accent."

"What difference does that make?" Laz asked.

The captain's lip curled. "I knew the Acadians would end up helping those French pirates in Louisbourg. What do you know about our expedition?"

"I don't know what you're talking about." Laz tried to remember why that name sounded familiar. His eyes widened as he recalled his grandmother wanting to take him to see the French fort of Louisbourg, a museum on the northeast shore of Cape Breton Island. Something about it being an important part of history.

The captain had been watching him closely and now said, "Of course you would say that. Let us dispense with lies, shall we? Why are you dressed so strangely?"

Laz swept his hair behind his ear and rubbed the back of his neck. "Why do you keep saying that? I just got here. How could I be wearing anything else?"

"Got here from where?"

"Halifax. Where am I now?"

Hawkins scowled at the map case then at Laz. "I know of no Halifax on this side of the Atlantic, though I've heard mention of the Earl of Halifax."

Laz's frustration bubbled up like a baking-soda volcano. "Does this have to do with that Cringle guy saying it was 1745? I'm sick of this pretending."

Hawkins blinked. "Precisely what year do you believe it to be?"

"It's 2017."

The man squinted thoughtfully. "So in order to distract me from your being Acadian, you pretend madness by claiming to be from a future time? I would suggest, young sir, you keep that nonsense to yourself lest the men decide you are devil-possessed, for surely only Satan could be involved in such devilry. Be assured, they would burn the devil out of you if it came to that." He stood, hand on his sword hilt, and studied Laz more closely. Then he paced around him. "The more I think about, devilry would explain your attire. Not even amongst Acadians have I seen such garb."

Laz blinked and thought, *Devilry? Satan? What has Dad gotten me into?*

He startled when Hawkins shouted, "Cringle!"

The man charged inside, sword extended, eyes wild. When he saw the captain and prisoner only standing, the sword point dipped. "Sir?"

"Get a kit from the slops. Charge it to me."

"Yes, sir." He sent Laz a dirty look and disappeared. Silence reigned in the five minutes he was gone. Laz imagined sending another message. (*Text to Ryder: crazy ppl in charge. Need straitjackets.*) Cringle returned with a pile of clothing and a pair of wooden shoes. At Hawkins' instruction, he set the pile by Laz's feet and retreated outside the door.

Hawkins pointed at the pile. "Put those on."

Laz replied, "Trade my clothes for those? You've got to be kidding."

With a swish, Hawkins pulled his sword. He shifted to the side and pointed the blade. "If by *kidding*, you are suggesting that I am jesting, I assure you, Lazare Berenger, that I never jest. I do not like your attire. I do not know what might be concealed under that strange garb, so you will remove it."

"No. I'm sick of you jerks pointing your toy swords at me." Laz grabbed the blade and pushed it aside.

Pain sliced into his hand and blossomed red as he dropped to his knees.

CHAPTER FIVE

Laz gripped the wrist on his bleeding hand and stared at the two slices in his palm. Panic filled his voice and made it quiver. "Real swords? You're crazy. Who are you?"

The captain wiped blood from his blade with a gray cloth. "I am Captain Elijah Hawkins of Portsmouth in the Royal Province of New Hampshire, loyal subject to King George the Second of England. And you, young sir, are a fool to grab a man's blade."

He disappeared for a moment and returned with a knife and square of cloth. He cut it into strips, folded all the pieces except one and laid them on Laz's palm, then used the final strip to secure them, tying a tight knot on the back of his hand. "Now, remove your clothes."

Confusion and fear crowded into Laz's mind. He searched the man's face for some sign that he felt sorry about the accident, but only saw a bully ready to squash him like a bug.

"I don't understand," Laz whispered.

Captain Hawkins' voice was clipped. "I apologize for the indecency of the request, but these are exceptional times. I insist you remove your attire."

A dot of blood on the makeshift bandage grew to the size of a dull pencil tip. Feeling like he had no choice but to obey, Laz got up and undid the buttons on his jacket with his left hand. He shrugged out of the coat and dropped it to the floor. Another glance convinced Laz he would find no kindness from this man, whose face was as wooden as the beams above his head.

It became too much for Laz. This man stayed in character every second. And he carried a real sword. Almost as if he actually believed he was Captain Hawkins of Portsmouth.

"What year is it?" Laz asked again, still whispering.

"You know the answer. It is the year of our Lord, seventeen hundred and forty-five. Or as you so churlishly said, 1745. Why pretend madness? Surely your people treat the mad as we do, manacling them, locking them away in fetid conditions. Why would you risk this?"

Laz worked his way out of his gray T-shirt and dropped it. "You're really going to make me do this."

"Regretfully, I must insist." Hawkins picked up the T-shirt and studied the cloth, the seams, and the Boston Bruins logo.

Reluctantly, Laz kicked off his shoes and removed one sock at a time. Hawkins picked up a shoe, frowned at the black canvas, and turned it over to study the black sole. Laz unbuttoned his fly, worked his jeans down with one hand, then stepped out of them. He hesitated with his hand on the waistband of his boxers. Shivers ran over his arms and legs, mostly because it felt like the weirdness scale had exploded.

Hawkins looked up, squinted one eye as if puzzled at the sight of underwear. He waved for Laz to continue. He pulled a white shirt over his head and whipped off his shorts. After sorting through the pile of clothes he asked, "Where's the underwear?"

"What do you mean?"

"There's no underwear. Can't I wear mine?"

"If you're referring to those odd small clothes, I do not believe I want you wearing anything of your unnatural attire. Surely you know how to dress."

Laz gave a frustrated sigh. "Pretend I don't. Tell me." He extended his arms to examine the shirt's sail-like sleeves. The shirttail reached halfway to his knees. It felt like wearing a dress and Laz knew Emeline would laugh if she saw him.

Captain Hawkins dropped the shoe and brushed his hands. He considered the pile of clothes with a frown that drew his eyebrows together. "Stockings, garters, breeches, waistcoat, shoes." After a pause, he added, "For your own sake, cease with pretending madness. You will be treated more kindly as a spy than a madman."

His solemn tone made Laz swallow, and he focused on getting dressed. The captain explained how to tie the garters above the knees so they would hold up the long stockings. The brown breeches had a baggy butt with laces on the back of the waistband, a button fly, and drawstrings at the knee-length cuffs. It felt like dressing for Halloween or a school play. Laz pulled on the breeches and started to button up the fly.

"Tuck in your shirt, Master Berenger."

"Whatever you say, Captain. Like I have a choice," Laz muttered and struggled to tuck in the shirt with one hand. *(Text to Ryder: breeches will nvr be cool)* Even with the shirt tucked in, the waistband was loose and there was no belt.

"You are a particularly useless young man." Hawkins stepped around Laz and cinched up the laces at the back. He spun Laz around and lifted his chain and medallion from under the shirt. "What is this?"

Laz had hoped the captain wouldn't notice the chain. "Don't touch that. My grandmother gave it to me. It's been in our family for hundreds of years."

"Indeed? What *is* it?" His fingers curled in the chain, and it bit into Laz's neck.

"A St. Christopher medal."

Hawkins' fingers tightened more and one corner of his lip curled. "Papist witchery." A hard tug broke the chain. Hawkins stepped back.

Laz snatched at the chain. The captain caught his wrist and twisted his arm, making his cut palm throb more and rocketing pain up to his shoulder.

"Give it back." Laz forced the words through clenched teeth.

The captain's grip tightened more and corkscrewed, until Laz groaned and his knees started to give way. With imposing strength, the captain kept Laz dangling in a knot of agony. "Listen carefully, young man. I am master of this ship. No one tells me what to do. I decide the fate of each man aboard." He released and Laz's knees hit the floor. He rubbed his shoulder and arm, trying to ease the pain. When he finally looked up, he felt the pleading look stamped on his face. The captain's lip curled.

He opened his palm, peered at Laz's medallion, then closed his hand back into a fist. "If it's that important to you, I will place the medal into safekeeping. Mayhap, if you are ever released, or in the unlikely event you earn my trust, I shall return your papist trinket." Hawkins nudged Laz's closest knee with his square-toed boot. "Now put on that waistcoat. I tire of seeing you half dressed."

Other than the shoes, the only thing left was a long, sand-colored vest with a raised pattern of swirling brown leaves and vines. Apparently it was called a waistcoat. After he swiped both eyes with the baggy shirtsleeve, Laz put on the waistcoat. Its hem was three inches above his knees. He felt like an idiot. More than anything he wanted to beg the captain to call his dad and end this. He thought, *But I can't give up this easily.*

Laz slipped his feet into the wooden clogs. "Happy?"

"Button up. Nothing about this situation makes me happy, Master Berenger."

"What's the point of this? Are you trying to break me? Make me obedient?"

"Obedience is a fine trait from which all young men benefit. In this instance, I simply desire to learn your identity and secure my ship's safety. While I see you feel uncomfortable in that garb, you look better, and the men will treat you more kindly if you are not so strangely attired." He settled back on the edge of the table and shouted, "Cringle!"

The man reappeared, sword in hand but not alarmed this time. He looked Laz up and down and nodded.

"I believe fetters are required, Cringle."

The man grinned. "Right away, sir."

They waited in silence for Cringle to return. Laz hoped fetters were some kind of food. Were they like corn fritters? His stomach grumbled. It seemed like the floor was beginning to rise and fall, barely enough to notice except for the slight queasy feeling it produced. Though Laz wanted it to be, none of this felt like a dream. Every second felt so real he wanted to scream the way Emeline did whenever she watched a scary movie.

The reflection of the captain showed in one pane of rippled glass. He had a skinny braid that hung below his collar. The door opened. In the windowpanes Laz watched Cringle cross the room in distorted waves. Cringle knelt in front of him and dropped something that rattled loudly. Laz startled to see a large iron cuff ready to clamp around one of his ankles.

"What are you doing?" Laz started to step back, but Cringle gripped his calf with a powerful hand. Laz struggled to free his leg.

When he wrenched out of Cringle's grip, Hawkins yelled, "Joseph!"

The silent man rushed in and Laz's heart began racing. He backed up but hit a wall of shelves. He groped behind himself for a weapon but only knocked books to the floor.

"Do not be difficult, Master Berenger," Hawkins said. "Surely if your community sent you, your leaders had to know capture was possible. You are big enough and old enough to suffer your incarceration like a man, however childishly you behave."

"Incarcer—" Didn't that mean being in prison?

Silent Joe grabbed Laz, and he started to twist and kick in earnest. Cringle grunted when one wooden shoe found his shin. He rose and sank his fist into Laz's stomach, making air whoosh out. Laz strained against Silent Joe's grip as his mouth opened and closed, but he couldn't swallow air. His eyes bulged.

Air rushed back with a loud gasp. Laz wheezed and took deep, noisy breaths.

He saw that one ankle was already shackled. Cringle secured the second cuff and passed Hawkins the key. Laz slid a foot to the side and the black chain between his ankles rattled.

Laz's voice went hoarse. "You're locking me up? *Please* don't do this." His calm flaked away like dried mud off rubber boots. "I won't talk about crazy things. Please. It's 1745. I'm Acadian. I don't know why that matters, but I'll say whatever you want. What are you doing?"

"I am taking you prisoner, Lazare Berenger. You are undoubtedly a spy for the French, and you will remain in irons until we reach Canso where my commanding officer will decide your fate."

CHAPTER SIX

As Cringle and Silent Joe took Laz away, Captain Hawkins said, "All the rowboats are ashore, Master Berenger. With those irons on, any attempt to escape will only win you a bed of seaweed on the ocean floor."

They shoved Laz into a storeroom and locked the door. Then the wind came up. Loose canvas and rigging flapped, ropes tapped the hull, and the ship bobbed and jerked in the now rough water. It felt like trying to sleep on a suspension footbridge with someone jumping on it to make it buck. Laz tossed and turned, and dreamed of drowning all night long.

He jolted awake, hoping he had also dreamed the ship and that he was in his own bed, or on the hotel suite's hide-a-bed. But the rocking and hard wooden planks crushed that hope. Laz groped around in the dark, found the wool blanket that the boy, Ben, had given him, and wrapped it around his shoulders. Because of the shackles, he couldn't tuck his frozen feet under him. He rubbed some feeling back into his toes before putting on the wooden shoes, and pulled his legs up against his chest as he leaned against a barrel.

His ankles were sore from the heavy iron bracelets. His tailbone ached, and so did the shoulder Hawkins had almost wrenched from its socket. His cut palm still throbbed, though not as badly as last night. The sea, the wood, and a faint whiff of tar combined with a few smells he couldn't identify. He had never felt so miserable.

If this was a bizarre adventure school for troubled kids, Laz couldn't figure out why hadn't they told him. There'd been no introduction or lecture about the rules. He couldn't believe his mom would agree to this. Arguing with his dad a lot didn't seem like a good enough reason to be sent to this place. Laz decided to watch for anything modern. Someone would have a cell phone, or there'd be a radio for emergencies, or they would stop in a port. He decided he would borrow a phone and call for help, because it felt like he had been kidnapped.

Laz tried to imagine the strange 9-1-1 call. *I've been kidnapped by pirates. We're on an old-fashioned sailing ship… somewhere along a coast. It's cold, so I think we're in Canada.*

He rubbed his chest, missing the St. Christopher medal. He'd had it for two years, and Hawkins grabbing it had felt like taking away a piece of himself. Why, he wondered again, had the medal been so hot when he'd first awakened in the cave under the tree?

Hand cupped on his chest, Laz dozed off. Minutes later the door crashed open and Ben stood holding a lantern. "Rise up. If we're slow getting into line, there'll be nothing but burnt dregs from the pot."

"We?" Laz rasped.

"Aye. Cap'n says I'm to show you around."

"And guard me."

"I'm not big enough for that. But if you give me trouble, I'll push you overboard and watch you sink." He grinned as if that were a hilarious thought.

He laughed when Laz grimaced, used the barrel to pull himself up, wrapped the blanket tighter around his shoulders, and stepped forward. The chain scraped and clanked on the wood.

"Leave the blanket. You look like my grandmother with her shawl."

"I'm cold," Laz replied.

Ben yanked the blanket away, and tossed it in the corner. "Don't be a molly." He gave Laz a little push. *Scrape. Clank.*

They made their way through the hold, up a ladder, and onto the deck, emerging close to one of two masts. With every step it was *scrape, clank.* The gray clouds and wind combined to slash at them with sideways rain that soaked through Laz's sleeves in seconds. Ben led him past several cannons to the front, which he called the bow, of the ship, up steep stairs to a higher deck, then past three more cannons and the front mast to a railing near the bow.

"What's this?" Laz asked.

Ben pointed. "The head. It's always by the bowsprit so the waves wash away the refuse. Have you not been on a ship before?"

"No." Laz studied the bowsprit, an angled pole emerging from below them, with narrow latticed walkways to either side of it. Laz noticed a raised box. On the other side of the bowsprit, a man sat on an identical box. He leaned forward with a look of concentration, blind to the world and even to the rocking surface below him, and Laz knew he was going to the bathroom. He shivered. "You expect me to use that?"

"Aye, well the cap'n's privy isn't for the likes of us."

Hearing the slosh of waves against the side of the ship was making Laz need to go to the bathroom. He climbed down the ladder—*scrape, clank*—and stood holding a waist-high rung. A triangular slice of rope netting stretched from the ship to farther along the bowsprit. To save a person who fell, maybe. He let go for a second, the boat rocked, and he grabbed hold again.

With his sore right hand hooked behind a rung, he did his business as quickly as possible. (*Text to Ryder: ship's head makes an outhouse seem fancy*) Meanwhile, the man had finished and Ben had taken his place. He yanked up his breeches, bounded to the closest ladder, and climbed up it. His head appeared atop Laz's ladder. "Come on, Molly. Time to break our fast."

Laz made his awkward way up the ladder. "Don't call me Molly."

"What should I call you?"

"Laz."

Ben scrunched up his face.

Laz shrugged. "My name is Lazare. Friends call me Laz."

"That's an odd name. Almost like Lazarus."

It was Laz's turn to give Ben a blank look.

"You know," Ben said, "from in the Holy Book. Lord Jesus raised Lazarus from the dead." He motioned Laz forward. "Cringle said you're a Papist. Don't Papists teach their children about Lazarus?"

"Papist?"

"Oh. I don't suppose you'd call yourselves that. What would you say? Catholic?" Ben tugged on each white sleeve, which were dirty along the cuffs. "We're Protestants, like all good New Englanders. Our minister said you Catholics are an evil lot, especially the French ones, and we need to be wiping that French papist fort off the face of the earth. He said the Lord will lead us into glorious victory."

Laz ignored the religious talk and wondered, *What fort is he talking about? Louisbourg or somewhere else?*

Ben stopped at the steep stairs above the main deck and watched Laz shuffle forward. "You don't look evil."

"What a relief." Laz could see that Ben didn't catch his sarcasm.

Ben gave him a small smile and zipped down the stairs. "Hurry, while the pottage is fresh."

"I can hardly wait."

There were a few people on deck, and they all watched Laz lumber noisily down the stairs. The captain stood on the raised deck at the stern, the back of the ship. Hands clasped behind him and feet planted wide, his beady gaze pelted Laz from a distance. Laz stared back, willing him to come and unlock these shackles. He didn't move. Laz felt like saying something nasty, but guessed that would get him tossed back into that storeroom. He needed his freedom to figure out what was going on.

So instead, Laz gave the captain a rough salute. He missed the sarcasm too. Instead of looking angry, he touched two fingers to the front of his tricorn hat. Ben grabbed Laz's arm and hauled him toward the door below the front raised deck.

"What's this place?" Laz asked.

"The forecastle," (he pronounced it *focsle*) "where the crew stays. We were on the forecastle deck, and this is the main deck. Cap'n Hawkins is on the quarterdeck. It's only for officers unless they give you permission, so best stay away."

Inside the forecastle, to the left, was a kitchen and heavy tables with rough benches. To the right, hammocks swayed above chests and assorted belongings. In the farthest corner, a few men were still cocooned in their hammocks. Wonderful heat welcomed the boys. A mix of smells—sweat, unwashed bodies, food, beer, a trace of tar—almost drove Laz back out.

The few people eating fell silent as the boys got some kind of porridge, weak tea, and a biscuit. They made their way to the empty table. *Scrape. Clank.* The men returned to eating. Laz raised his biscuit.

"No!" Ben grabbed his wrist. "That's hardtack. You'll break your teeth. Do this." He banged his biscuit against the table then dunked one corner in his tea.

"Why—" Laz stopped when the crumbs that had fallen to the table wiggled. "What are those?"

"Weevils." Ben drew the biscuit out of the tea and took a bite.

Laz felt his stomach flop. He handed Ben his biscuit and stirred his pottage, which was a mix of grains. Some lumps looked like fish, which Laz thought was a disgusting thing to put in porridge, but better than insects. Laz used his left hand to spoon the nearly tasteless goop into his mouth. His right hand was an upturned rooster foot, talons curled inward, protecting the blood-dried bandage staining his palm. The ship's rocking caused his bowl to shift, but the table's raised rim kept it from crashing to the floor.

Ben finished first. He sprang up. "Stay here. I'll get a new dressing for that." He pointed at Laz's hand.

As soon as he left, Cringle thunked his metal bowl down and sat across from Laz. In daylight his hair, pulled back into a ponytail, was more dirty than brown. Pockmarked cheeks bulged with pottage. He soaked his biscuit in his tea and watched Laz with open hatred. He swallowed and said, "How's the French pig this morn?"

Laz felt words knocking against his teeth again, trying to get out, and knew they would earn him another swat. Guessing that was what Cringle wanted, he kept quiet.

"Doesn't he speak English?" one of the sailors from the other table asked.

"He does. He speaks like some great man, an earl or some-what," Cringle said.

"Those Frenchies have sly tongues," came the reply.

Cringle snorted again and bit off half his biscuit. He chewed and watched like a cat in a staring contest. Laz was afraid to turn away and his stomach was getting jittery, though that might have been from the pottage.

Ben returned and laid out a fresh cloth, a knife, and a bowl of water.

"Don't let 'em grab that knife, Ben. Stupid Frenchie doesn't know which end is for holding." Cringle grinned when the men behind him hooted and laughed. He moved tables.

"I feel so special," Laz said. "If you aren't guarding me, someone else steps in."

Ben flushed, which made his blond hair look even lighter. "Orders from Cap'n. You cannot be left alone unless locked up."

"I'm really dangerous." Laz flexed his cramped right fingers and winced.

Ben slid the bowl of water toward him. "Surgeon said to soak off the old dressing." He untied the bandage's knot and motioned toward the water.

Laz lowered his hand, palm up, into the water. With a shout he tried to remove it but Ben held it down. He was small but strong. Laz gritted his teeth and asked, "What's in the water?"

"Naught. It's only salt water. The old hands say wounds heal faster this way."

Laz swore under his breath.

Ben's eyes grew wide. He whispered, "Do not let Cap'n hear you spew blasphemies. Men have gotten the lash for less."

Laz searched his face for any sign he was faking, but he only saw was worry. "Why would you work for him?"

"He's a good man, and fair."

"Aren't you too young to be working?"

"I'm old enough, thirteen. Father apprenticed me onto *Constance*'s crew a year ago. I'm too small to be useful on the farm, and truth be told, I love this ship." Ben continued to hold Laz's hand under the water. "How old are you...Lazare?" He said the name slowly.

"I'll be thirteen in about a month."

He looked thoughtful. "I wondered if you were close to my age, though you're tall enough to be a king's guard. What's your trade?"

"No trade. I go to school."

"That's right uncouth, unless you're training to be a physician or somewhat."

Uncouth? Didn't that mean to act rudely? Lazare wondered what it meant to Ben.

The boy began picking at the cloth bandage. The stinging had eased but was still prickling Laz's palm. He wasn't sure dirty salt water was good for his cuts and wanted to say so. Before he could, Ben removed the bandage with a final tug. Laz hissed as one section of the deeper cut started bleeding again.

Ben swished Laz's hand around and drew it out of the water. He dabbed at the blood with a corner of the discarded bandage. "There. Now for the new dressing."

"Are you the surgeon's assistant or something?"

"I don't have enough learning for that. But I watch him. I watch everything." Like the captain had, Ben made a pad with several strips of cloth, laid it on Laz's palm, then secured it with the last strip. He dropped the dirty bandage in the water and tucked the knife away. "Let's go on deck and see if the storm is breaking."

On the forecastle deck the boys settled on two coiled piles of rope beside the railing that overlooked the main deck. Laz's sleeves hadn't quite dried in the warmth below deck, and the cold cloth slapping his arms in the wind made him shiver. Ben had a coat and a red tuque (a knitted cap), so Laz asked him if there was any way to get his coat back.

"No. Cap'n sent Silent Joe back to shore with orders to burn it all, and to not show anyone what he carried. He was ill at ease over those clothes." Ben looked Laz up and down. "They were right uncouth, but so is everything about you."

Laz realized that *uncouth* meant strange. He agreed that this whole thing felt highly uncouth. Out-of-this-world uncouth. "I can't believe he'd burn my clothes. What a jerk." (*Text to Ryder: forced to cross-dress. DM gone too far*)

Ben gave Laz an alarmed look and shouted to a passing sailor, asking about outer vestments for the prisoner. The word made the shackles feel heavier to Laz. He adjusted them so a strand of rope took some of their weight off his tender ankles.

The man returned with a ratty brown coat and a red tuque like Ben's. Laz thanked him. The coat was too big, but it helped a lot. The wool tuque refused to fit over Laz's wavy hair and kept inching upwards as it tried to shrink to its original size.

Feeling warmer, Laz decided sitting was better than clanking around like the ghost in *A Christmas Carol*. The morning passed with him searching the horizons of the bay and the water for signs of modern life. Ben dozed.

Laz asked a sailor who was returning from the head, "Where are we?"

He walked over, adjusting his dark red breeches. "Being Acadian, and near to home, why would you need to ask?" When Laz turned up his palms, silently asking the question again, the man squinted at the shore. "We delivered goods to Fort Anne after the French and Mi'kmaq attacked last August. Asked some locals about harbors and such. They said the Mi'kmaq talk about fishing in summer on a big bay they call Chebucto. The captain thinks that's where we are." He kicked Laz's wooden shoe. "You tell me, Acadian, is this Chebucto?"

Laz searched his memory, trying to recall where he had heard that word. Then he remembered his mom giving directions from the airport into downtown Halifax. She had said to turn onto Chebucto Road. Laz's stomach turned queasy. "Why did you stop here?"

"Driven by a storm. You were delivered to the ship with the eye of the storm above. It's almost spent. Now we wait for the tide to turn."

The first day in Halifax, Laz and his family had arrived in early afternoon, and they had gone on a harbor tour on an old ship. The tall ship, *Silva*, had three masts and a motor. It had gone toward the ocean, around an island with old fortifications, then had come back through the Narrows, almost to the first bridge. Beyond the bridge they had seen a large natural harbor, thick with ships. The tour guide had called it Bedford Basin.

Laz stood and squinted at the shorelines, taking in the shape of this bay, then peered at the narrow exit to the sea. "Is there an island down that channel?"

"Aye. If not for the captain's good sailing we would have wrecked on it when the storm drove us inland. So, Acadian, is this Chebucto?"

This bay had the same shape as Bedford Basin, the same narrow entrance. Laz's mind churned. Chebucto, the local tribe's name for the bay in 1745, was echoed by a road's name in modern Halifax. Laz rubbed his chest, remembering the heat of his medallion—St. Christopher, the patron saint of travelers. An idea hit Laz: Had he traveled through that battlement tunnel, not to a place, but to a *time*? He wanted the question to be wrong, but it felt right.

"Well?" The voice startled Laz from his thoughts.

Dread became an iron band that squeezed Laz's chest, making it hard to breathe. He inhaled slowly. "I hope not, but...I think it is."

CHAPTER EIGHT

Laz suddenly felt very sick, and he just managed to drag his chains to the side of the ship before he doubled over the railing and heaved. Pottage spewed down the planks and splattered a window. He sagged onto the nearest cannon barrel and cradled his head in his hands.

This couldn't be 1745, he thought. *But everything fits*, a stubborn voice inside replied—the way the captain had treated him, the real swords, the food, the way no one ever sounded modern for even a second, and no signs of anything modern, not even a jet trail in the sky.

His stomach lurched again, and he fell against the rail but only sour spittle came up.

A hand gripped his shoulder. Ben said, "Are you ill, Lazare?"

"Don't touch me!" Laz pushed him away and crumpled to the deck. He leaned against the rail and interlocked his fingers behind his neck. His cut palm pulsed under his ear.

"You look pale," Ben said, "as if you've seen a specter."

Laz squinted at him. "A 250-year-old one." He closed his eyes and silently begged it to not be real. (*Text to Ryder: need rescue by Doctor Who*)

"Mayhap I should fetch the surgeon?" Ben sounded worried.

"Keep your surgeon. I just want my life back."

"Don't be like that." Ben sat down. "I thought we were becoming friends."

"Right. Shackles are a sure sign of friendship." Laz wanted to take the words back when he saw Ben's hurt expression.

"I'd unlock the irons if I could. But Cap'n doesn't listen to lowly sorts like me. I'm guessing he wants the men to all know you're a prisoner, and be wary."

Laz peered between the rails. On the shore, the bonfires had burned down to black mounds. Men pulled rowboats into the water and piled in. There had to be a few hundred of them, with more coming out of the forest.

An expedition, Captain Hawkins had said. Laz's father had been in the military, and this looked to him like an army on the move. He watched the rowboats get pushed away from shore by men gathered there. "What happened in 1745?" He asked himself and spat to the side, hoping to get rid of the taste of vomit.

"What do you mean?" Ben asked. "This is 1745. Look around you."

Laz pointed. "I'm looking. What's happening?"

"Those are the militia we're transporting to Canso," Ben said. "They're such landlubbers that they camped in that sodden forest rather than ride out a few waves."

"Why did the captain arrest me for being Acadian?" Laz wondered.

"You must know King George's War against the French started a year ago. Lots of New Englanders think the Acadians will help the French, even though they said they won't. And now here you are, spying on us."

The man in the dark red breeches, who'd asked about Chebucto, stopped beside the boys. "Sounds to me like you're helping him spy, Ben. Will you tell him our whole plan?"

"I don't know it," Ben replied, eyes wide.

"A good thing. Get to the quarterdeck. Captain wants you." The man braced one leg on the railing and crossed his arms. "Ben's a trusting soul. You hurt him, Acadian, and the whole crew will be begging to serve up a share of lashes to you."

Lips pressed together, Laz gave a nod. He wasn't going to hurt the only person who was being nice. The rowboats surged through the lessening chop, bringing the militia closer with every turn of the oar. *What was King George's War?* Laz wondered. He couldn't recall if it was something he'd learned in school. If he had, he'd forgotten it, like most history.

Rowboats bumped into the side of the ship. Men scrambled onto the main deck; slower ones dragged themselves over the rail and fell to the deck to be helped up by laughing friends. At least two-dozen men milled on the deck, their packs piled beside the main mast. There was more laughter and loud comments. Some men pointed at Laz, which made the band around his chest return and squeeze.

Red Breeches stayed beside him. No one came up the stairs beside Laz, though a few ventured up the other stairs, disappeared to the head area by the bowsprit, and returned the same way. *Do I have the plague?* Laz wondered. Hoping it wasn't still around in the 1740s, he decided the men had been told to leave him alone.

Three rowboats delivered more men. There were around fifty now, plus the crew, so maybe seventy men all together onboard. The other ships were smaller, but Laz guessed there had to be more than 500 gathered on these dozen ships. That sounded like enough militia to cause a lot of trouble.

A wave of longing crashed over Laz. He wanted to be home. No matter how much he argued with his dad, being put in irons was never a punishment. Laz rubbed his stocking-clad legs above their shackles and studied the fetters, as the captain had called them. Inner hinges curved around to the bulky cylindrical locks. The chain was welded on to the back of the cuffs.

"You can't pick those locks," Red Breeches said. "Attempted escape will earn lashes too. Ever tasted the cat? Nine tails with nine claws that rip your back to shreds in no time at all."

Laz licked his lips. His suddenly dry mouth sharpened the taste of vomit. "Could I get a drink of water?"

Red Breeches shouted, "Ahoy, militiamen. Our Acadian prisoner is thirsty. Any of you have a canteen on you?" He narrowed sky blue eyes. "One canteen enough, Acadian?"

"Stop calling me that," Laz said. "I have one Acadian grandmother. My father works in Boston and we live in Newtown. I'm not what you think I am."

"Newtown?" With a doubtful snort, he called, "Anyone come from Newtown near Boston? That's where this Acadian claims he hails from. Says he isn't really Acadian. Only has an Acadian grandmother."

Someone replied, "Aye, that's like King George saying he isn't English." The laughter that followed had a mean edge. Laz licked his lips again.

A dozen militiamen broke away from the group and stomped up the stairs closest to him. One spoke up. "Cooper here says he's from Newtown. Stand up so he can look at you."

Before Laz could move, two of the men grabbed his arms and hauled him up. Laz was slightly taller than the hook-nosed, scrawny man who stepped forward to study his face. His fishy breath clogged Laz's nostrils. His stringy hair and smudged jaw made Laz wonder if he ever bathed.

He spat on Laz's shoe. "True there be eleven hundred souls in Newtown now, but I've delivered wood to most of 'em, and I never seen this one."

"That's a lot of people for you to be so sure," Laz said quietly.

"Aye. It's a number of folks, but hear you talk. There's not a soul who speaks like that in Newtown or any town around. Funny sounding, to be sure."

"Aye," said the man holding Laz's left arm. "Might be what a Frenchie sounds like if he speaks English. "Look at him, lads. Dark-eyed and skin that looks as tan as mine after a summer of working in the fields."

"Olive-skinned they call it," Red Breeches said, "probably because of olives that grow in the south of France and Italy and those hot places." He was enjoying getting the men upset.

The man on Laz's left grabbed a handful of his hair and yanked his head a quarter turn. "Look at this dark, curly hair. Not English hair. Lots of Frenchies have dark hair."

"A Frenchie nose too," Cooper said. "Straight as a stiff rooster."

Laz stared over their heads and tried to ignore their comments. As Ryder would say, he needed to keep his mouth shut. But it was hard.

Cooper leaned close and his foul breath fogged Laz's senses. "Say something in French, Acadian spy. Come on." He grabbed Laz's jaw and wrenched his head to face him. Then he started whispering awful things, insulting Laz over and over.

Several men chuckled when Cooper said, "Milk-livered Frenchie."

The insults got meaner, and started attacking Laz's family. He cried, "*Ferme ta bouche.*" (Shut your mouth.)

Cooper stepped back, arms raised in victory. The men holding Laz's arms kept him still. Cooper faced the other militiamen. "See, boys? As French as the day is long."

"What did he say?" Red Breeches asked.

"Don't know. Don't sound very polite, though." Cooper stepped to the side and sneered at Laz. "What say we give the Frenchie a lesson in manners, boys?"

"Huzzah!" Several fists pumped the air.

"What should we do, Cooper?" the one holding Laz's right arm asked.

Silence fell while Cooper studied him with a mean squint. "Didn't this start because the Frenchie wanted water?" He pointed toward the front of the ship. "Let's give 'em water."

"Can't toss 'em overboard," Red Breeches said. "Captain Hawkins wants to deliver him to Commander Pepperrell."

Cooper grinned, showing a smile with a missing tooth and two blackened ones. "Then we'll just use 'em for bait."

Laz tried to yank free, but both men held firm. Someone dragged the thick end of coiled rope he'd sat on earlier and handed it to Cooper. He looked Laz up and down then grinned again. Laz hated that grin.

"I'm not good with knots. Who wants to make sure our bait doesn't slip off the line?"

Red Breeches stepped forward. Cooper pointed at the chain and Red nodded. He tied a complicated knot through the center link of the chain connecting the two ankle cuffs. "Don't do this," Laz whispered.

"Be at ease, Acadian. We're only having a little fun." He wiped his hands on his jacket and nodded at the men holding Laz. "Take off his coat and shoes. Captain will be angry if we lose any of his kit."

The men peeled off the worn jacket. As one bent over to pull off his shoes, Laz kneed him in the forehead. He straightened and boxed an ear.

Laz's head was ringing as they dragged him around the cannons to where the forecastle deck curved toward the bowsprit. They bent Laz over the rail. The waves slapped the ship over two decks below. Then someone held his wrists together and tied them.

Laz yelled, "No!"

They dumped him over the edge. He flopped down several feet and jerked to a stop. Bumped against the ship. When he tried to twist to look up, grinning faces lined the rail. Someone out of sight anchored the rope.

He called, "Pull me up! Cooper!"

The grinning man leaned over the rail, raised his hand and brought it down. The rope played out, lowering Laz in jerks and jolts. Stomach in his throat, heat pooling in his head, he yelled for them to stop. He twisted and strained. Saw men on another ship watching.

"Help me! Help!"

The downward movement quit when Laz was a foot above the waves, His head and heart both thudded like a rapid drumbeat. The iron cuffs scraped at the tops of his feet and heels, but they held. Laz tried to calm down and breathe slowly as he waited to be raised back up. Red said they were just having fun, he reminded himself.

Laz felt a notch of upward movement. A few inches. A few more. He closed his eyes and whispered, "Thank you."

The rope went slack.

Laz plunged under the water.

CHAPTER NINE

Liquid ice encased Laz. It seemed to press down and crush him as it tried to enter his mouth and nose.

With his arms tied, he thrashed but couldn't swim. Murky light waved above him, but he couldn't reach it. Rope floated down and his legs followed, dragged by their iron chains. Gravity pulled him deeper.

His lungs ached with their need for air. They expanded. Collapsed. Burned.

Lights strobed on the edge of his vision, a rainbow of nothingness. Laz knew he was almost out of air. He needed to fight. Instead, his body went limp.

Then his feet rose past his face, and his body twisted. The fighter in him woke up, and he struggled to hold his breath a little longer. The water grew lighter, and he felt a faint burst of hope. Then his lungs exploded. He gasped and water flooded into his throat. With a swish and splash, air brushed his cheeks, but he gaped like a fish, unable to feed his lungs.

Everything went black.

Laz woke on the deck, barfing saltwater onto the captain's boots. His lungs wheezed in air. Over the grating he heard voices, quiet, fading in and out, then louder.

A voice said something about fun. The captain's voice filled with fury that boomed over Laz. "This young man is not a source of entertainment. He is a prisoner. He is not *my* prisoner, he is the king's prisoner—the king's property—in the king's war. Do *any* of you pudding-headed fellows understand this? Would any one of you durst face the king, or even Commander Pepperell, and tell him you destroyed his property FOR A DRAM OF ENTERTAINMENT?"

In the silence, the only sound was air rasping into Laz's hungry lungs. His limbs began shaking.

Captain Hawkins, voice still vibrating with anger, said, "Turner, I expect better of my own men. You are on report. Kitchen duty until I say otherwise. As for you militiamen, your commanders will deal with you as they see fit, but while you are on my ship, you will have half rations, including rum."

A groan rippled through the men. Hawkins ordered four men to carry Laz down to lie beside the kitchen fire, where the warmth lured him to sleep. Twice he jerked awake, sure water had filled his lungs. Both times, Ben sat beside him with the firelight painting a worried look on his face.

The third time Laz woke, he felt the rocking of the ship beneath him, the creak of timbers; and he heard the flap of something in the wind. His cracked lips barely moved when he whispered, "Water."

Cool metal touched his chin. A hand lifted his head. Ben said, "Take a small sip."

Laz did, followed by another. After half a dozen sips, he took the stein's handle, downed the contents, and held the metal cup out for more. After the second cup, Laz flopped onto the pillow made from a rolled-up blanket. "This place is going to kill me," he whispered. The firelight showed it was night and he wondered how long he had slept.

Ben sat cross-legged by his knees. "You seem inclined to beckon trouble, Lazare Berenger."

"Huh," Laz said with a snort. "Do you know what made those men almost drown me? I was thirsty, so I asked Red Breeches for some water." He left out the part about arguing how much Acadian made a person Acadian.

"Red—do you mean Turner? He does have a liking for red breeches." Ben smiled. His smile dropped away. "If only I had seen what was happening sooner. Cap'n had me helping the militia officers get settled. You'd think they was dukes, the way they bossed me around."

"You saw it, not Hawkins?" Laz asked.

"Aye. When I saw them dragging you to the rail, I raced into his quarters. Cap'n was worrying over his maps. He started ripping strips off my hide with his tongue. I had to shout at him. Shout at my cap'n. I almost voided on the spot. When I hollered they was drowning you, he shot out of that room with a roar, like an angry mother bear."

"I wouldn't mind seeing that. Some other time."

Ben seemed shocked at the suggestion. "I would tremble if he came at me like that. A mama bear charged me once when I was six. I was too afraid to even move. My uncle's musket ball pierced her eye, or I'd have been ripped to pieces."

"Davy Crockett to the rescue," Laz said with a small smile.

"Who?"

"No one. He's probably not born yet." Seeing his puckered brow, Laz changed the subject. "Did I miss eating?" Who knew almost drowning was so tiring a person would sleep all day?

"We saved you food." Ben popped up and reached into a cubbyhole set into the fireplace above the mantel, then headed to a counter.

When Laz shifted to lean against a table leg, he wiggled his toes and wondered why his feet felt odd. He ripped off the blanket. The shackles were gone. So were those itchy stockings. Laz touched the raw, scraped skin on the tops of his feet and ran a finger near the ragged tear of skin on the back of his heel. (*Text to Ryder: never use leg irons to hang upside down*) Dread crawled over his skin, and he wondered how he was going to survive this place.

Ben returned with tea and a plate of stew with a biscuit sitting in the middle of it. "I knocked the weevils out for you."

The boy wore the same hopeful look Emeline always used on Laz. He wanted to roll his eyes, but instead he said, "Thanks." He broke off the top of the stone-hard biscuit and buried it in the stew to soften. He was so hungry he decided to not look for bugs. "Did the captain free me?"

"You're still a prisoner, but we're at sea now so there's nowhere to escape, unless you swim like a fish."

Laz shuddered. "I've given up swimming for a while."

"Aye. A sound plan. And you're safe now. The law has been laid down, and no one is to lay a finger on you."

"It's only right. I *am* the king's property. George, isn't it? George the what? Two? Three? Seventeen?" Laz spooned stew into his mouth, and his eye twitched at the saltiness of the meat. At least it was still warm. As he chewed he remembered the captain had said he was a subject of George the Second.

"Do not jest, Lazare," Ben replied. "You have it right, but that only means the only one who can kill you is the king, or in this case the commander of the expedition."

"You're a serious little dude." Laz broke up the biscuit and mixed it into the gravy.

"What is a dude?" Ben asked.

Laz paused, spoon almost to his mouth. "Ah. Where I'm from it means guy, man."

"So it's French?"

Laz's eyebrow raised and he said, "Sure."

He dropped the spoon onto the plate when Red Breeches stumbled into the kitchen. He pulled his legs out of the way as the man fiddled with the fire, stirred the embers, added wood, and jabbed it with an iron poker that had a nasty hook near its point. Red straightened and turned around, poker aimed in Laz's general direction, which made him stiffen.

Red yawned and leaned the poker against the fireplace. "The cook put me on fire duty instead of banking it. We had to keep the prisoner warm," he said. He scrubbed his face with both hands, as if still trying to wake up, then pulled a three-legged stool over to sit between Laz and the fire.

"What do you want, Turner?" Ben sounded almost hostile,

which amazed Laz. Turner looked equally surprised.

"I mean no harm, Ben. I only..." Turner rubbed his nose with the back of his hand. "I wanted to apologize to the Acadian."

"For almost killing me?" Laz ate some more stew and watched the struggle swirl over Turner's face.

"I thought Cooper was jesting, that he'd lower you down, maybe get your hair wet, then reel you up," the man said. "But they let out a good twenty feet of slack all at once and down you went—"

"I remember that part. It was being hauled back up I'm fuzzy about. Maybe because I had water in my lungs and I'd passed out." Saying it made Laz want to deck him. Except everyone in this place was stronger than him and he knew he'd get hammered. They all worked hard every day of their lives, where Laz used to call his mom to have her pick him up at a door rather than walk across a mall parking lot.

"I'm sorry, Acadian. Truly, I am," Turner said.

"That's why you let them hassle me, isn't it?" Laz said. "Why do you hate Acadians so much?"

"They're French." Turner rubbed his nose again and squinted at nothing. "I lived near Portsmouth, in a little fishing village on the coast. Last year French raiders attacked the town, emptied a warehouse of salt fish, and burned down a few buildings, including one family's home. A mother and young child perished. My house stood two doors down. It could have been my family." He searched Laz's face. "So I moved them to Portsmouth and signed on to the *Constance* crew."

"To fight a war."

"Not then. We were only running supplies. Governor Shirley organized this over the winter, and named Commander Pepperrell to lead us."

"Lead you where?" Laz asked.

Turner gripped his chin and narrowed his eyes. "Commander Pepperrell will be the one to decide how much you should know, Acadian."

"Yeah, I'm such a dangerous spy, or so I've heard. If you want me to accept your apology, you have to do something."

"What would that be?"

"Stop calling me Acadian. My name is Lazare Berenger. Call me either one."

After a moment, Turner nodded. "Might I ask something... Berenger?" Laz nodded and Turner said, "What did you say to Cooper in French?"

Laz replied, "I told him to shut his mouth."

Turner rubbed his nose. "I doubt many people are so bold, not even his commanders."

The way Laz had said it had been rude, and he wondered if being polite would have saved him a swim. He decided not. His short experience with Cooper showed him to be bone-deep nasty, and a good man to avoid. But in the meantime, Laz had a bed by the fire. After today, that was better than a new phone, and he planned to enjoy it as long as possible.

The night was too short, as it turned out cooks are early risers. Since Laz was awake, more or less, he offered to help and was handed the job of stirring the pottage. He didn't mind because it kept him by the fire. He found out that hardtack biscuits were made ahead of a voyage and could last for months, which explained a lot. He was amazed weevils could bore through them at all.

Another advantage to helping the cook was eating first. Laz tried his biscuit dipped in tea, which made it taste like chewy cardboard. After he ate, he left the forecastle and its sickening mix of smells, which were worse with food in the belly.

Militiamen crowded the main deck, where they'd apparently camped. Only one sailor, who was examining the rigging, was on the more exposed forecastle deck. So that's where Laz settled, right where he'd been tossed over the rail. Ben said the captain had ordered the men to leave him alone, so Laz figured staying there would remind the men of that. And Laz felt as if he needed to face the spot. It was like getting back on a horse after it had bucked you off. His Grandmère had said that before, and he only now understood it.

Laz spent the morning searching the water and sky for signs of 2017. The longer he searched, the more trapped he felt. How was he supposed to get home? If the way home was through that tunnel, it was hopeless because he didn't even know what direction they had sailed from Chebucto. He kept hoping it had something to do with his St. Christopher medal—why else had it been hot against his skin after?

After that...he'd slipped through time? He recalled what he had thought was a dream, sliding down a black spiral. He wondered if it had been a wormhole, which sounded crazy.

Could he be locked in a twenty-first-century psych ward and imaging this? But how could he come up with so much detail when he had never been interested in, or read anything about, 1745?

As the afternoon wore on, Laz began stalking the perimeter of the forecastle deck. He marched past the main deck railing, turned right past the left (port) railing and cannons, turned right past the front railing overlooking the head and bowsprit, turned right past the right (couldn't remember what it was called) railing and cannons. Over and over. With hands in his pockets and red tuque jammed over his ears, he was at least partially warm.

Pacing held the cold at bay, but it also kept the black shadow of panic flapping behind Laz from landing and digging in its talons. He usually had a snappy answer, and a quick reaction time, but now his mind was blanking. He felt so uncertain. All he wanted to do was curl into a ball and whimper. (*Text to Ryder: if u find my guts, fedex them to me*)

A sail snapped in the wind and Laz ducked then chided himself to get a grip. He resumed pacing, until someone stepped in his path. Red Breeches—Turner—scowled at him. With his stringy blond hair, green eyes, and days-old stubble, he reminded Laz of an actor, but he couldn't think who. *If only he is one*, Laz thought. He sidestepped to go around, but Turner placed his hand on Laz's chest to stop him.

"The cook demands the clomping cease, or he will be coming up with his cleaver." When Laz didn't react, Turner sighed. "And Ben is worried about you, Acad—Berenger. He called to you several times, yet you failed to reply."

Laz couldn't think why it mattered that Ben was worried, not when he was trapped in a world where he didn't belong. He blinked at Turner like the man was talking another language.

Turner said, "Some of the crew are starting to whisper that you're mad."

Laz worked his jaw then replied, "Maybe I am."

Turner's fingers curled in the loose jacket material and he pulled Laz close. "Madness, like witchery, comes from the devil. They will toss you overboard in chains again, without an anchoring rope, before inviting calamity by allowing madness onboard."

Iron clamped around Laz's ribs. "No," he whispered. "They wouldn't."

"They would. And Captain Hawkins wouldn't stop them."

Laz tried to swallow. He realized Turner was attempting to help so he told the man half the truth. "Thoughts keep going round and round. I can't stop them. I feel trapped."

"A person cannot outrun his own thoughts. Being a prisoner must be a hard thing, but you have to find peace. Mayhap if you found something to do."

"Like stirring pottage? That'll only give me more time to think and I'll freak out completely," Laz said.

Frown in place, Turner tilted his head. "You Acadians have uncouth turns of phrase."

"Trust me, so do you." Now that he'd stopped moving, Laz's feet started to ache. Wooden shoes were not made for comfort. He asked, "So what could I do?"

Turner smiled. "Mayhap the cook would release me from kitchen duty if I told him you are willing to help me mend sail."

"Sew? You want me to sew?"

"It takes concentration to do a good job. It might still your restless thoughts."

After a long pause, Laz managed a weak nod. "A good thing there won't be pictures. I'd never live it down."

CHAPTER TEN

Turner led Laz into the hold, where a spot had been cleared and two men sat in a circle of four lanterns, repairing a sail. "Lads, I've brought a lubber willing to give a helping hand."

The men groaned and shook their heads. Turner got two short stools, widened the circle, and unrolled a bundle of tools. He motioned for Laz to sit and said, "Storms are hard on gaff-rigged ships. Our sails aren't sleek like a Bermuda sloop's, but we're fast when the wind is up. Two of our forward sails were damaged in the storm's shifting winds, so here we be. Our favorite task, right, lads?" They groaned again but didn't look up.

"Why are we down here?" Laz asked.

"The wind is brisk enough to make repairs on the forecastle deck difficult. And the main deck is occupied by militiamen. I should think you've had enough of them."

Not waiting for a reply, Turner began teaching Laz how to mend a sail. He had imagined the cross-stitching with tiny needles his mom did some evenings. "Girl's work," he'd told Emeline when she'd said he should try. But these tools looked like a shoemaker's. The oversized needles were triangular and dull, so they didn't rip the canvas. Turner was right that it took lots of concentration to follow his directions.

The rest of the afternoon, some of the evening, and all the next morning, Laz holed up with Turner and the others in the dim light, doing repairs. His shoulders and hands were sore, but he refused to admit it. Ben popped in occasionally, always with a big smile when he saw Laz working, and a declaration that they'd make a sailor of him yet. (*Text to Ryder: if I can't get back I might take to the sea. It's a pirate's life for me.*)

Laz didn't mind being at sea—the motion didn't bother him—but not returning to his life at home was too awful to consider. No pizza or spicy Thai food? Never going to the movies, texting with friends, driving into Boston in forty minutes, or flying to Moncton in a couple hours to see Grandmère? And never using a flush toilet again? Ben had no idea how much Laz hated using that head, balancing on a rectangular box set on a triangular spit of wood to go to the bathroom into the ocean. He had to get home.

They went for lunch, scraped the bottom of the pot, which peppered their pottage with charcoal flecks. "This is disgusting." Laz studied the congealing mess on his spoon then washed it down with lukewarm tea.

"Never let the cook hear you complain," Turner whispered, "or you'll end up with rotten meat in your next bowl. Gives a nasty bout of flux."

Ben bounded into the forecastle. "We're almost to Canso! They've struck the forward sails and are racing to the top." He bolted toward the deck.

Plates and spoons clattered as the men hurried to follow, so Laz did too. Outside, all the militiamen were gathered on the main deck, craning their necks to watch two sailors race up the ropes and rigging to reach a small square platform above where the big lower sail normally billowed out. Laz joined Turner and Ben on the forecastle deck with the other sailors, all loudly cheering. It was like the 100-meter Olympic race, over in seconds it seemed.

Laz asked, "Why didn't they get onto the platform through its hole near the mast. That looks easier than getting on it over the outside edge."

"That's the Lubber's Hole," Ben replied. "No sailor would embarrass himself by using it."

"The safe way?"

"Aye. For lubbers and the like."

They watched two more races, then Turner challenged Cringle. Laz yelled himself hoarse for Turner to win, but it was so close no one could tell. The captain gave the race to Cringle. "Because he's been on the crew longer," Ben muttered.

One of the militiamen said that he wanted a go. At the back of the group, Laz peered between the heads of the sailors, certain the voice was familiar. It was Cooper, the man who'd tossed Laz overboard.

"Well?" Cooper shouted. "Is no one brave enough to take me on?"

"Yer a lubber," Cringle replied. "Even Ben could beat you with one hand tied behind his back. It's not a fair race. Most lubbers can't climb halfway before they start to tremble."

"I've built houses and barns and can climb rafters with the best of 'em. Come on. There must be one amongst you who doesn't mind losing to a militiaman. Winner's side gets the other's rum rations. There's more of us so you'd each get two extra rations."

Laz had been watching how the men had climbed. It was parkour on ropes.

He yelled, "I'll do it."

Men stepped back, forming an aisle, and Laz made his way to the front, where Captain Hawkins stood with arms crossed and scowl firmly in place.

"You are not one of my crew," Hawkins said.

"I've been sewing your sails for two days," Laz replied. "Besides, this makes it a fair race. Lubber against lubber."

Hawkins didn't immediately refuse. But Cooper spat onto the boards. "You told us we couldn't touch him, yet you'll let him climb and probably die from a fall?"

"I'm not going to fall. But if you're not brave enough to take me on..."

Cooper sneered. The captain snorted. "If you race, you follow our rules." Laz nodded. Cooper glared at him but also nodded. Hawkins said, "A clean win is over the futtock shrouds, not through the lubber's hole."

Laz kicked off his shoes and stripped off his stockings and garters. He added the tuque and outer jacket to the pile, then started to unbutton his waistcoat's dozen buttons.

"Will you race naked?" Cooper's perpetual sneer deepened.

"The sailors raced without their waistcoats, so I'm going to as well." Laz dropped the long vest on top of the coat. He held out his arms. "Where I come from, naked means without clothes. I'm not naked."

"You're indecent," Cooper said.

"And you're ugly," Laz replied.

"No need to be boorish, young Berenger," said Hawkins.

"Sure there is. A man dumping you in the water makes you all kinds of boorish."

Cooper spat again. "No less than a spying scab deserves."

The captain ordered them to silence. Laz rubbed his palms on his thighs, glanced at his cut palm, healing enough that blood no longer stained the bandage. A climb might change that.

Hawkins noticed the glance. "Are you up for it, Berenger?"

Laz nodded and took his place at the base of the shrouds, the vertical ropes that were anchored below. Evenly spaced thinner lines were fastened horizontally to turn the shrouds into a rope ladder. The trick, from what he'd seen, was to keep one hand on the outer shroud, not on the thinner lines, and you could shift your hands upward more quickly.

Cooper kept on his shoes and long vest. He glared at Laz from the base of the facing shrouds.

The captain extended his sword horizontally. His blade slashed down and Laz shot up. The ropes dug into his feet but he climbed so fast they didn't have time to hurt. Both groups of men shouted below. Laz only looked up as he kept moving.

The shrouds tapered to their anchor point through the lubber's hole. About four feet down from that he came to the shrouds that ran from an anchoring arm up and over the edge of the platform. He swung onto those. His feet lost their grip and his legs dangled. A gasp rose up from below. Rather than flail, Laz climbed the angled rope ladder like monkey bars. When his knuckles brushed the platform he reached three rungs up and hauled himself over the edge, high enough to set his knee on top and push up to stand. The sailors below cheered, throwing tuques and tricorns into the air. Laz grinned.

Gripping the shrouds, he leaned over the edge of the platform to see Cooper, red-faced, making his way up the inverted incline just below the platform. "Nice view from up here," Laz said. "You should come on up." Cooper's face took on a purple hue. Laz grinned then looked around.

The ship was approaching a harbor formed by some islands to the right and mainland to the left. Farther along the coast was a scattering of small islands. There were already at least fifty ships in the harbor, all flying the same colors as the *Constance*, a red flag with a red cross and a smaller British flag in the top left quadrant.

"An invasion force," Laz whispered. From this high it looked like a forest of masts dotted by red flowers.

A hand seized Laz's ankle. Startled, he looked down into Cooper's sneering face. His one arm was woven through the rope rungs of the shrouds and his feet were still below the platform. Without thinking, Laz offered his hand.

Cooper grabbed it and yanked. Laz flew off the platform.

CHAPTER ELEVEN

In the air, everything seemed to move in slow motion. Cooper had pulled Laz off the platform in line with the wooden arm that usually anchored the top of the big sail. Laz grabbed the diagonal rope that ran from the mast above him to the end of the arm.

He swung almost full circle around the rope. His shins cracked against the wooden arm and he almost lost his grip. He clutched the sail rolled up on top of the arm. His heart jackhammered in his chest and ears. People below were shouting, but he couldn't hear them.

Laz straddled the arm and caught his breath. His knuckles were white from gripping the rope that had saved him. Cooper sat on the platform, hatred distorting his face. He pivoted on his butt, dangled his feet down the lubber's hole, then started down the shrouds.

Not wanting to be anywhere near Cooper, Laz worked his way along the arm, almost to its end. People were shouting for him to go back to the shrouds. Instead Laz leaned over and grabbed some rigging that ran diagonally from the end of the arm he sat on to where the foremast's boom met the mast. (*Text to Ryder: need zipline. Send ASAP.*)

Firmly gripping the line with both hands, Laz swung off the wooden arm and worked his way down, hand over hand, legs swaying. Gravity tried to speed him up, and his neck and shoulders trembled with the effort of keeping a steady pace.

When his feet touched the boom, Laz stood on the thick wooden arm and held onto the diagonal rope. Hawkins regarded him with raised eyebrows. Laz smiled. He felt like he was in *Pirates of the Caribbean*. He gave a small bow. "Permission to come aboard, Captain?"

"Don't be pudding-headed," Hawkins replied. "Above my ship's deck is still on my ship. Get down here, Berenger."

Laz jumped the six feet down to the deck, landing in a crouch like his dad had taught him years earlier. He straightened, spotted Cooper, and started forward.

Hawkins blocked Laz's way and grabbed him by the shirt. "A prisoner who attacks any member of this expedition will feel the lash, Berenger. You do not want that."

Laz jabbed his finger at Cooper. "Did you see what he did?"

"From down here, we saw you bend over and lose your balance. How or why is your word against his." Hawkins' grip on Laz's shirt stayed firm.

"The man's a, a—" Laz tried to think of an old-fashioned word. "A rabble-rouser."

Hawkins' eyebrows lifted slightly. "Or you are clumsy. One thing for certain, you are an impertinent fellow who would rather divert the crew than see to his own safety."

Laz sputtered. He'd never been clumsy. Hawkins almost smiled, apparently pleased with Laz's irritation, then released him and ordered Cooper to return to the main deck. The captain approached the rail overlooking the militiamen. "All hands will remain on board today and tonight, while your captain and I go ashore to report to Commander Pepperrell and to make arrangements for your quarters there." He pointed toward the quarterdeck. "My second-in-command, Lieutenant Sherwood, is in command of everyone on board this ship until we return. Failure to obey him will be punished." He clasped his hands behind his back. "On a kinder note, I would like to thank Mister Cooper for generously donating all your rum rations to my sailors. Enjoy your evening, gentlemen."

The militiamen began grumbling. Laz's grin almost split his face. Cooper would not be treated nicely by the sounds of it. (*Text to Ryder: revenge is sweet*)

Laz turned to find Ben, whose eyes were like CDs. "How did you do that? You were born to be a sailor, Lazare." His eyebrows scrunched together. "I wish we weren't enemies. Then you could list with *Constance*'s crew. Cap'n likes you, even if you do give him cheek somewhat."

Turner clamped his hand on Laz's aching shoulder. "Can't be calling you a lubber, Berenger. You might want to see to your hands, and get in the forecastle out of sight of those militiamen. They will blame you as much as Cooper for losing their rum."

They insisted Laz soak both hands in saltwater, and ignored him when he suggested plain boiled water. Mild rope burns scored his left palm. The cuts on the right palm broke open again, but weren't bleeding as much as they first had, so Laz figured they were healing despite his abuse. Someone brought his clothes and shoes and patted him on the back. Laz shrugged into the waistcoat but left it unbuttoned. Over the next few hours, almost every sailor gave him a pat or gentle punch on the arm.

After a festive supper—pottage with meat *and* beans—someone pulled out his fiddle.

The men sang and jigged and laughed. The rum came out. Lieutenant Sherwood banged down a cup on the table in front of Laz. "There you go, Berenger. Your tot of rum plus two."

"Um. But I'm the prisoner," Laz replied. "Do prisoners usually get rum?"

"Of course not, but you won it for us, so drink up."

Sherwood raised his own stein, so Laz did the same. He nodded. "Cheers."

Laz responded with the French, "*Santé*," which earned him a doubtful squint.

They both drank. Laz only took a sip, but the rum seized his throat then burst into flames and flushed into his stomach. His mouth opened and closed, opened and closed. Finally, he coughed and managed to get some air into his lungs.

Sherwood laughed and joined the circle around Cringle, who was jigging like a crazy person. Laz pretended to sip more rum. He dipped his fingers in the alcohol and sprinkled some on his cuts, then waved his hand to soothe the stinging.

Laz listened to stories, slapped his thigh in time to the music, and pretended for a night that he was part of the crew. It was a good feeling. He'd set down his cup but when he checked, it was magically empty. He was relieved to avoid drinking the rum.

Much later Laz fell asleep to the drumming of shoes on the floor and the high-pitched joy of the fiddle, and dreamed of his Grandmère dancing the jig and calling him to join her.

Someone shook Laz hard, and wouldn't quit shaking him. He swatted at the arm and got cuffed on his ear. He rolled onto his back. "Leave me—" Captain Hawkins scowled down at him. "Oh. Um. Morning, Captain," Laz said. He had stayed up too late and felt exhausted.

Hawkins straightened. "Wake up, boy. Commander Pepperell wants to interview you."

Fog clung to Laz's thoughts. "Who?"

Hawkins leaned over again. "Pepperrell. The commander of this expedition. And the man who will decide your fate, Lazare Berenger."

Worry slammed into Laz and he had the sudden urge to vomit.

CHAPTER TWELVE

Hawkins led Laz to his commander like a dog on a leash, holding onto rope that bound Laz's hands instead of his neck. And he'd left off the shackles. Laz thanked him for that.

There were no docks, just charred remains, so two sailors rowed them to shore. Laz was so nervous that the motion of riding the waves left him feeling queasy. He threw up into the water.

"Did you have too much rum, Berenger?" Hawkins asked. Laz shook his head.

The sailors dragged the skiff onto a grassy shore. The freshly trampled path led up a hill to the burned skeleton of a fort. Scrubby bushes and the odd clump of evergreens littered the hillside. Everywhere men carved out space for campsites.

"Where are we?" Laz asked. He felt a headache starting.

Hawkins surveyed the hillside and peered across the bay, where the blackened remains of a village crouched against the browns and yellow-greens of early spring. "Canso."

He spoke the word firmly, as if Laz should know it. When Laz shrugged, Hawkins pressed his lips together for a moment before he said, "Last May, French from Louisbourg overtook this fort, pillaged the town, made prisoners of the men, and shipped everyone else to Boston. You cannot tell me this is news, even if you are from a very isolated Acadian community." His eyes narrowed. "Which community are you from? Given where we found you, I assumed you came from the settlements north of Annapolis Royal, Grand-Pré maybe."

Laz's Grandmère lived on the west side of the Bay of Fundy. Since he didn't know if Moncton existed in 1745, he nodded and faced the fort. "Was anyone killed?"

"One, I believe. A few were wounded. The French caught them unawares so they surrendered without much of a fight." Hawkins resumed the uphill walk. "Odd that you wouldn't know this if they sent you to spy on us."

"Odder than you will ever know," Laz muttered. Since the captain was talkative, Laz asked, "What's the army for? Going to invade something?" Hawkins fell silent and walked faster. Laz tugged on the rope, making Hawkins falter for half a step. "Come on, Captain. Who can I tell? I'm your prisoner. Even if I could escape, I wouldn't know where to go because I don't have a clue where Canso is."

Hawkins cast Laz a puzzled look. They reached the top of the hill, the highest in the area, which made it a good site for a fort, though it hadn't saved this one. The fort looked to have been mostly wood, even the outer walls. *Great firewood*, thought Laz. Hawkins led him to a huge canvas tent set up close to the burned-out fort, on what seemed to be the sheltered side.

"Nice of you to deliver me, Captain. Makes me feel special," Laz said.

"I brought you because I wish to be present for the interview."

Inside the tent, a man leaned over a table examining a map. He was dressed in red—breeches, waistcoat, jacket—with white stockings and black buckled shoes. A real Santa Claus, but one with a thing for buttons. Gold buttons ran the length of both his long waistcoat and his jacket, and buttons even decorated the jacket's cuff which folded back almost to his elbow. Frilly lace on his shirt cuffs and necktie, and a puffy white wig ensured that Commander Pepperrell won the prize for snobby twit, Laz thought.

When the man didn't look up immediately, Laz peered at the map. It looked like a piece of a larger map. On the near edge, a cluster of islands was clearly marked Canso Islands. The man in red was studying a place farther north. When he straightened, he flattened his hands on either side of where he'd been looking, and Laz saw the name: Louisbourg. On the walk up, Hawkins had mentioned the "French from Louisbourg." So it had to be the reason for this expedition.

"Getting a good look at my map?" the man asked.

Laz snapped his gaze upward but didn't say anything. Then he noticed a man in a plain outfit, standing silently in the corner. A slave, Laz guessed, by his dark skin and lowered gaze. He thought that might even be worse than being a prisoner. He felt slightly ill, realizing these men thought slavery was fine.

The man in red moved to a wooden chair, sat down and propped his feet on a matching footstool. He rested his elbows on the chair arms and interlocked his fingers over his stomach bulge. He looked Laz up and down, very thoroughly. Laz felt like he was inspecting a new lawn tractor, deciding whether he wanted to buy it. Finally, he invited Hawkins to sit in the chair facing him.

Laz wasn't invited to sit. The rope looped from his wrists to Hawkins' hand where two strands coiled snuggly over his knuckles. Laz couldn't run anyway, not with two men outside the tent holding flintlock muskets. Years of living with a military dad interested in family history meant Laz knew old muskets and rifles.

Hawkins explained where they'd found Laz, what he'd been wearing, and why they'd burned his clothes. Laz missed those comfy Vans. His wooden shoes were giving him blisters. Hawkins explained about questioning Laz, but made no mention of his claim it was 2017.

Pepperrell might have dressed like a fool, but his expression was very shrewd. He watched Hawkins a bit, and Laz a lot.

When silence took over, Pepperrell let it simmer for a minute while he continued to study Laz, who ended up looking over the commander's shoulder. The band had returned to hug Laz's ribs. Feeling uneasy made his headache thud more rapidly.

"Well," Pepperrell said, "there's no doubting, from your name and appearance, that you are French."

"Acadian," Laz corrected. His grandmère would have fits if he said he was French.

"A quibble. Your ancestry is French." He steepled his fingers in front of his double chin. "What should I do with you, Lazare Berenger?"

The band tightened more as Laz said, "I'm not a spy."

"Oh. There is no doubt you are a spy. Protestations will earn you only contempt, boy."

Laz released a slow breath, trying to ease his tension. "You could let me go."

The man tapped his index fingers together then touched them to his chin. "That is most certainly not an option. If you were a French officer, I would allow your freedom within my camp, for I know your word would be sure and you would not flee. But Acadians are a rough lot, peasants who mixed with local tribes from what I've heard, and as such you are not trustworthy."

Laz felt his jaw go slack. He snapped his mouth closed.

"Regardless, this is a different situation, is it not?" Pepperrell said.

"How?" Laz asked.

"You are not a regular officer in enemy forces. A man convicted of spying during wartime is subject to death by hanging. And you, being an Acadian living under British domain; well, your spying is treason. Also a hanging offence."

Laz backpedalled until the rope on his wrist grew taut. He could barely breathe as the iron shackle on his lungs squeezed. He shook his head. "You can't mean that."

Pepperrell sat straighter and gripped the arms of his chair. "I do mean it, young sir. You do not have neckwear, but soon you will, and it will be a hangman's noose."

CHAPTER THIRTEEN

Laz's vision blurred. He couldn't believe this was happening. He was going to wake up and it wouldn't be 1745, and this jerk in tights wouldn't be sitting in front of him like a red space slug, saying he was going to hang Laz. For being a spy.

I'm not a spy, Laz thought. *I'm a stupid kid who had a stupid fight with his dad and stomped into a stupid tunnel where I fell through a stupid hole in time.* He gulped air. This couldn't be how it ended. He had to get back. He'd do anything, promise anything, so long as he got home.

Laz felt like the noose was already choking him. He gasped, desperate for air. Pain radiated up his arms, through his shoulders. "Berenger!" He blinked at the sharp sound of his name and Captain Hawkins' face came into focus.

Hawkins approached Laz, winding the rope around his fist as he did so. In his retreat Laz had pulled it so tight that it dug into his wrists. Hawkins talked quietly, as if to a spooked animal. "Calm down, Berenger. Don't shake your head at me. You must remain calm. All will be well."

Be well? They were going to hang him, but it was going to be *well*? Laz started to retreat again but Hawkins' massive hand clamped onto his shoulder and held him immobile. Hawkins faced Pepperrell. "Sir, I respect that you are the commander of this expedition, but you cannot simply hang someone without a trial. The king would never do such a thing."

Pepperrell stood and clasped his hands behind his back, which made his stomach round out. "We are mounting an attack. We do not have time to dally with trials."

"With all respect, sir, I suggest we hold him prisoner until after the attack, at which time we will have time for a trial. He is from an Acadian settlement near Annapolis Royal, an area under British rule. As such, he must be accorded the rights of a British citizen."

This logic irritated the commander, which loosened the iron shackle around Laz's chest enough he could breathe more normally. Pepperrell said, "And if he escapes?"

"He is a mere youth, a man in size but not in temperament. He cannot harm us. I doubt he could even make it to Louisbourg to warn them. It's a long distance on foot, and first he'd have to get to the island, what do the French call it? Île Royale?"

Listen to him, Laz thought.

Pepperrell looked down his long nose. "What would we do with him in the meanwhile? I suppose you think he should be left in your hands?"

"I would say yes, Commander, except you've assigned the *Constance* to join the ships blockading the fortress' shipping lanes. Having a prisoner along would be ill-advised."

"Indeed. I shall have to find a militia unit willing to watch over him, and mayhap put him to work. Which militia units were on your ship? They might be a good choice."

Hawkins cleared his throat. "I would suggest looking else-where, Commander. One of the militiamen onboard took a particular dislike to Berenger."

"That could be ideal. He would be certain to keep a close eye on our prisoner."

"No," Laz said. "You can't leave me with Cooper. He almost killed me twice." He wrapped his fingers in Hawkins' jacket lapel and begged. "You have to take me with you. I'll sign onto your crew. Please. I'm good on a ship, you know I am."

"Unhand me, Berenger."

Laz felt the black wings of rising panic swoop through the tent. He tightened his grip. "I have to stay with you. You're my only way home." His breathing came in rasps.

Hawkins uncurled Laz's fingers. "It's been decided, Berenger. I've saved you from a quick noose. Stay away from Cooper and you shall be fine."

Laz clutched his wrist before he could lower it. "Then give me my medal back. Please. I need it. Without it, I...I'm trapped."

"What is he blubbering about, Captain?" Pepperrell's tone was sharp.

"When I captured him, I took a papist trinket he was wearing."

The wings flapped around Laz's head and he tightened his grip. "My St. Christopher medal. I have to have it."

Hawkins cut through him with a steel glare. Laz took hold of the rope so he wouldn't grab the captain again. He wanted to shake his medal out of hiding.

"You are *demanding* this trinket? I will remind you that you are a prisoner, young sir. You may demand nothing." Pepperrell's expression turned sly. "When Captain Hawkins returns from blockade duty, we will consider your *request* for this trinket to be returned. Of course, our decision will be based upon your good behavior as a prisoner."

Worry stamped Laz's forehead. "What if his ship is sunk by the French?"

Pepperrell sniffed. "You'd best hope it isn't."

The interview wrapped up quickly, with Pepperrell issuing orders. Outside the tent, Hawkins handed Laz's rope to one of the guards with instructions from Pepperrell.

As he started to walk away, Laz called, "Stay safe, Captain Hawkins."

He spun around. "I will, Berenger, but not for the sake of your trinket. I will stay safe because I am a fine captain on a fine ship."

Laz hoped so. He nodded and gave Hawkins his imitation salute. The captain touched two fingers to his tricorn and strolled down the hill.

CHAPTER FOURTEEN

Laz decided that for Pepperrell and company, "good behavior" apparently meant slave labor. They had arrived at Canso on April 4, and for almost three weeks he worked alongside militiamen, rebuilding port defenses.

His hands blistered then grew calluses. Men's faces bloomed red and Laz's turned brown, which made them heap insults on him about being French or Acadian. Laz laughed them off because he wasn't the one with painful, peeling cheeks and necks and arms.

Militia units took turns working for an engineer who kept them to his plan. Laz was assigned to the engineer's camp and was treated as a servant there as well. He swore he'd never complain again about the few chores his mom made him do.

Those units not rebuilding defenses were constantly drilling in the open areas. Having sat through his dad's military parades, Laz could see those men weren't professional soldiers. Half the time they didn't even try to march in step. But most of them were good shots. What Laz hated most was walking past the men doing bayonet practice. Every *thunk* of every blade pushed into a dummy wearing a blue coat, made his stomach muscles twitch.

A few times a week, the engineer released Laz early—he had begged for the favor—and he went for a walk. Closer to the other end of the island was a rise with a gravel bluff that fell into the sea. Laz tramped down a path that came out at the base of the small cliff.

Laz treasured those few minutes alone a few times a week. There were over 3,000 men here, between the island and the mainland, so being alone was rare. But the problem with being alone was that his thoughts started up. Mostly he wondered if time was going by at the same rate back home that it was here. He hoped that it was like in that book his mom had read to him and Emeline, *The Lion, The Witch, and the Wardrobe*, where days in Narnia were only minutes in their regular world.

Otherwise, his mom would be upset; even his dad might be worried; but Emeline would be frantic. Laz knew he wasn't always a good son, but he *was* a good big brother. Emeline and he were close, and thinking about her flipping out over him being missing ripped his guts into shreds. Laz hoped and prayed she was okay, actually prayed, because he figured any help was better than what he'd gotten so far.

Laz sat on a mound of dry pebbles that had been warmed by the sun, and watched two ships head toward the harbor. The near one, he now knew, was a sloop. The far one was hard to identify because they were sailing so close together.

They were almost out of sight when Laz started stripping. One reason for his walks was the chance for a private place to swim. He'd been spotted doing it, of course, and everyone expected him to sicken and die. Bathing so often was unnatural, he'd been told countless times. (*Text to Ryder: not bathing won't kill u but u'll smell dead*) Laz preferred taking chances with a dip in icy water than living with his own stench.

No one else seemed to care, and those filthy bodies could even stink up a campfire. Laz had noticed the smell on the ship, but had put it off to no space and no bathtub. That was another thing he'd never take for granted again: showers and warm water.

Laz charged into the surf, dived under, swam fifty feet and back, then got out. It was so cold he shivered violently as he made his way to his pile of clothes. He dried off with his dirty shirt and pulled on his clean one. The engineer had scrounged an extra one for him. He scooped up some sand, waded out to his knees, and did his best to scrub his dirty shirt.

At home, Laz had complained when his mom had told him to toss a load into the washing machine. Just drop clothes into a machine, dribble in some soap, close the lid, and press a few buttons. *Those were the good old days*, he thought, which made him sound like his grandmother.

His legs were almost blue when he retreated to the pile of smooth stones. He dropped the shirt, which he'd rinse back at camp to get out the salt. Then he rubbed his shins and calves, until his fingers and legs were tingling, and patted them dry with the outside of his jacket. He wrapped his feet in his breeches, draped the jacket over his legs, and enjoyed a few minutes of not being bundled up and tucked in and buttoned down.

The sun broke through clouds a short distance above the horizon and Laz closed his eyes to enjoy the sunlight's warmth.

"Lazare!" a voice called from above.

Laz twisted to look over his shoulder. "Ben!" He jumped up and spun around. "There's a path by the shore just down the hill." He pointed to the west.

"Aye. Get your breeches on. No one should see a man so naked." He raced along the hill's sheer drop, his laughter carrying on the breeze.

Laz stepped into his breeches, making sure the shirt was tucked all the way under his butt, almost like underwear. He wondered when it had been invented. He sat back down and was securing the stockings (beige and getting darker every day) with their tie-up garters, when Ben arrived. It was so good to see a friendly face that Laz jumped back up and hugged him. They were both surprised by that.

"Tell me 'Happy birthday,'" Laz said.

"It's your birthday?" Ben asked.

"If it's April 23."

"Aye. Then a happy birthday to you, Lazare."

"Thank you." Laz sat back down and motioned for Ben to join him. "It's good to hear that from someone who doesn't want me hanged as a spy."

"From a friend?" Ben wiggled his rear to shift the pebbles.

"Yes." Laz smiled and squinted at the horizon. "Though you're a fool to let anyone think we're friends."

"Men regularly name me a fool."

Laz laughed.

Ben passed him a flask. Laz raised his left eyebrow in a silent question. Ben nodded. "My double ration of rum from the captain, for being on the crew that captured a French sloop. Did you see her?"

"You mean the closer of those two ships that came in while I was swimming? I couldn't tell that the *Constance* was the escort ship. Congratulations." He pretended to take a sip of Ben's rum and winced from the smell alone.

They joked back and forth, and Ben told Laz about blockading the French port from far enough away they couldn't be spotted by Louisbourg sentries. The most dangerous part, he assured Laz, was avoiding ice flows. That gave Laz another thing to worry about: hoping the *Constance* didn't pull a *Titanic*. Ben insisted Hawkins was too good a captain to hit an iceberg.

Sunset was approaching, and the low sun lit up some sails on the southeast horizon. Laz pointed them out to Ben. He leaped up with a whoop. "The navy is here!"

"What are you talking about?" Laz asked.

"I heard Cap'n talking. Word's come that the British are sending proper navy ships to join our colonial fleet." Ben waved his arms wildly, though they were too far away to see a whole fort, never mind a single boy. "We'll soon be taking the fight to those scurvy French in Louisbourg."

"Let's go tell Hawkins," Laz suggested. Maybe it would put him in a good enough mood to return his medallion. Laz thought of bayonets slicing into practice dummies' stomachs, and knew he didn't want to stick around for a fight.

CHAPTER FIFTEEN

Hawkins brushed Laz off and said they'd talk later, that he'd had an idea he needed to consider. Four days later, a militiaman showed up where they were building a new block-house and said he was there to escort Laz to Commander Pepperrell's tent.

Laz had successfully avoided Pepperrell for three weeks, and Cooper, too, except when his unit had construction duty with the engineer. In daylight, with people around and Laz staying focused on his work, Cooper hadn't been able to do much more than insult and threaten him. When he became particularly vile, Laz had stared at him and thought, *You're dead, Cooper. You've been dead for at least 250 years.* Cooper usually fell silent under Laz's glare. Once though, he'd attacked Laz and two men had pulled him off. He'd gotten kitchen duty for that.

Pepperrell was different. He didn't make threats. Hawkins had convinced him to wait until they had more time for the luxury of a treason trial, but Laz didn't want to give him any reason to change his mind and move up that date.

He immediately became very, very worried.

As they made their way up the hill, the bustle everywhere was a reminder that something was ready to happen. It had been like this since the British had arrived on Laz's birthday. They'd only stopped for water and the latest news, then sailed past Canso to join the blockade. But their arrival had obviously signaled something to Pepperrell.

Laz's stomach churned, and he tasted acid in the back of his mouth. The militiaman held back the tent flap and Laz stepped in, immediately aware of his filthy clothes in this tidy place. It felt like walking across his mom's newly washed floor with muddy sneakers.

Pepperrell was seated and waiting. Hawkins stood behind the other chair, hands clasped behind his back. His broad face didn't look angry, which Laz took as a good sign. He nodded to the captain.

"See here, young sir, why are you so filthy?" Pepperrell asked.

"I've been digging defensive ditches by the new block-house," Laz replied.

"Good of you to volunteer to assist the men."

Laz's eyebrow shot up. He forced it down with a scowl. "You define *volunteer* the same way my father does."

Pepperrell pressed his fleshy lips together for a moment. Hawkins gave a slight warning shake of his head. Laz shrugged. "No big deal. It'll wash off."

"Yes. I've heard of your uncouth habit of bathing in the ocean." He pulled his head back, as if in judgment. It made his double chin pop out more. "You seem able to adjust to new circumstances with reasonable skill."

"My mother says I'm resilient, something I got from moving around a lot," Laz said.

Pepperrell eyed him like he was a swarm of bees. Laz decided he wasn't interested in actual responses, so he fell quiet.

Sheltered from the breeze, with the sun heating the canvas walls and roof, the inside of the tent felt stuffy. Some trickles of sweat ran along Laz's hairline, in front of his ear, then down his neck. He pushed his tangle of hair behind his ear.

After a few minutes of examining the boy with scientific intensity, Pepperrell said, "Captain Hawkins seems to think that you could do the king a service."

"The king?" Laz swallowed, mouth dry. "He's not coming here, is he? Or are you sending me to London?"

Pepperrell snorted. "I thought you said he was clever, Hawkins."

Hawkins' lips pressed together briefly. "All that means, Berenger, is that people in service of the crown could use your talents. In this case, us."

"You've kept me prisoner for three weeks. Haven't I been helping?" Laz couldn't keep the irritation out of his voice.

Hawkins rested a hand on the back of the chair. "You have had considerable freedom these past weeks, and you have not betrayed our trust. Which is why I believe you could be trusted with more."

"What do you think I can do?" Laz far preferred talking to Hawkins. He was honest. Pepperrell came across as shrewd, even sneaky. Laz guessed he didn't care about the men he used to get things done, where Laz knew from experience, and from Ben, that Hawkins was loyal to his crew.

The captain's broad face was serious. "We want you to get inside Louisbourg to sow doubt, discord, and a bit of mischief."

Laz's jaw tightened and he forced it to unlock. "What kind of mischief?"

"Do not use that tone with my officer," Pepperrell interrupted.

Laz ignored him and raised his left eyebrow. "Well?"

"Merely a few simple acts of sabotage," Hawkins said.

Laz's eyes bulged. "*Merely?*" he said, astonished. "Why would I do that?"

"For one," Hawkins replied, "as a British citizen, it would balance out any accusations of treason if you aid in our victory."

"It doesn't do me much good to be cleared of treason if I get killed by the French."

"You won't. They won't suspect an Acadian boy. You speak the language. You will be able to blend in, move around as you please. The risk to you is small. The rewards, great." Hawkins reached inside his dark green jacket. When he pulled his hand out, Laz's St. Christopher medal dangled from his index finger.

Laz inhaled sharply. Hawkins didn't know he was taunting Laz with his ticket home. He reached out.

Hawkins flipped the medallion up and closed his fist around it. "Are you interested?"

The repaired chain looped down from his fist. Eyes on it, Laz thought. "If you want me to enter a French fort, a *papist* fort, then I should be wearing a *papist* trinket, don't you think? Give it back to me and I'll do your dirty work." Although Laz knew he'd return to his own time once he put that chain on, so he'd never see the inside of any fort.

"Ah, Berenger, therein lies the rub." Hawkins put the chain and medal back into some inner pocket. "It is obvious how desperately you wish your trinket returned. That makes it the ideal surety."

"Ideal what?" Laz asked.

Hawkins squinted over Laz's shoulder. "Warranty. Or bond. I don't know what the French word would be."

"*La guarantie?*" Laz's fists clenched. "It's your guarantee I'll do what I'm told. You'll keep it until I'm done your mission, and then I get it back."

Hawkins inclined his head.

Laz's ribs felt squeezed. This wasn't a trip to the corner grocery for milk he was suggesting; it was walking to a store in the middle of a neighborhood you had been warned to stay out of because a gang war was heating up. Head down, Laz ran his left index finger along the twin scars on his right palm. "And if I refuse?"

"If you refuse, young sir," Pepperrell said, "I will make time on the morrow for your trial."

Laz's heart blasted into mach speed. He searched Hawkins' square face. "You said no trial until after the fort was taken."

"That is what I suggested." Hawkins' shoulders lifted slightly. "But the commander has the final say in everything."

"Right. And what kind of a trial will I get in the middle of this camp? A five-minute show then declare me guilty and find some rope?" Laz felt angry but helpless.

"Are you suggesting the commander would fail to give you a fair trial?" Hawkins said.

Laz snorted. "Fair? When his army is getting ready to launch an invasion? Not likely."

"Decide." Pepperrell said the word with such force that Laz shivered.

"Getting hanged in the morning isn't a choice, it's a threat." Laz's brow folded down as he glared at Hawkins. "You knew as soon as you came up with your plan that I'd agree to it. Your so-called deal guaranteed it."

"I do not deserve your scorn, Berenger. I am doing my level best to give you the chance to redeem yourself."

"I don't want to be redeemed. I want to go home."

"One will only come after the other."

Laz squeezed his eyes shut to fight back unexpected tears. No way was he going to show any weakness to them, not ever. But with eyes closed, all he could see was Emeline's worried face. He opened his eyes, and, in French, whispered, "*Grosses bêtes.*" (Big idiots.)

He stalked out of the tent, shoved past the guard, and made for his sliver of beach. Footsteps sounded behind Laz but he didn't look back. Instead of taking the path along the shore, he hiked up the rise, keeping close to the gravel cliff. He stopped at the top and faced the open ocean to the southeast.

Laz wondered what would happen if he never got back. He'd never let himself think that before, but walking into a fort that was going to be attacked changed everything. Suddenly it was way too real. Laz rubbed his thumb over the scars on his palm but didn't look at the reminder of how real this was.

Real swords. Real muskets. Real cannons. Real flesh.

He inhaled the fishy, salty scent of the ocean, imagining it also smelled of calmness. He had wanted to learn parkour.

It was about balance, knowing your body's center, finding it, using it to move through your environment. He wished he'd had lessons, because he'd never felt so off-balance.

Whitecaps skimmed over the water and disappeared into the depths. This same ocean washed up in Boston. Was his dad back in his downtown office, standing at the window and looking down Long Wharf to the harbor? Was he thinking about his son? He'd always expected more from Laz than he could give, but right now, Laz would do anything he asked. Anything. Because that would mean Laz was there. Not here.

"You love the ocean," Hawkins said from behind Laz's right shoulder.

"Except when I'm thrown into it wearing shackles."

"That was unfortunate."

"So is this." Laz bit off the words, resenting the captain's quiet tone and the way it sliced through his frayed calm. Laz's knees quivered, so he sank down to sit cross-legged.

Hawkins sat beside him, propping himself on one hand and resting the other on his upraised knee. "I do not claim to know French, but I would hazard a guess that what you said in the commander's tent attacked our honor."

Laz shrugged and tugged up his sagging left stocking. "What would you call someone who uses blackmail to force a person to do something?"

"Blackguard, mayhap. But this is war and it does not signify."

Laz brushed his hair out of his eyes to squint at the captain. The wind blew it back across his face.

Hawkins searched his outer pockets and produced a leather strip. "Here. Your hair has grown. Tie it back. A man should be able to see his surroundings."

Laz took the leather, combed his hair back with his fingers and tied it into a thick, stubby ponytail.

"Better. Now let me see how your hand is healing." Hawkins took Laz's wrist and peered at the scars, one longer than the other, but both looking as if a slender white cord was embedded under the skin. "You've kept it clean. A feat considering the manual labor to which you've been forced."

"I kept it bandaged as much as possible." With Hawkins' bare head bent over, Laz noticed the sun gave a reddish tint to his brown hair. Onboard ship, he'd always worn his tricorn while on deck.

Laz asked, "Why are you acting concerned?"

Hawkins released the hand. "Mayhap I am."

"Right. Got to make sure your saboteur is healthy."

"No, Berenger. I happen to admire your spirit. And Ben likes you. He's near a son to me. He would never forgive me if I allowed something to happen to you."

"Then don't send me into an enemy camp," Laz said.

"It's the best way to keep you alive, given how other captains are pressing Commander Pepperrell to deal with you harshly, as a lesson to all Acadians under British rule. Fortunately for you, the commander is reluctant to hang someone so young, though he will if pressed."

"This isn't fair." Laz raised his hand to silence Hawkins. "Don't say life isn't fair. I know that way better than anyone around here."

Hawkins looked puzzled. "Of what do you speak? Of getting captured?"

Laz couldn't answer that. Down below, high tide was almost brushing against the mound of stones he used for a chair. Even from here he could see the indent he'd created to make it more comfortable. "I'm not sure I can fool the French. I'm not very sneaky. More like...mouthy. Impudent is one of my dad's favorite descriptions."

"Impudent." Hawkins almost smiled. "I like that. You will need to be impudent, and daring, to walk into Louisbourg. And I am certain your impudence will bring you success."

On the far side of the island, artillery practice began. The cannons boomed, launching their cannonballs at targets along the shore. Laz plucked at grass and let the wind carry it from his outstretched hand. He caught a whiff of Hawkins' sweat. "Why are you sure I'll succeed?"

"Our initial interview showed your mettle. But when that militiaman pulled you from the top—"

"Wait? You *saw* what Cooper did?" Laz almost yelled.

"Indeed, but I could hardly take the side of a prisoner."

Laz snorted. "Nice."

The near smile appeared and disappeared again. "As I was saying, when you flew into the air, yet managed to save yourself, more, managed to turn near disaster into a rousing bit of entertainment, I knew you were a survivor of the first order." Hawkins squeezed Laz's shoulder. "As you did in my riggings, so you will land on your feet in Louisbourg, Lazare Berenger."

Laz shrugged away the compliment. "What about my St.

Christopher medal? Even if I get inside, that doesn't mean I'll be able to do whatever you expect me to."

"I give you my word, as the captain of the *Constance*, that I shall return your trinket when we meet after."

"After what?"

"After you have attempted your task, whether successful or not. All I ask is that you try." He offered his hand. "Will you accept my terms, Berenger?"

Long seconds passed. Laz's father had always insisted that a handshake was a contract. If you shook on something, you did it. Period. Hawkins' hand and his gaze held steady. After sucking in a lungful of ocean air, Laz shook his hand. Firmly, the way his dad had taught him.

Hawkins smiled.

CHAPTER SIXTEEN

Laz left that night, shortly after midnight, in a twenty-foot shallop. Since he didn't know anything about sailing, Hawkins' second-in-command, Lieutenant Sherwood, manned it. He tried to teach Laz a few basics as they sailed, so that it would seem possible that he'd arrived alone on the shores of Île Royale, which Laz was pretty sure was modern Cape Breton Island.

After a few hours, Sherwood encouraged Laz to sleep, but that wasn't going to happen when they were sailing across twenty-five miles of open water in a shallow, oversized rowboat with a single sail. Sherwood assured him they would get there safely, that he was the best man on Hawkins' crew when it came to sailing by the stars. He said they had to pass a smaller island on their way to Île Royale, but they couldn't get too close in case their sail was spotted. Laz had seen no sign of it. Feeling uneasy, Laz spent most of the night peering into the darkness for signs of ice—a small iceberg or even a chunk of bay ice could easily crush the shallop.

The long night gave Laz time to review the story Hawkins and he had come up with. He'd traded the flowery waistcoat for a plain walnut-colored one that looked suited to a poor farmer. Hawkins also insisted Laz wear heavier stockings that had a homespun look to them. Laz got to keep his red tuque and baggy brown jacket, which was nearly red beside the dark brown vest. His wooden shoes had toughened up his feet so Laz was happy to keep them.

The crescent moon would be a slice of nothing in a few days. The dim light skipped on wave crests and shimmied in a rippling line from the shallop to below the sliver in the sky. Breaths escaped in fog plumes.

"Land ahoy," Sherwood whispered.

Laz tucked his numb fingers under his armpits and squinted ahead. A ribbon of black slashed across the dark gray water, closer than expected. Laz whispered, "I don't see lights. Are you sure this is Port Toulouse?"

"Aye. When we get past the headland you'll see lantern light. The sky will be lighter when we beach so you'll see the palisade silhouette then."

"Are you sure you can get away?"

"Aye. It will mean a hike of five or six miles to where another shallop will pick me up tomorrow night, but that won't be a problem. I do regret having to leave this shallop with you, but the French have to see how you arrived, and they will undoubtedly claim it. I'll be well along the shore when those Papists begin interviewing you, and they won't look for anyone else unless you tell them to."

"I made a deal with Hawkins and I'm going to keep it," Laz said. What would happen to him here? He expected they would take him prisoner and send a messenger to Louisbourg.

"What's the word of an Acadian worth?" Laz heard the sneer in the man's voice. They both fell silent.

The night breeze pushed the shallop through the water, closer to the growing mass of black, formless land. When they slipped around a headland, Laz spotted tiny lights straight ahead. They cut through the waves like an arrow shot at a target. The familiar iron band returned to hug Laz's ribs, and he focused on the cold air slapping his face and the mist of saltwater kicked up by the bow.

Maybe half an hour or more passed, but it felt to Laz like only minutes when Sherwood whispered, "Get down and brace for a hard beaching."

He ran the small boat aground without slowing. It scraped rock and creaked loudly. Laz sat up as Sherwood jumped out of the shallop, slung his canvas bag over his shoulder, and said, "Don't betray us." He sprinted down the rocky beach and into the first clump of trees he reached.

No turning back, Laz thought. The idea that he'd never see Hawkins again sucker-punched him. He liked Hawkins. The man was protective, though in a backhanded way, and supportive. Not always pushing, pushing, pushing like his dad. Laz sat for a few minutes clinging to Hawkins' belief he could do this. Someone believed in him. "Impudent," Laz whispered. He stepped over the oarsman seats to stow the sail. Sherwood had taught him the steps, and he recited each one under his breath as he worked.

Ten minutes after he began, he heard someone approaching. The sky was gray and getting lighter. The land took on shape and substance. They had beached on a gravel bar with a few larger rocks, and one had damaged the shallop. A small rise to a mostly grass slope led to another bluff with an exposed gravel face. Atop that bluff were the man-made earth ramparts of Port Toulouse. Beyond the ramparts were some rooftops and a single spire. Did this place even exist in modern times? The name wasn't familiar.

Four silhouettes of soldiers, carrying long muskets made longer by bayonets, advanced down the hill in pairs. Laz stepped out of the shallop and strained to pull it farther out of the water.

"Identify yourself," one soldier said. In French, of course. Laz had to forget his first language was English. French only, like the summers on Grandmère's farm.

"Lazare Berenger," Laz replied. "Help me, please. Papa sent me to warn you."

They reached the shore and spread into a semicircle. Four bayonets pointed toward him. In his mind Laz heard the sound of blades slicing into practice dummies at Canso. He retreated a step, and one bayonet motioned him forward. "Up the hill. You are our prisoner until our captain decides otherwise."

Prisoner again. *These guys are all the same*, Laz thought. "Please. Can I get my bag?" He pointed to the boat.

"Jacques, get his sack. You, Berenger, move."

They marched Laz up the hill into a small fort with a cluster of three or four buildings then locked him in a cellar below the barracks. The dank air seeped under his clothes, but even shivering couldn't keep him awake. He slept until midmorning when they herded him into the biggest building and into an office.

The soldiers who'd brought Laz up from the beach and the ones with him now were all in blue stockings, breeches and jackets, with black tricorns. The man at the desk wore a red waistcoat with a white shirt. Off to the left, a blue coat with wide red cuffs hung from a wall hook. He was definitely dressed fancier than the others.

He leaned back. His droopy eyes and long nose reminded Laz of a bloodhound. After he had eyed Laz up and down for five minutes, he emptied Laz's bag onto the desk. A ratty blanket, a small knife, a bit of dried meat, and stinky cheese wrapped in cloth, and his extra shirt. The belongings of a poor farmer's son. The captain swept it all onto the floor. "Who are you?"

Laz pulled his red tuque off and clutched it in both hands. "Lazare Berenger, sir."

"Yes, yes. I was told that. From where and why are you at my fort?"

"I'm from the west. I sailed—"

"From the settlement on Île Saint-Jean?"

"Yes. I came—"

"Port-la-Joye?"

"Papa has a farm west of Port-la-Joye." Where was Port-la-Joye? Laz had never heard of it and hoped it was too far to send someone to check his story. "We—"

"Why is your father not with you?"

"I am trying to tell you." Laz clamped his mouth shut, waiting for the interruption. The captain waved his hand for Laz to continue. "We sailed to Canseau." He put the French inflection into Canso. "We knew our soldiers had burned the town last year, and were hoping to find..." Laz shrugged. "Useful building materials, nets, anything left behind."

"Scavengers." The man sneered. Laz studied the long fingers splayed on the desk and resisted replying. This was why Hawkins had him dress in a poor man's clothes, so he would be thought of as unimportant. The man said, "Did your father fall overboard? Why are you here?"

"He...he stayed there to—" Laz swallowed hard. Nervous wasn't hard to fake when you suddenly were. He twisted the tuque. "We saw ships. He stayed to keep watch and sent me." Laz sighed. "I am not a good sailor. I think I damaged our shallop."

The captain clasped his hands together on the oak desk. "Ships. What kind of ships? How many?"

This was like being in a play. Laz purposely widened his eyes and searched the man's face, as he kept his voice to a whisper. "British. The bay was full of them. Hundreds."

"What kinds?"

"Many schooners, many sloops, Papa said he saw a brigantine and a frigate."

"Are you telling me you saw an armada?"

Laz nodded vigorously. "We thought they might be coming here, so Papa sent me ahead. He hopes to find a way to report to you if they leave Canseau."

The captain studied Laz for several more minutes. He continued wringing his tuque. It seemed like a habit a poor person might have. The man leaned back and sighed. "I knew they would retaliate for last year's raid." Another sigh. "But if you're telling the truth, that is too many ships for an attack on our minute garrison. They must be planning an attack on Louisbourg."

"Louisbourg?" Laz widened his eyes again. "That's impossible."

"Is it? Still, we must get you to Louisbourg so you can report what you saw directly to Governor Duchambon."

"But I damaged Papa's shallop," Laz said. And he was glad of it.

"We will keep it here and repair it. I have some Mi'kmaq guides who can take you in their shallop today."

"Today?" The band encased Laz's ribs again. Things were happening too fast.

"Yes. Time is important. There have been rumors of British ships spotted in the waters off Île Royale, perhaps a blockade, but no official word has reached us. Perhaps because no ships have broken through."

"But if we go in a boat, won't a British ship stop us, if there is a blockade?"

"No. My Mi'kmaq guides are natural sailors. They use a small shallop. The sail is hard to spot and they stay close to land so they can run aground if a larger ship gives chase. A larger ship's draft keeps it out of shallow waters." He waved his hand at the floor. "Collect your belongings. My men will find you some food. I will make arrangements so you are on the water before noon."

Laz found that being in a boat with four silent companions was a boring way to spend a day. At home he'd always been listening to music, checking his phone, playing games, texting. But out here: nothing. There were only his thoughts and the water and the endless shoreline.

Two of the Mi'kmaq apparently spoke French, but they hadn't proved it. All four were dressed traditionally, in animal-skin clothing. They'd given Laz a hide, moose he guessed from its dark hair, and he'd used it as padding in the bow of the shallop, as out of the way as he could manage. Two barrels and a small bundle of furs were piled in the middle by the mast, probably for trading in Louisbourg.

Laz searched the shore for an hour or two, hoping that Sherwood was watching and would tell Hawkins he was on his way. When boredom and tiredness ganged up on him, he wrapped up in the hide and slept.

Late afternoon cast long shadows from the shore across the water when Laz woke. He'd been dreaming about walking the streets of Newton with Emeline, from home to the school to the mall. His chest ached and his throat closed as the hurt of missing his little sister rose from deep inside. Waking up to the slap of waves and the silence of the Mi'kmaq guides deepened his loneliness.

He faced forward to avoid curious eyes. A murky shore on the left and open water on the right, and no sign of life except a hawk soaring above the trees. The smell of animal hide and saltwater stung his nostrils. Behind him, one Mi'kmaq said something to his companions in his own language, and chuckles rose up. The sound of human voices was like quenching Laz's thirst. He was glad he didn't know if they were laughing at the young Acadian.

With a glance back, Laz asked, "How far to Louisbourg?"

The fellow at the tiller replied, "*Demain.*" (Tomorrow.)
"*Merci.*" (Thanks.)

They sailed until it was nearly dark then put into an ice-free cove. One man left and returned with fresh water. Tiller Man handed out dried meat. Another pulled some fish from the water that had been strung from the boat and filleted them with a few strokes. Apparently they'd managed to fish while Laz had slept. The fourth lit a small fire and oversaw the cooking. After they'd eaten, the four men rolled up in skins around the dying fire. So Laz did too.

If not for those two words—*tomorrow* and *thanks*—he could have been starring in a silent movie. But he didn't feel like the star, more like the red-shirted ensign from *Star Trek* who was going on a suicide mission. The Red Shirts never survived. (*Text to Ryder: quick. Beam me up.*)

Day two was a replay, right down to their two words of conversation. Laz guessed that Tiller Man had a different definition of *tomorrow* than he did.

On the third day they rose with the sun and returned to the water after sharing dried meat and water. With no wind, the four Mi'kmaq men used the oars. The shore inched by. But an hour or two later, the breeze started rising. Soon they hoisted the sail and the shallop began skipping over the waves.

The sun was past noon when one of the men spoke and pointed out to sea. Laz squinted at the horizon, trying to spot what he'd seen. Then he saw a sail.

The sail grew bigger, took more form, and became a double-masted ship like Hawkins' schooner. It was getting closer and

Laz searched for the flag. Was it a French ship or British? It didn't seem to be flying one.

Tension crowded into the shallop as the ship changed course and began angling to intercept them. Tiller Man changed course, taking them closer to shore. The other three Mi'kmaq took their places on the rowing benches. The men fitted the oars into their locks and held them above the waves. Everyone watched the ship as it drew closer.

The ship's flag unfurled. Red, like the ships in the fleet at Canso. British. Heading for the shallop, a whale looking to catch a minnow.

Tiller Man yelled for Laz to take the helm. Heart crashing, he climbed past cargo and the over benches. He stumbled onto the tiller's bench. Tiller Man grabbed his wrist and placed his hand on the arm of the helm, then said, "Hold strong."

With the sail still up, the men began to row. Facing the stern, they could all see what was behind them. Laz looked over his shoulder and the leader yelled to not move, to hold strong. He had aimed the boat toward the shore and now he directed Laz, "Right, right more," which steered the boat to left. With the bow pointing straight at shore, he stopped rowing, loosened one rope and tightened another so the sail shifted to catch more wind.

They rowed with all their might, faces stern, eyes never leaving the hunter chasing them. Laz's air huffed out in time to their strokes. He glanced back. The ship was much closer. Its prow sliced through the water, bowsprit looking like a spear.

Is it going to catch us, or ram us? Laz wondered.

Thunk. Thunk. The bow slapped each wave. Skimmed the surface. Behind them, the heavier craft parted the waves. *Whissssh.* Steady. Fast. Laz's heart hammered. Tiller Man spoke in Mi'kmaq. They all clenched their jaws. Rowed harder.

"Ahoy!" An English voice stretched over the waves. "Strike your sail, and heave to. We are taking command of your shallop."

Obviously not understanding, Tiller Man scowled over Laz's shoulder and kept rowing. Laz couldn't say anything or the Mi'kmaq would realize he spoke English.

"Faster," he breathed out in French. "Faster."

The Mi'kmaq grunted as they rowed. Splash. Lurch forward. Splash. Lurch forward. The shore drew closer.

From behind, slightly quieter, the voice yelled, "Surrender and no one will be harmed."

Laz risked another look. The ship tacked right. Three wooden portholes opened. Black muzzles poked out.

Gasping for breath, Laz faced forward. "*Le canon! Le canon!*"

CHAPTER SEVENTEEN

The British ship prepared to fire its cannons at the shallop.

With each pull of oars, the Mi'kmaq surged closer to shore, straight toward a boulder. Laz yanked the rudder left. They veered right.

Boom! Laz dropped to the deck.

Whoosh! Sploosh. The cannonballs fell short. Water splashed into the shallop. Waves pushed the boat forward. The keel scraped rocks.

All four men bailed over the sides and pushed and pulled the boat higher out of the water. Tiller Man yanked Laz's sleeve. "Follow. Quick."

Laz scrambled out of the boat into knee-deep water. Splashed ashore. Raced behind a tree. Braced against it. Tiller Man hauled him upright. Shoved his bag into his hands. Waved for him to come. Laz jogged after him.

Another barrage. Trees crashed and cracked. A limb shot past Laz and buried itself in a tree trunk. Laz ran.

He followed the Mi'kmaq, who were brown streaks flashing through the forest. Over logs. Through snow clumps. Around trees. Under them. Over rocks. Up hillocks. Maybe half a mile in,

Tiller Man called a halt. He passed his water skin around. One of the other men dropped a long oilskin on the ground and unrolled it to reveal muskets. He passed them to each of the others and kept the fourth for himself. He handed Laz a spear with three prongs. Laz doubted it would be helpful.

Tiller Man urged everyone to drink more water. It felt stupid to keep thinking of him like that, so Laz tapped his chest. "My name is Lazare." Nearly black eyes met his. The man nodded and said something in Mi'kmaq. Laz shrugged in confusion. In French, the man said, "Captain calls me Paul." He didn't introduce the others, just turned and started walking.

They fell into single line, Laz in the middle. The land was boggy in places, rocky in others. They zigged and zagged through the forest, following a path he couldn't see. They stopped once to drink and relieve themselves. (*Text to Ryder: moss makes ok TP*) They chewed on dried meat as they walked.

With no sign of pursuit, Laz breathed easier. Their pace stayed brisk. Once in a while he saw blue glinting through the trees. They skirted around a lake, past at least two miles of gravely, sometimes boggy shore, with trees and shrubs crowding up to the water's edge.

By the end of the afternoon, Laz was glad for his long days of labor at Canso, because Paul and his friends didn't slow down for anything. Late afternoon they reached the shores of a large bay, and a fishing village.

Paul kept in front and approached a man on the first dock they reached. The others held Laz back. Paul talked with the man, their conversation too quiet to hear. The man, who'd been mending nets, shook his head. Asked something else, he shook his head again.

Expression clouded, Paul stalked back to them. He spoke rapidly in Mi'kmaq to the others, who replied, then left the way they'd come. Paul crossed his arms, musket in one hand. Laz said, "What's happening?"

"The fisherman will not sail us to Louisbourg. There is no room to stay here." His expression darkened more, and Laz realized the man probably didn't want a Mi'kmaq under his roof. Paul nodded at his retreating friends. "They will see if the boat remains. And our furs." He pointed at Laz, then himself. "We walk."

"To Louisbourg?"

"Yes."

So they walked, parallel to the water. Ice pushed up to hide the shore like a white crumpled sheet, and floated out in the bay. Maybe that was part of why the fisherman refused to take them, Laz thought. But only part.

The swooping bay made their path three times longer than sailing across might have been. Clouds moved in to hang low over the water and brought an early dusk. At one point, when it was almost dark, Paul struck out across ice clogging a smaller cove. They hiked quickly, not wanting to be caught on the ice in darkness.

When they were under trees again, and barely able to see, Paul called a stop. Laz unslung the bag from his shoulder and pulled out the thin wool blanket. Paul unrolled a small skin. Neither were enough to keep them warm. Paul tramped about a bit then called Laz.

He had to feel his way. With no moonlight, the darkness was funhouse black. Paul had found a bed of moss. It was cool, but dry. They both burrowed in. Laz shared the dry bread and cheese from his bag then took a trip into the darkness to relieve his cramping stomach. After more water, they slept.

The night was cold. Laz tossed and turned, startled awake several times with the thunder of cannons in his ears. His breath huffed out as he shivered and wished for warmth, for relief from this new reality, for family, for home. But mostly, for escape from the thought worming into his brain in moments of quiet—the thought that whispered he'd never get back.

This was his life now. Crapping in the forest using moss, eating moldy cheese and infested bread. No electricity or heat or cars or computers or phones. No friends except a boy on a ship he might never see again. No family.

Laz pressed his hand over eyes that were trying to tear up.

In the dark, Paul said, "We are safe, Lazare. And tomorrow, Louisbourg."

He'd heard. Laz sniffed, whispered, "I miss my family."

"Yes. I also want to be with my family."

"Your father and mother?"

"No. My wife. My baby. Soon, he walks."

Laz guessed Paul was twenty at most. "I'm sorry I took you away from them."

"Captain pays. Gives tools for fishing, sewing. This is good."

Above, the sky was dark gray against the black treetops thrusting upward. Air frosted Laz's cheeks. "Is it too soon to go?"

"We will walk by the ice until light comes."

So they packed up in the gloomy half-dark. Paul led with the musket propped on his shoulder. Laz followed, using the spear as a walking stick. Along the shore, the ice melted from gray to steel blue to pale pink. When the sun rose, light bounced off the stark white surface. Eyes almost squinted closed, Paul and Laz hiked into the sunrise.

Ice creaked and shifted out in the bay. It hissed and inched forward near their feet.

Maybe an hour later, Paul pointed out a finger of land almost completely hidden by the ice, then angled away from the shore. Again the land was a jumble of rocks, frozen bogs, clumps of grass, brush, and snow. Only scattered stubby trees dotted the semi-barren land. Ice crackled under their feet. It smelled of rotting wood and dried grass.

The ground rose, giving a view of the bay. White islands, varying from the size of rowboats to bigger than schooners, floated on the tide. Paul shielded his eyes and scanned the horizon beyond the bay, so Laz did, too.

The British ships were out there. Laz knew it from being in Canso. That included some big naval ships called men-o-war. The biggest was Commodore Warren's sixty-gun ship. Laz was thankful it was just a schooner that had chased them to ground yesterday, though he couldn't imagine a man-o-war giving a full broadside of thirty guns to a puny shallop. He ran fingers through his hair and retied his ponytail. He'd never realized until now how much knowledge he'd picked up from listening to the militiamen in Canso. How much could he tell to the French in Louisbourg?

"Come." Paul interrupted his thoughts.

They topped the rise and Laz halted, mouth open. He snapped it closed. Stared.

Paul returned to stand by his side. He pointed. "Louisbourg."

"Yes," Laz whispered. He'd seen the destroyed fort at Canso, and the undamaged one at Port Toulouse. Laz knew Louisbourg was bigger. He'd imagined something the size of the Citadel in modern Halifax.

But Louisbourg was no fort.

It was a town, with massive walls and rows of rooftops. And beyond the town, a jungle of ships' masts. There had to be thousands of soldiers and sailors. It was a French army on the edge of the wilderness.

There was no way that untrained colonists could take this town.

Laz realized he was spying for the losing side.

CHAPTER EIGHTEEN

An hour later they had picked their way down the slope and across the open plain to the base of the wall and bastions that stuck out like teeth. Sentries shouted down, asking their business. Paul replied that he brought a messenger from Port Toulouse.

They swung left, following a path at the base of the wall. Laz ran his fingers over the rocks of various sizes held together with mortar, and imagined the American colonials charging toward it. He guessed that a lot of them would die if they tried.

Laz did not want to be here. He had thought the Citadel looked pretty cool, but this was life and death. These walls had been built because the French and English liked killing each other. He remembered watching a movie with his dad about the American Revolution called *The Patriot*. Cannonballs taking off legs. A head—

He braced himself against the wall as he suddenly realized that if that ship's cannons had hit their boat... His stomach squeezed, and he swallowed hard.

Laz had never cared much about history, but now he was caught in it. He closed his eyes and rested his forehead against the stone. His friends had always been impressed that he'd try almost anything on a dare. But that was just for fun. This was real. Too real.

He wondered how you faced a cannonball blasting your way. A musket firing at you. A bayonet sinking into your stomach.

A hand clamped onto his shoulder. "Come, Lazare. The sentries will not let us enter if they think you carry disease."

Laz thought that might be a good thing.

But they continued on. The zigzag of the wall curved to the right. The path narrowed as a frozen pond crowded near the wall. Laz noticed a small door tucked into a fold in the stonework. The wall immediately jutted out more teeth and turned a corner. They took a narrow bridge that spanned the pond and cut to the road beside a sprawling bay.

To the left were a few houses, maybe fifty yards along the shore. Paul and Laz headed right, toward slat gates, and past a small red sentry box the size of a British phone booth. A guard startled Laz when he stepped out.

"Where did you come from?" he demanded.

"From Port Toulouse," Paul replied. "I bring a messenger."

"You walked?"

"No. We sailed. A big boat chased us to shore."

The sentry turned to Laz. "You don't look like a messenger."

Impudent, jumped into Laz's thoughts. *I can do this*. He pulled his shoulders back. "I am a witness to important events. The captain at Port Toulouse sent me to inform the governor."

"Where are you from, messenger?"

"Île Saint-Jean."

"So give me your message."

Laz raised one eyebrow. "You don't look like the governor." His stomach cramped.

The guard glared and thumped his musket stock on the ground. Laz didn't move. The guard marched over a red bridge. The last six feet was a drawbridge. They followed, their footsteps echoing. They stayed back while he spoke to another guard at the gate, which had both studded doors propped open. The guard called to someone behind him, and ordered that second guard to take them to the captain.

They entered a canyon of stone, with cobblestone floor and walls rising up on either side. The guard entered a door on the left. Paul stopped Laz with a hand on his shoulder. "You are in Louisbourg. I go."

Laz extended his hand. "Thank you."

Paul scowled at it for a few seconds, then nodded and shook hands. "Be well, Lazare."

"Safe travels, Paul."

He nodded again, took back his spear, and strode into the town.

Laz wanted to call him back. But when the guard tugged his sleeve, he stepped into a guardroom where a few men relaxed near a fireplace. The guard led Laz to a man reading in a chair beside a window, introduced his captain, and explained Laz's presence.

The captain waved Laz to sit. When he did, his legs started to quiver. He tried to remember when he'd eaten or drunk anything. He looked up at the guard. "Water, please?"

The man agreed only after his captain nodded. He fetched a mug of water and Laz took small sips.

"What did you see that Port Toulouse sent you here?" The

captain sounded bored. He picked up his tricorn from the table and began to fiddle with it.

Laz stared and thought. He looked more than bored. He looked sullen. Another of his dad's favorite descriptors of Laz: sullen. Not just grumpy. Cheesed off.

"Well?" His irritation cut through Laz's thoughts.

Be impudent. Be bold. "You don't look like the governor, either. I'm not supposed to talk to a sentry, or a captain of the guards, or the mayor. I was told to talk to the governor. Where is he? I'll go find him if you don't want to help me. It's your neck."

He slammed the hat onto the table, crushing it. "Are you threatening me?"

"No. But he will be upset that you didn't bring me straight to him." Laz shrugged and downed the rest of the water. Then matched his action and banged it down on the table. This was almost fun.

The captain muttered, "Filthy little rat," under his breath, and pushed to his feet. He snatched up his tricorn. "You want to talk to the governor? Fine. I will take you there and he can eat you for lunch." He stalked out, not looking to see if Laz followed.

The road passed between low harbor walls and the higher walls of a mini fort bristling with cannons. A bastion, Laz knew from his father's teaching him about military forts, a stronghold protecting this part of the town. Most of the ships anchored in the bay looked like merchant ships. They had cannons, but not massive numbers of them.

Half a block past the bastion, they reached a fence and a stone house with wood trim. Ahead was a tall yellow gate that opened onto the docks. But instead of heading for the center of town, the captain swung right, down a side road, with the backs of buildings and fences on the left, and a swath of grass and the fortified wall on the right.

The road was wet, and though Laz tried to avoid puddles, dampness seeped through his wool stockings. On the left, a building took up the whole block. Laz shuddered at the sight of bars on the windows. They passed a small building, hiked up a rise, and angled across a lawn between most of the town and a long stone building with red shutters, a dozen chimneys, and a low steeple. A beaten path sloped back down to a wall and gate with squared-off posts topped by cannonball-sized stone decorations.

The yard beyond the gate had what Laz guessed was another guardhouse, then a bridge over a trench with water. A tunnel through the building had studded doors at either end. Beyond that he saw a parade ground inside another bastion.

They'd passed only a few people, probably because it was lunchtime like the captain said. Now a guard inside the tunnel asked their business. When the captain explained, the guard rolled his eyes. "He is eating with his officers. White door, up the stairs. Someone will direct you."

Laz had the weirdest sensation of walking through a living history museum, with everyone in costumes. Except, he had been in a living museum for almost a month, and it stretched from Chebucto to Louisbourg, and everyone carried real weapons. He silently ordered himself to stay calm; now was a bad time to freak out.

They clumped up wooden stairs and were pointed in the right direction. The captain stepped into a dining room with windows overlooking the parade square and outer battlements. He came to attention, clapped his musket stock onto the floor, and angled it out like a gate to keep Laz from advancing.

A man, rounded and slightly slug-like, laid down his utensils, dabbed at his mouth with a napkin, and leaned into his tall-backed chair. He gripped the armrests. The captain addressed the man as Governor Duchambon.

All the officers peered at Laz as the captain explained, again, why he was here. One, a man who had to be over fifty, looked amused, where the other officers looked irritated at being interrupted. Duchambon seemed the most irritated of all, with fleshy lips pressed together. His white wig gave him a stuffy look. A bit like Pepperrell, Laz decided. He breathed out slowly, hoping Duchambon wasn't so quick to threaten a trip to the gallows.

Finally, the governor brushed some crumbs off his gold waistcoat and said, "A settler from Île Saint-Jean, is it? Tell us your news then, boy."

Laz pulled off his red tuque, gave his name, and explained about going to Canso.

The governor said, "Why would you scavenge a destroyed fort?"

Laz shrugged. "It was a hard winter." The governor looked well fed and doubtful, but several of his officers exchanged odd glances, as if some of them had also had a hard winter. Beside Laz, the captain snorted quietly, agreeing with the knowing looks.

Then Laz described seeing the British ships and his father staying to spy on them, and Port Toulouse sending him here, and what had happened along the way. The older man rested his arms on the table and leaned forward. He said, "How many ships?"

"H-hundreds. They filled the bay."

"Morpain," the governor said, "this is my interview."

The man inclined his head but kept leaning toward Laz, his interest keen. He was lean, with gray hair and amber eyes that reminded Laz of a wolf.

"Hundreds, you say?" Skepticism filled the governor's tone.

Laz nodded. Morpain interrupted again. "Describe the ensigns."

"The what?"

"The flags, boy. Describe the flags. There must have been flags." He touched a button on his light gray jacket. "They would have insignia on them, like my buttons."

Laz squinted one eye, picturing the flag on Hawkins' ship. "They were red. With a smaller flag in the top left corner. The small flag had two red crosses, white and blue background."

"That small one is a British flag. Are you certain? Were there no full-sized British flags?"

"No. Just the red ones. But very many."

"Hundreds of ships," Morpain said, "but all colonial ships." Laz shrugged. Morpain said, "You just described the colonial ensign. These ships are not from the British navy."

"A mob of colonists," the governor said then burst out laughing. "The colonists are useless, a rabble. They have not been able to stop our privateers from raiding their coastal towns, and now they think to bring an attack to us? Here?" He burst out laughing again.

"But," Laz said, "There are so many." Undermine their morale, Hawkins had said, by exaggerating the size of the force headed their way. Laz didn't think this was the reaction Hawkins had expected.

Another officer said, "No force can touch us here. Our harbor is defended so strongly it will never be taken."

Morpain narrowed his eyes and swept his gaze over his fellow officers. His lip twitched. Definitely wolf-like. Laz was glad he wasn't in charge. He focused on Laz, making his mouth dry up. Laz looked away and kept his attention on the governor.

"That's all you have to tell us?"

Laz nodded.

"Leave us. You have interrupted our lunch for no good reason."

When Laz hesitated, the governor flapped his lace-cuffed hand. The captain beside Laz spun him around and pushed him out the door.

Minutes later Laz stood alone at a muddy crossroad, the governor's residence behind him, and the town in front. Uncertainty yawned inside him as he realized he had failed. And he had no idea what to do next. Hawkins had explained a few simple sabotage acts he could commit, but until he knew his way around, he couldn't do anything. He knew he needed to look around, do something, but he couldn't seem to get his soggy feet moving. The governor's laughter kept ringing through his head.

A throat cleared.

Laz spun and took a hasty step back. The wolf, Morpain, stood before him, cloaked against the weather, wearing a gold-trimmed tricorn that turned his eyes a matching bronze.

He swept back his storm-gray cloak and rested his left hand on his hip, above his sword. "Tell me the truth, boy. Do you even know how to count?"

CHAPTER NINETEEN

Did he know how to count? Laz wondered what kind of question that was. Morpain held Laz captive with amber laser-eyes, expecting an answer, and it made Laz nervous.

He licked his lips and swallowed. Laz tried to hold his gaze, which should have been easy since they were the same height, but he found it very hard. "Of course I can count. I'm good at mathematics." He focused his attention on the officer's square-toed shoes.

Morpain huffed. "I suppose you will tell me next that you can read."

Laz's head jerked up. "But I can." He clamped his mouth shut, realizing his mistake. A poor farm boy in 1745 wouldn't likely be able to read. He rubbed his eyes and was hit by a second of wooziness.

Morpain grabbed his elbow. "You are pale. Have you eaten today?"

Laz squeezed his eyes shut then opened them. "A piece of dried meat. At dawn."

"You should go to an inn and eat. Do you have money?"

Laz dug into his jacket pocket for the few French coins Hawkins had scrounged from someone in Canso. He showed them to Morpain.

The man huffed again. "Two *deniers* will get you a few scraps, if that. Come." Still holding Laz's elbow, he steered him toward a street between two wooden houses. The buildings were a mix, some wood with colored trim, one painted stone, several natural stone buildings with colored shutters framing the windows. Straight ahead stood that tall yellow gate that opened to the harbor. It had a gray roof shaped almost like a helmet.

A few people passed them. Women in long skirts, aprons, and white caps. Men in clothing similar to Laz's, but neater and newer. Even a nun in black with a white collar and head covering. A few children dressed like miniature adults skipped by. Morpain touched his tricorn and greeted each adult. He paused to tease a boy, then urged Laz to keep walking.

"This isn't a fort," Laz said. "It's a town. I thought it was a fort."

"It is a fortified town."

"How many people live here?"

"Around 2,000. That increases when the port is busy of course."

At the intersection in front of the gate, they turned right onto a wide frontage road, the busiest one yet, with some carts and men hauling sacks or carrying buckets or baskets. They passed the corner building with a sign reading, "Hôtel de la Marine." Morpain led Laz into the second building. The low-ceilinged room had tables with white tablecloths, white-ridged walls, and windows with yellow trim.

Morpain greeted people as he guided Laz to a table at the back, near the kitchen. It was warm. He stripped off his cloak, tricorn, and jacket. Brushed at his long blue waistcoat, and sat. Laz dropped his bag, took off his jacket and tuque, and sat across from the man. The smell of fresh bread and some kind of stew made his stomach growl loud enough that Morpain smiled.

He called over the waitress. "Suzette, two bowls of soup, some bread. And...do you have any coffee?"

"No. It is long gone. Though I think the hotel still has some hidden away for officers." She sniffed.

"That's fine. Spruce beer, then. And hurry before my companion faints from hunger."

She cast Laz an alarmed look and scurried into the kitchen.

The warmth coaxed the cold out of Laz's bones. It was the first time he could recall being decently warm since Canso. He slipped his damp feet out of his wooden shoes, hoping they'd dry a bit. He noticed how filthy he was. His fingernails were caked with dirt, and he rubbed them while they waited. He couldn't think of anything to say.

Suzette returned with a wooden platter of bread, then two pewter bowls and spoons. When she started to turn, Morpain clasped her wrist gently. "Surely you have some butter?"

"It costs extra." She sent Laz an uncertain glance.

"I am paying for the meal," Morpain replied.

She nodded, and returned a moment later with a knife and small bowl of butter, and with two large steins. She set them down. "Anything else, Port Commander?"

"This is fine, Suzette."

After she left, Morpain watched Laz devour half the bread and all his fish soup. The warm, filling broth relaxed him. When he was done his bowl, Morpain traded, and nodded. Giving a return nod, Laz started on the second bowl.

With that bowl half gone, Laz slowed down and took a sip of the beer. "This is awful."

"It has its uses. It keeps scurvy at bay, and the flux," Morpain said.

"The flux?" Laz asked.

He half smiled. "The water here is swampy. Surely you noticed since you walked across some of the land. People who drink it seem prone to falling ill with the flux."

Laz realized he meant diarrhea. Maybe that was why his stomach had been cramping all day. Not fear, not much, but the water Paul had given him. Paul was used to it, but Laz wasn't. Laz sipped more of the bitter beer.

"What will you do now?" Morpain asked.

"I don't know. I will have to wait until Papa comes for me, unless there is a ship sailing back to Port Toulouse," Laz said.

"What of your Mi'kmaq companions? Can they take you back?"

"Three turned around at that village on the big bay."

"Gabarus."

Laz shrugged. "The other one left me at the guardhouse with that so helpful captain."

"Then you are stuck here until I send a ship to Port Toulouse."

"When will that be?" Laz drank some more beer. He thought it might be numbing his tongue, since the taste was improving.

Morpain ripped off a chunk of bread and handed it over.

He buttered the heel and bit into it. "I'm not sure." He spoke around the bread. "There have been rumors. Ships beyond our horizon, perhaps a loose blockade, but no one knows." He ate the rest of his bread and wiped his mouth. "Your story of being forced to beach supports that. It isn't proof, but it is one more hint that something might be happening. I won't send out ships until I know."

Laz shifted on the hard bench. "You don't believe me about Canseau."

This time Morpain shrugged. "A boy with big eyes could see far more ships than were really there. Hundreds might only be twenty. A raid with Port Toulouse as its target, perhaps, to repay the one at Canseau last year."

"No. There were more than twenty. More than a hundred." Feeling much better, Laz leaned forward. "I *can* count. And multiply and divide and do fractions and even algebra."

"Truly? Are you an engineer?" Morpain smiled. "If not, you should be. Who taught you such skills on remote Île Saint-Jean? There are no nuns running schools there that I know of. And as Port Commander, I know a lot." He said it casually, but Laz heard his warning. He thought Laz was lying.

"My father taught me," Laz said firmly.

"And he taught you to read?"

"No. That was my mother."

"A farmer's wife who can read? She must have married below her station."

That almost made Laz smile. "Grandfather certainly believed that."

Morpain laughed. But mentioning Grandpa tore open the wound of missing Mom and Emeline. Laz frowned at the butter dish and felt like he was bleeding inside.

"What happened to her?" Morpain asked.

Laz hesitated. Adults usually couldn't tell if he was lying or telling the truth. Fists clenched on the table, he squeezed his eyes shut and said the first lie that came to mind. "She died giving birth to my little sister."

Morpain's hand covered his. "I'm sorry. Both my parents died when I was young. It sent me to sea."

"Thank you," Laz whispered.

"Did the baby survive?"

Laz nodded. "She...is being cared for by a neighbor." He breathed out her name, "Emeline," and hoped she didn't mind being connected to this insanity. He couldn't pretend she didn't exist. Somehow, he felt better, giving her a fictional life in 1745.

"You adore her. I hear it in your voice." Morpain removed his hand and smiled. "It is good to have family to care for, yes?"

Laz agreed. "I want to go home. Now. More than I can say." Inside, the bleeding continued, as if kindness were a knife that was widening the wound.

Morpain turned into a bobblehead, with a sort of side-to-side nodding that wasn't quite nodding, but wasn't a headshake, either. "But here you are. And here you will stay until you can go." He shrugged. "You might as well make the best of it, yes?"

Morpain's casual attitude hit a detonation button Laz didn't know was there. He jumped to his feet and the bench tipped over with a thud. "No! I've been making the best of it for a month. A horrible month!" Laz grabbed the stein by its rim and thumped it down. "Every." Again. "Step. Every single step has taken me farther from any hope of getting home."

Laz knocked the stein off the table and charged out of the restaurant, almost bumping into a man herding geese down the road. His geese honked as Laz veered around them toward the yellow gate. To the right of the gate was a single post, over six feet high, on a platform. He grabbed the post then slid down to sit and lean against it. He rested his forearms on his raised legs and stared blindly through the open gate, to the port and the ships at anchor.

He thought he had been doing okay, getting through each day. But now, all the days had piled up. It had been a month since the tunnel. He jerked his head back, banged it against the post. And again.

Laz wanted to curse Hawkins. He liked the captain, and he knew Hawkins liked him, but not enough to offer him an easier way out. Not enough to just return his medallion. Laz had thought he could do this, go to a place where there was going to be a battle, but he just wanted to go home. He'd never wanted anything so badly in all his life, no matter how angry his dad might be.

Eyes closed, Laz soaked in the bit of warmth the sun offered and tried to calm down. A *thunk* startled him. He cracked his head on the post, accidentally this time. Morpain stood before him, holding his jacket and bag. He had dropped the wooden shoes by his feet. Laz glanced at his filthy stockings, then Morpain.

Laz blew out a breath. "I'm sorry. You were nice to buy me lunch. Thank you."

"I had to pay extra for Suzette to clean up your mess," Morpain said. "If you don't like spruce beer, that is no reason to spill it everywhere." He sounded amused.

"I'll pay you back." Laz narrowed his eyes against the glare on the water and watched two fishermen carry their catches through the gate. He recognized mussels in one basket, but couldn't identify the fish in another.

"With your two *deniers*?"

Laz shrugged. The fishermen walking by gave him an odd look. One shook his head.

Morpain sat on the edge of the platform and set down Laz's belongings. "Something I said upset you, and for that it is I who am sorry, Lazare. If I may call you that."

"I'm not lying. The British are going to attack here. Not Port Toulouse. Here." Laz couldn't look above Morpain's neckwear, all neatly tucked and folded instead of ruffled. "And I don't want to be here when it happens."

"The way you faced the governor and his officers, you did not strike me as a coward."

Laz stiffened. "I don't think I am. I don't mind taking chances. But staying here to be target practice for a bunch of religious fanatics doesn't seem very smart." *Papist this, papist that. God will give us the victory.* It was all Laz had heard at Canso.

"A big word from someone who seems younger than his size indicates. Do you know so many British colonists that you know they are...fanatics?" Morpain looked amused again.

"They're all crazy, what's the word, Protestants, aren't they? That's what I've heard."

He laughed. "Come here."

Laz slipped into his shoes and followed Morpain to the reinforced wooden wall that stretched in both directions from the yellow gate. It ran the whole length of the waterfront. They both rested their arms on the wide top and surveyed the port. The docks were at least ten feet below them, and by the way the water lapped close under the wooden slats, Laz guessed it was high tide.

Morpain pointed past ships to an island on the right, almost in the middle of the mouth of the bay. "That is Battery Island and it is fortified with cannons." Beyond it, a lighthouse stood on a spit of land.

Then Morpain pointed left. "And see that building on the inner curve of the bay? That is the Grand Battery. Another fort, also with cannons. And the Dauphin Gate, where you encountered your helpful captain, is guarded by a semicircular battery. All three of those batteries work together to create what we call a field of fire. In this case, the whole bay is covered. There is no way to get at the town without taking extensive damage."

That did not sound good for Captain Hawkins, or Laz's medallion.

Laz realized he had been frowning, because Morpain clamped a hand on his shoulder. "You are safe here, Lazare, until we can get you home. I promise you that."

Honesty seemed to roll off the man in waves. Laz had the feeling he was the kind of man who inspired confidence. And Laz wanted to believe him. More than anything.

But he knew that promises get broken all the time.

CHAPTER TWENTY

Laz knew about broken promises first hand.

Last fall, Emeline had wrangled a promise from him that he would take her and her friend to a nearby mall on the Saturday after her ninth birthday. A magician was going to perform and she was crazy about all kinds of magic. Happy that he'd given her a birthday present she had claimed to "absolutely adore." Laz had promised to take her. That morning, Ryder had called, and Laz had immediately taken off to the skateboard park. He didn't get back until late afternoon.

Their parents had both been busy, so Emeline had been forced to stay home because the mall was too far for her to go to alone. When Laz returned, he thought he had stepped into the end of the world, the way Emeline was sobbing, and apparently had been sobbing all afternoon. Her face was red and blotchy, smudged, and tear-streaked. But that wasn't what got to Laz. It had been the look in her eyes. Trust broken.

He was grounded. And Emeline didn't talk to him for two weeks. Since then, Laz avoided making promises. She could ask him for almost anything, but he ran from promises like a six-year-old boy avoiding kisses at recess.

Yet now Laz stood, on the steps of a wooden house, facing

Morpain, who said, "Promise to serve me as best you can, and that you *will not* leave Louisbourg without my permission."

Morpain had arranged for Laz's lodging, and was paying for it out of his wages. Laz didn't understand why, but Morpain had hired him to be his messenger. It occurred to Laz that this was great cover to go anywhere in the fortress. Morpain, it seemed, was a sucker for a sad story. Although, Laz's story was partly true: he did want to go home.

When Laz recoiled slightly at the word, *promise*, Morpain offered his hand and said it again. "Promise me, Lazare."

Laz wanted to say no. Instead, he shook hands. It felt like shaking Hawkins' hand. They were both good men, and he liked them.

Morpain kept hold of Laz's hand and clamped his left hand onto Laz's right shoulder. "I'm a hard master, but I never ask anyone to do what I cannot. We will be a fine team, Lazare Berenger."

"Thank you, sir."

A smile crinkled out from his eyes. "I am not a sir. If you must, you may call me Commander, or onboard ship say, Monseuir Morpain. I most often answer to simply Morpain. But not Pierre. Only my wife calls me that. It is Saturday, so you can report to me on Monday. I have a room and desk in the King's Bastion barracks where you faced the governor, though I'm often aboard my frigate, the *Castor*. The guards at the King's Bastion will know my whereabouts, and if they don't, my manservant Georges always knows."

Morpain strode toward the waterfront. Behind Laz, the door creaked open. A boy, maybe nine years old, stepped outside. He smiled up at Laz. "You're so lucky. You get to work for a pirate.

"Really? Morpain is a pirate?" Laz grinned. (*Text to Ryder: working for* un corsaire, *a pirate, dude. Beat that.*)

The boy started to reply but his mother called him inside. Morpain had brought Laz to the home of a widow with six children, a servant, and a slave. The house was wooden, two and a half stories high. The half was an attic where the servant slept, and so would Laz. The slave had a room in the small barn, with the goats. The thought made Laz shudder.

Madame Richard had a large garden and had continued her husband's spice business. Spices and chocolate and goat cheese—a weird combination. She explained it had been a hard winter, and her stock was low, with no sign of ships bringing more. Her eldest daughter was sewing for soldiers, and now she had a boarder, Laz.

He learned all that in less than five minutes after Morpain introduced them. What she missed saying, her children happily filled in. Laz told Madame Richard that he was going for a walk to learn the layout of the town. The boy offered his services and his mother agreed. So his guide, Jacques, showed him the town.

On Sunday, after Laz was made to attend church, he explored more on his own, always looking up at all the interesting roofs, thinking how they'd make great parkour routes, and wishing he had gotten to do that introductory course. Mostly, the town was laid out as a grid, roughly seven blocks by six blocks. And it had walls on every side.

Monday morning breakfast was served just after dawn. Everyone ate together, in a noisy free-for-all. Laz was half asleep when he stumbled down the stairs to use the outhouse, but by the time the meal was over, he was wide-awake with a headache.

The servant was a girl near his age named Isabelle. She had been the only quiet one and had given him a small smile as he'd left the table.

Laz's job was to shadow Morpain, fetch and carry, run messages. His *manservant* was actually a slave who took care of personal stuff, and he had a clerk to help with his paperwork. The clerk liked no longer running errands, so every time Laz stopped by his desk, he offered a smile and a sliver of chocolate. Louisbourg was almost out of chocolate so Laz made sure to always thank him.

On Wednesday, they rowed to Morpain's frigate and he outfitted Laz with a navy jacket that fit better than his baggy brown one. Laz kept that one as a spare. And Morpain found different shoes, square-toed things with buckles and no left or right feet, but they fit. Laz kept the clogs too. He hoped his growing wardrobe would soon include an extra pair of breeches and stockings. Even his suitcase in Halifax had had more clothes than he now owned.

Laz decided that living in the past was fine for rich people, but being poor sucked worse than having to wear knee-length pants and stockings. At least everyone wore those.

Friday dawned warm and sunny, so Laz left his jacket on his bed, which was a stuffed mattress on the floor. He'd seen plenty of men working in Louisbourg without jackets or waistcoats. When he caught up with Morpain, he received an unimpressed look. Laz checked his vest buttons but they were all fastened.

Morpain said, "Always wear your jacket when reporting to King's Bastion. The military has standards. You are a messenger, not a fisherman." He rested his hand on Laz's shoulder as they walked. "But for today, this is fine."

They stopped on the outer wall in the northeast corner where a small bastion jutted out. It faced a finger of low swampy land surrounded by crisscrossing waves, and beyond that, open ocean. The air was fresh, tinged with warmth in the breeze that fluttered Laz's billowing sleeves. He braced his hands on the wall and inhaled deeply.

"With these spring winds, all the bays will soon be clear of ice." Morpain leaned sideways against the wall and squinted at the horizon. "How are you fairing at Madame Richard's?"

"Isabelle, the maid, smiles at me every morning. She seems nice. The family mostly leaves me alone."

A smirk settled on Morpain's mouth. "Probably because of your strange request to bathe once a week. Very odd, coming from a farmer's son, if you ask me."

Laz cleared his throat and changed the subject. "Why are we up here?"

Morpain opened his jacket and pulled out two wooden cylinders trimmed with brass from under his sword belt. He handed one over. Laz telescoped out the collapsible spyglass, revealing smaller sections of all brass. He turned it over, pushed it closed, and lengthened it again. *Pirates of the Caribbean* popped into his mind. "Jacques said you were a pirate."

Morpain swept into a courtly bow and straightened. "With a king's commission to harass any and all British ships I encountered."

Laz's eyes widened. "And did you?"

"I did. Some I harassed until they sank, though mostly I captured ships, claiming them for King Louis. And now I serve his majesty as a port commander." He extended his spyglass. "We are here to search the horizon. The townsfolk are growing concerned at the absence of ships. Supplies are dwindling, and the events over the winter—" He lifted the telescope to his eye. "Look for the smallest hint of a distant sail."

What events? Laz almost asked, but it was obvious Morpain hadn't meant to say anything. They spent the rest of a boring morning scanning the horizon. Morpain left and returned with bread, cheese, and spruce beer. They sat and leaned against the warming stone to eat, then returned to their searching.

As they worked it struck Laz how comfortable he felt in Louisbourg. Part of that was probably no longer being a prisoner. But everyone here simply accepted him. He was merely Lazare, the boy from Île Saint-Jean, and Morpain's trusted messenger. The slow rhythm of the town reminded him of summers at Grandmère's farm. Everyone worked hard, but no one hurried. They played hard, too, with evenings spent laughing and drinking and making music.

Two hours after they ate, Morpain startled Laz with a loud, "There!" He lowered his spyglass and pointed to the south-southeast. "A sail."

It took a few minutes for Laz to locate what he'd seen. They continued scanning the rest of the horizon, but mostly focused on that single sail. They both saw when a tiny cloud puffed out from the sail.

Laz lowered the spyglass. "Was that—?"

"Cannon. Yes. There is another ship out there."

Now they watched with urgency. Laz felt Morpain's tension. Once Laz thought he saw what might have been a second sail, but it vanished. Morpain started to pace. The first sail continued to grow and angle toward Louisbourg. In the late afternoon Morpain announced they should go to his ship and wait.

On board his three-masted frigate, the *Castor*, he resumed pacing. Abruptly, he started shouting orders. Laz stayed out of the way on the quarterdeck as his commands brought the ship to life. Morpain sailed the ship out of the bay and anchored off the point. "We must know if we are greeting a friend or attacking a foe. Watch for the ensign, Monsieur Berenger." On board ship he always called Laz that.

Half an hour later, they both spotted it. "French," Laz said.

"A merchant ship," Morpain replied. "Good. Very good." He issued more orders to raise anchor and turn the ship around.

When the merchant ship came within hailing distance, Morpain had one of his men use flags to instruct the ship's captain to report to the *Castor*. As they reentered the bay, Laz struggled with growing dread. He had promised Morpain he'd stay. He had also promised Hawkins he would try to sabotage the French. Part of him wanted to break both promises and escape. Both men trusted him, and another part of him didn't want to let either one down.

The captain of the merchant ship came aboard and reported to Morpain on the quarterdeck. The man looked pale, with white brackets around his thin lips. He gripped both lapels of his green jacket as he spoke. "Port Commander, we were attacked, almost within sight of Louisbourg."

"Yes. By whom?"

"The British."

"A single ship?"

"I engaged a single ship, but two others were sailing into the fray when we caught a timely breeze and outran them. One of the ships was a man-o-war."

Hands clasped behind his back, Morpain inhaled noisily through flared nostrils and exhaled slowly. "A blockade it is then."

"Without a doubt," the merchant captain replied.

Morpain's bobblehead nod-shake seemed to confuse the man, but Laz had come to recognize it as a sign he was thinking. Morpain faced Laz. "Monsieur Berenger, it seems you might have been correct that the British have mischief on their minds. If you were also correct about numbers, their fleet will soon arrive and our defenses will be tested."

"Do you still think we will be safe?" Laz asked.

Morpain looked surprised. "Without a doubt."

The merchant captain added, "God is on our side."

Laz had heard that before, from the New England men in Canso.

Morpain clamped his hand on Laz's shoulder and grinned widely. "Your first true battle, Monsieur Berenger? Are you not excited?"

Laz grimaced. "That's not the word that comes to mind."

CHAPTER TWENTY-ONE

Louisbourg seemed to hold its breath as they waited for the enemy to swoop in. Fear was a cold front that chilled conversations and hushed voices.

The next few nights, Laz went to Grandchamp's Tavern, which was beside the restaurant where Morpain had fed him that first day. He liked the boisterous singing and laughing that had spilled into the street the first evening he'd passed by it. But now it held whispers and quiet ballads by a man who played guitar for a few *deniers*.

The people in the tavern didn't have the same confidence as Morpain. They were worn out by the winter and lack of supplies. People spoke about rationing. A few soldiers mostly whispered among themselves and shot angry looks at anyone who glanced at them. Laz knew he was missing something but couldn't figure out what.

He had gotten used to staying out as long as he wanted. Thirteen was considered practically a man here, and he enjoyed the freedom. He returned to Madame Richard's close to eleven o'clock. As he turned down the Richards' street, Laz met the sergeant on night patrol, with musket slung over his shoulder. His crude lantern, a wood frame and glass box with a candle, swayed back and forth. He greeted Laz in a quiet voice and he replied the same way. It wasn't a night for loudness.

The house was silent, but as she had the last five nights, Isabelle sat in a chair by the fire. She stood when Laz entered and asked if he wanted to warm himself. He refused, took a candle, and excused himself upstairs, knowing it would take her a few minutes to bank the fire.

In the attic, heat still radiated from the central chimney. Laz retreated into his corner, created by wooden partitions the way some offices used half-walls to create cubicles. He stripped down to his long shirt, which not so magically turned into his nightshirt.

After a long day of running messages all over town for Morpain, Laz started to drift off as soon as he crawled under the blanket. Isabelle whispering his name jolted him awake.

"What?" Laz asked.

"Has Commander Morpain said? Will we be safe?"

Laz half sat up and peered at her candle-lit face. He nodded. "He insists we will be."

She smiled. He realized he'd gotten used to it, and her. He smiled back. "Thank you for waiting up. It's nice."

Isabelle blushed and nodded, then disappeared behind the partition.

Before he reached the guardhouse, Laz remembered to do up all his buttons. He brushed off the navy jacket and reported to the guard. "Is Commander Morpain in the bastion this morning?"

He stared as if Laz were a raving idiot. "Of course. With all the officers on the walls, watching the British land."

Laz jerked back a step. *Where could they be landing?* Laz couldn't get the question out. He stuttered, "Th-the British?"

"Well it isn't King Louis come to pay us a visit."

Laz shot toward the tunnel entrance into the bastion like an Olympic sprinter. His shoes clattered over the stone floor, and he raced onto the parade square and toward the ramp that accessed the outer walls. A soldier partway up the ramp blocked his path. Laz lunged at the slope, grabbed a post above him, and pulled. He rolled onto the grassy flat, sprang to his feet, and charged toward the crenellated wall and the row of cannons facing outward.

Beyond a grouping of three cannons, the governor, Morpain, and all the other officers were gathered, facing the land beyond the walls. They were arguing.

Between two cannons, Laz veered to the wall. Twenty or thirty ships were anchored in the bay a few miles west. They looked like miniature toys. Skiffs were dots rowing toward shore.

Laz's heart thudded like it was trying to kick its way out of a locked closet. He gripped the wall and tried to understand what he was seeing. This wasn't an attack using ships like Morpain had expected, but a land attack. Laz didn't think they could do any damage to this massive fortress. They couldn't get close enough to fire their weapons without the fortress being able to fire back.

Could they?

Twenty feet away, the officers' argument was getting louder. His back to Laz, Morpain shouted, "You have to repel the attack! We cannot permit them to gain a foothold."

The governor looked ready to fall apart. He searched the faces of the other officers, and one said, "We are safe behind the walls, Governor. Why risk men for nothing? They will never get their cannons through the morass out there, and their muskets are like shooting peas at a man-o-war and expecting it to sink." Another said, "They are colonists, not even regular army. They will sink their cannons in the mud, give up, and go home."

The arguing continued like this for twenty minutes at least, Morpain growing more agitated as time passed. One officer hung back, but remained close to Morpain, as if giving him silent support.

Almost an hour after Laz arrived, Morpain demanded, "Give me 400 men. I will repel them."

The group fell silent. The governor fidgeted for several minutes then said, "I don't think...No, no. We cannot spare that many. No."

Morpain threw his arms into the air and spun around. His frown was ferocious. Again Laz was reminded of a wolf. But his anger wasn't with Laz, so he pointed to Morpain's waist, mimed using a spyglass. Morpain tossed it to him then spun back toward the governor and officers. Their argument dropped into restless murmurs.

Laz took the spyglass and trotted down the ramp and across the parade ground. In the access tunnel, he entered the barracks, and with only two wrong turns, found the staircase up to the bell tower above the center of the long building. A soldier was already there. He made room, recognizing him as Morpain's man. They both aimed spyglasses at the bay to the west.

From higher up, Laz had a better view of boats delivering men and equipment to the shore, though they were small even in the spyglass. More ships entered the bay. Laz studied them, hoping to spot the *Constance*. He wondered if he could sneak away, rejoin Hawkins, and get his medallion. Go home.

It was too far to pick out details. One of the schooners was gaff-rigged, but the rectangular sails were almost all Laz could make out. These spyglasses were not the high-powered scopes of the twenty-first century.

On the wall, the endless argument continued. Laz glanced down occasionally, but the activity on the bay was magnetic. The boats were like ants advancing in orderly lines from food back to the anthill. Rising land and scattered clumps of forest hid from view the boats actually beaching. Military procedure was something Laz had avoided learning about, given his dad's military past, so he couldn't imagine what the men on shore were doing. No smoke rose from campfires. And everyone kept out of sight below the ridge.

A soldier arrived in the tower, got a verbal report from the man beside Laz, and thundered back down the stairs. The man jogged across the square to the ramp, up it, then saluted and repeated what he'd been told. Laz lifted the spyglass again.

At Canso, more than 3,000 militiamen had gathered. Laz remembered hearing that number. Were they all landing on that one beach? Slow clumping announced the messenger soldier's return. He was red-faced and looking winded. He pointed at Laz. "Berenger, Commander Morpain said to report downstairs to him immediately."

Laz collapsed the spyglass and glanced down. Morpain was no longer in the cluster of officers.

"Now!" The soldier barked.

Laz startled and squeezed past the man, who cuffed the back of his head as he passed.

In the access tunnel, Morpain paced. When he saw Laz, he grabbed his arm. "Come, my young messenger. We must prepare to mount a counterattack."

"A what?" Laz tried to pull away. "I'm not a soldier." Apparently Morpain had won the argument.

"Of course you are not a soldier. You are my messenger. My runner. I will have need of you to keep contact with Captain La Boularderie in the field."

Shaking his head, Laz said, "I can't do that."

"Why not?"

Laz stared as the iron band returned to hug his ribs for the first time in many days.

Morpain grabbed Laz by both shoulders. "Men like you and I, we are made for moments such as these." Laz felt his brow wrinkle in confusion. Morpain continued, "Today, history is unfolding. And we will make our mark on it. We must face this challenge. Face it and win, Lazare. You and I are not ones to skulk. *Carpe diem.* Seize the day! We will be recorded as the men who repelled the British colonists." His voice fell to a whisper. "Not such a hard task, in the end. They are untrained buffoons."

Win—the word echoed through his brain. Laz hated losing. But this? The clamp on his ribs didn't ease. Morpain guided him outside the bastion. "We must prepare with all haste. Time is the real enemy, Lazare."

He continued on, praising the virtues of action, as he marched Laz past the guardhouse. The band loosened as Morpain talked. He made it sound more like an exercise. Here was something more challenging than parkour, something that his dad might even approve of. And then Morpain said, "We must keep our families, our town, safe."

Laz thought of Isabelle, how she had seemed like a friend last night. And the town. Louisbourg had become a place he liked very much. He fell into step with Morpain, who must have sensed the change for his hand dropped away and he strode toward the troops' barracks in the neighboring bastion.

For Laz, the next few hours were a blur of delivering Morpain's orders. Rushing, rushing. It wasn't until they were ready to march out the Dauphin Gate that Laz took time to look around. He tapped Morpain's shoulder. "This doesn't look like 400 men."

"The governor wouldn't release 400. Our victory will be all the sweeter," Morpain said, face glowing with excitement.

"So how many men do we have to repel the landing?" Laz asked.

"Eighty."

Morpain swept Laz alongside him as the other officer gave the order to march.

Eighty. Against thousands.

CHAPTER TWENTY-TWO

They marched out in a column, three men in each row. Morpain and the other officer, Captain La Boularderie, were safe in the middle of the column, so Laz kept close. Also trailing right behind Morpain was his slave, Georges, carrying some gear. Laz guessed he was in his thirties. It was obvious he was very dedicated to Morpain. That seemed to Laz to be most people's reaction to him. *Me included*, he thought. Laz still couldn't believe he was doing this, but it was like every day of the last six weeks. One day at a time. One step at a time. Moments like this felt so unreal to Laz that it was hard to think of them as anything except playacting. His mind blanked as the red gates swung open for them.

Not thinking might be best, he decided.

There was something grand about being part of the column, a living, breathing weapon. All the off-white jackets with buttons glinting, muskets dark and deadly. Marching in step, which Laz found was harder than it looked, especially over uneven ground when they left the road.

Morpain nudged Laz. "Take one of my pistols." He held it out as they walked.

"I don't even know how to load it," Laz said.

"It's loaded. All you have to do is cock the hammer, aim, and pull the trigger."

"I won't hit anything. I've never fired a pistol," Laz protested.

Morpain pressed the pistol against his chest. Laz clenched his fingers around the curved handle, nowhere near the trigger, and kept it against his body so the barrel rested on his upper arm. The weight of it tugged at his wrist. "What do you do with it after you fire the musket ball? Drop it?"

"Use it as a club. That's what the metal butt plate is for. Do *not* drop my pistol. It's been my constant companion when boarding enemy vessels, and is a fine weapon," Morpain said. "Use it if you get attacked at close range. That won't happen. Our muskets will keep the enemy at bay."

Oh good, a useless weapon. Laz kept his thought to himself and his attention on the ground to avoid tripping over rocks or sprawling into a puddle.

They trekked nearly three miles over rocky and marshy ground toward Gabarus Bay, where the colonists were landing. It gave Laz lots of time to think that he should have bolted back to the fortress before the gate had closed. The men cursed and muttered under their breaths. Morpain and La Boularderie ignored the hushed complaints.

The smell of wet earth and rotten plants was overridden by human sweat whenever a puff of breeze swept over the small force.

They arrived very suddenly. Shouts and the noisy chaos of boats being unloaded carried on the wind. The sergeant called a halt a football-field short of the hill that was blocking the noise. He ordered formation of two lines. Laz and Morpain were on the right flank, close to a stand of trees. The sergeant crept toward the low hill to get a look at the enemy.

"Why aren't they taking cover?" Laz asked Morpain, feeling again like this wasn't real.

Morpain's look was puzzled. He drew his sabre. Laz scanned the area, as his nervousness grew. Then he realized they were going to stand in the open and wait for the enemy to walk onto the field, like they were two football teams at the start of a game.

Movement caught his eye. Laz searched the trees and long, afternoon shadows, spotted a few men, crouched low, working their way closer to the French.

The feeling of unreality disappeared and Laz's heart started galloping. He tapped Morpain's shoulder and pointed toward the forest. He said, "What? You need to urinate? Now?"

Laz leaned close and whispered, "There are men with muskets in the forest."

"No. You are imagining things." Morpain didn't even look.

They were maybe 200 feet from the trees. Laz wondered how accurate a musket was. He imagined he heard the sound of flapping, black wings of fear in his mind.

He edged backward. The soldiers loaded their weapons and waited. Finally, the sergeant returned, reported to Captain La Boularderie, then they both came over to Morpain. A few words drifted beyond their tight circle: superior numbers, entrenched, retreat.

Yes, please, Laz thought. The officers separated, La Boularderie tight-lipped and frowning. The sergeant returned to his position and issued orders. To advance. Laz's feet wouldn't move. What was he doing? He wasn't old enough to be in battle. He thought of Ben.

The line of men took four steps. A ragged row of colonists rose along the crest of the hill, muskets aimed. No one fired. The French advanced. Laz still hadn't moved. The flintlock pistol dangled from his fingers and brushed his thigh.

He noticed more movement in the forest, and turned. Men in civilian clothing stood up from behind bushes, stepped from behind trees, muskets pointed at the French soldiers. One musket swung toward Laz and lowered. The man tilted his tricorn back and stepped into a triangle of light. Even from this distance his hooked nose and rat-like features were clear.

Cooper. The man who'd almost drowned Laz. The man who'd tried to pull him off the foremast's top. Cooper pointed at Laz then raised his musket and aimed it.

Laz still couldn't move. Dark wings blurred his vision.

Orders echoes across the field. Then: "Fire!" Shouted in French and English.

Puffs of smoke appeared among the trees.

Something whooshed past Laz's shoulder. His knees buckled. He dropped to the ground.

He remembered being seven, and standing in Grandmère's field. His father had been trying to teach him to shoot a pistol. There had been two crows on a fence, watching them.

Laz had refused to try, had cried that the pistol was too heavy and it hurt his fingers. When he had dropped the weapon and ran toward Grandmère's house, his father had shouted, "Little coward! Get back here!"

Laz's lungs screamed painfully, *Breathe*. Finally, he gasped in air. He was flat on the ground, Morpain's pistol still in hand, but the memory of his father's words fresh in his mind. He'd never remembered that before. Maybe it hadn't happened, he thought. But it had. He knew it. Hand trembling, Laz released the pistol. Rolled away from it.

Battle sounds claimed his attention. People shouted. Muskets fired, sounding like overly loud spitballs. *Pfft. Pfft. Pfft.*

Smoke stung his eyes and turned figures into shadows.

An English voice Laz recognized said, "I think I got the little French scab. I knew he was one of them." Cooper.

Someone shouted, "What are you doing?"

"Going to finish him off. See if Frenchies bleed red or blue." Cooper's voice sounded closer.

Laz knew he had to get away. He rolled onto his knees. Smoke hid the battle, and drifted between him and the trees. He started to push up. Morpain stumbled from the haze, sword in hand. "Lazare! There you are. I've called retreat. Come."

Laz stood. Cooper stepped out of the smoke, bayonet aimed at him.

CHAPTER TWENTY-THREE

Cooper lunged at Laz with his bayonet. He jumped aside. When Cooper came at him again, Morpain slashed at the bayonet with his sword. "Run, Lazare!"

Laz took a step. Pivoted and bent to grab Morpain's pistol. Above him, steel clanged against steel. He dived, rolled, and popped to his feet. Georges bowled Cooper over and swept Morpain away. Laz followed then passed Morpain and Georges.

Here was something Laz knew. He jumped over rocks, ducked low when shots rang out. He sped up when he heard steps behind him. The sound of wheezing made him glance back, then he slowed for Morpain. The way he leaned on Georges made Laz think he'd been injured.

Laz heard shouted orders to hunt down the French and said, "They're hunting us."

"How do you know?" Morpain asked.

Laz almost said he had heard them, then he realized they'd spoken in English. "I saw some following us."

Georges pointed toward the forest and Morpain nodded. "We'll take cover."

The trio headed toward the nearest trees, ducked under branches, and crouched on mounded moss as they scanned the field. Dusk and smoke joined to shadow the clearing with early darkness. "You must rest," Georges whispered to Morpain. "We will stay in the trees."

"Why not head back to Louisbourg?" Laz asked.

Morpain replied, "With dark, I fear our sentries will shoot at anything that moves."

They crept under sweeping branches. The ground sucked at them and tried to trip them. As everything faded to darkness, Georges scouted for a hiding place. Now would be the perfect time, Laz realized, to make his way to the beach and ask to report to Hawkins on the *Constance*.

But Cooper had seen him, and Laz knew he'd report it. They'd believe he was fighting with the French. Cooper would never let him reach Hawkins, Laz was sure.

So he stuck close to Morpain's side. When the half-moon rose, it let them see again. They skirted the forest, sticking to the protection of shadows.

Finally, they stopped to rest. Laz was so thirsty he could barely swallow, but no one had a water bottle. Some of the soldiers had carried glass bottles with stoppers in little fitted baskets that attached to their belts. Laz tried to not think about them.

He passed the pistol back to Morpain, who said, "Foolish boy. I almost didn't get my blade in the way when you reached for this. Why didn't you use it?"

Laz remembered his memory and said, "I can't shoot. Please don't ask me to."

Above them, branches rustled. Morpain sighed. "My pride led to that disaster."

"What do you mean?" Laz asked.

"La Boularderie wanted to retreat. He was right that even 400 men would not have been enough. Eighty was foolishness. Those colonists were more prepared than I expected. And worse, they do not know the rules of combat."

"You mean sneaking through the trees?" Wasn't that normal? Laz thought, but realized it probably wasn't normal in 1745. He asked, "Doesn't anyone fight that way?"

Morpain harrumphed. "Our Mi'kmaq friends steal through the trees in that manner."

"Will the Mi'kmaq help us with this battle?"

"Yes. They are loyal to their friends." Morpain groaned. "I am too old for skulking in the dark. I must sleep for a few minutes."

"You are injured, Master. Let me tend your wound," Georges said.

Laz stood up. "I can keep watch."

"Thank you, my friend."

When Georges finished his first aid, he covered Morpain with a blanket of leaves. He was snoring in minutes. So far as Laz knew, the three of them were alone. Georges joined Laz for a minute.

"Do you like being a slave?" Laz asked, realizing it was a stupid question.

"I dream of freedom," Georges whispered. "Until then I have the best of masters."

"Yes, he is," Laz replied.

Georges settled down to sleep, giving Laz another opportunity to leave and find a way back to the *Constance*. All he had to do was sneak past sentries and a few thousand sleeping men, steal a skiff, and row into the bay in the darkness, hoping he could find the right ship before a musket ball found him.

Laz felt helpless. He knew Hawkins would never return his medal after Cooper poisoned him with reports of betrayal. He didn't know how to fix that because it was true. He had been helping. *My friend*, Morpain had called him.

Someone snorted in his sleep. Laz thought about the battle, and the memory that had hit him like a hammer blow from Thor. That seven-year-old Laz had known that his dad had been drunk. How had he known that? His father *never* drank. Laz rested his head against a tree. Maybe his dad never drank *after* that incident. Maybe it had scared him too.

And crows had watched them. That was why Laz always felt like fear had black flapping wings. Realizing that seemed to make the wings feel less dangerous.

Laz snuck out from under the trees. Knee-high ribbons of fog trailed across the ground. A slice of horizon faded from black to dull silver. He shivered. It grew still lighter as Laz scanned for movement in the area. The outline of Louisbourg became visible—the spire over King's Bastion, the square posts at the Dauphin Gate topped with armor-like sculptures, the steep rooftops dotted with chimneys.

A hand rested on Laz's shoulder. He stiffened, realized it was Morpain, and relaxed.

"She is beautiful, is she not?" Morpain whispered.

He meant the town. Laz nodded.

"Come. We are not far from the bayside road. We need to return," he said.

Laz was glad to be moving. His stomach growled. Neither of them commented, since they had no food. Georges walked behind them. They reached the road halfway between a scattering of buildings along the shore and the fort Morpain had pointed out on Laz's first day in Louisbourg: the Grand Battery. Morpain studied the situation in the growing light, his head bobbing and shaking in silent conversation. Georges stood behind him with arms crossed, looking like he wanted to get moving but saying nothing.

"This is not good." Morpain pointed to the battery. "The cannons in there are fixed. They only face out to the water to protect from sea assault. But with those underhanded colonists on land, how will we protect the battery?"

Laz hoped Morpain didn't want an answer. His stomach growled like a dog protecting a bone, long and low and persistent.

Morpain laughed and started toward the houses and Louisbourg. He tried to hide a limp. He knocked at the first door and invited themselves in for breakfast. The one-room cottage was dark, barely touched by the firelight and two candles on the table. A dank smell of wet wood hung in the air, made it thick and harder to breathe. In one of the dark corners, Laz thought he saw a tangle of bodies. Children, maybe.

After Morpain explained the situation, the man of the house set down two tumblers without glancing at Georges. "Brandy. To warm you after a night in the forest, Commander."

Laz stared at his pottery cup. Morpain nudged him. "Drink."

Laz touched one finger to the cold surface. "My father stopped drinking when I was seven."

Morpain tilted his head. "Tell me about it sometime. Now drink."

Laz took a swallow. Fire burned down his throat. He inhaled air in a noisy attempt to quench the flames. Shaking his head, he passed his cup to Georges.

The man smiled across the table. "Not the expensive stuff you find on the governor's table, but it does the trick."

Laz pressed his fist against his breastbone as heat unfurled like a ship's flag. He ate some dark bread and stinky cheese while Morpain explained to the man that he had to move behind the walls.

"But I must protect my home." He splayed broad fingers on the rough wood table.

Morpain shook his head. "We have to burn it down. This and all the houses outside the walls." Horror widened the man's eyes. Morpain reached across the table and cupped the man's wrist. "We cannot leave those British colonists any kind of shelter so close to Louisbourg. There are too many to fight off."

The man looked crushed, but he didn't question or argue with Morpain. Laz had noticed that people here always gave in to those they considered their betters. Louisbourg was a military town and the chain of command was always obeyed.

So after drinking their brandy and eating their food and telling the farmer his house would be burned down, they left. It was all very polite. Laz understood Morpain's reasoning but knew he'd hate getting that kind of news. He felt far older than thirteen.

They stopped at each house. There were only six. Every time Morpain delivered the same verdict. Be out by noon. Then soldiers would arrive to burn everything.

A child had run ahead with news that Commander Morpain had survived the battle. When Morpain, Laz, and Georges reached the small outer gates, soldiers held them open. Usually Laz walked beside Morpain, but when they stepped onto the bridge between the two gates, he fell back to walk beside Georges. The walls above the second, main gate were lined with soldiers waving their tricorns and shouting a welcome.

Inside the gate, more soldiers greeted them from the walls of the Dauphin Battery on the right, and still more crowded the roadway. They shouted and clapped their backs and cheered Morpain for the grand act of staying alive. The wall of the battery curved away, and in the green space between the battery and the town's buildings, all sorts of townsfolk gathered, from fishermen to innkeepers, even nuns with a cluster of children.

They surrounded the trio and cheered and welcomed them. Welcomed Morpain. Laz knew they included him because of Morpain. Even so, warmth Laz had never felt, except at Grandmère's, spread through him—much better than cheap brandy. He had moved so often as a kid, that he'd never felt at home anywhere but the farm. But Louisbourg, after only two weeks, felt like home.

"Lazare! Lazare!"

He searched the crowd for whoever was calling his name. People stepped aside, and Isabelle, mobcap askew, dark hair in an unruly braid, ran up to him. "I'm so glad you're safe. I was worried."

They shared a smile that cemented their friendship.

Morpain's hand slapped onto Laz's shoulder. "Come, Lazare. We have work to do. Messages to run. A fortress to prepare."

Laz stared blankly for a long moment then shook his head. A few of the closest people gasped. Morpain's eyebrows drew together. Before a lecture could begin Laz held up his hand. "Please. You slept last night, for a few hours. I kept watch all night. You need to let me get some rest or I'll be no use at all."

Everyone close enough to hear fell silent. Laz glimpsed wide eyes, a few open mouths. Horror. He lifted his chin and held Morpain's surprised gaze. Then a smile started to tug on the man's lips. "You are right. I can do without you for the morning. Georges will help. Report at noon. Isabelle, see that my young messenger gets some rest."

Isabelle walked with Laz and told him about the town's horrified reaction when Morpain did not return, and the relief they all felt this morning. Her voice kept Laz moving. Back at the house, he fell asleep so fast he didn't feel her drape his blanket over him.

Noon came too fast for Laz, and the rest of the day passed in a weary blur, as he spent it running messages from Morpain to every part of the fortifications. He had taken over the defenses, apparently with no objections from any of the officers, not even the ones whose jackets were trimmed with red, which signaled they were nobles, by birth or King Louis' decree.

The governor was a mess, distraught that Captain La Boularderie was either captured or dead. Most of the men had returned
safely to the fortress. They had all thought Morpain and Laz were
dead or captured too. Laz realized it was a good thing that Morpain had survived, because none of the other officers seemed to
know what to do. Or they were scared spitless like the governor.

Nightfall finally gave Laz a break from endless errand running. Madame Richard had left food warming for him—a fish
broth and a slice of dark bread. Not much, but Morpain had
ordered everyone to ration their food supplies. Laz washed it
down with some cheap wine she'd left out. He drank it because
thinking of well water and its gift of flux was enough to make
almost anything taste good. *I'd give a week's wages for a root
beer*, Laz thought.

The sound of Madame and her children drifted from the
back sitting room. They were having a Bible reading like they
did most nights. Soon they would start their prayers. Isabelle
came out of the dining room, which served as Madame Richard's store. "I have a bath waiting. The water is still a bit warm."

"Thank you." With shutters closed and half a dozen candles
lit, the room worked well for Laz's baths, which still hadn't been
the death of him, to everyone's surprise.

She flashed her nicest smile. "Good night, Lazare. You're
very brave."

The bath water was barely lukewarm. Laz quickly scrubbed
off dirt and grime, massaged soap into his hair and rinsed it. He
snuck upstairs with only his long shirt on, which would have
given Madame fits if she'd seen. Again, he fell asleep instantly.

It seemed only minutes later that Morpain stomped into his room. "Wake up, Lazare! Didn't you hear me calling from below?" He nudged Laz's shin. "Get dressed. I'll wait for you outside so I don't inconvenience Madame Richard any further." He lit a candle on the small chest in which Laz stored his clothes, and left.

When Laz reached the street, Morpain was leaning against the building, arms and ankles crossed. Morpain started walking and Laz joined him.

Laz was struck by the thought that a life working for Morpain and living in Louisbourg might be his future. Maybe he could be one of Morpain's sailors. He liked being on ships. Except for the maggoty bread.

That other life was becoming more like a dream, a ridiculous dream full of nonsensical things Laz could never explain to anyone. This busy day-to-day slog felt more real than memories of texting and watching movies and sitting in front of a computer. His hands and feet were callused. He was lean and fast. He had come to 1745 a boy, but Laz knew that was changing fast, even if he was only thirteen.

They stopped. Laz had been walking blindly, lost in thought. The yellow gate that opened to the harbor loomed above them. He asked, "What are we doing?"

"You, Lazare. What are *you* doing?"

Laz shivered in the frosty night. "I don't like the sound of that." When Morpain only shrugged, Laz gave in and said, "Fine. What am *I* doing?"

"You are delivering a most important message for me. A skiff waits."

"To one of the ships?"

"No," Morpain replied. "You must deliver a letter from the governor to Commander Thierry in the Grand Battery." He handed over a rolled paper sealed with a wax blot that looked black in the darkness.

Laz's thumb explored the shape of the seal. "Wouldn't going by road be easier?"

"We cannot know if the road is safe. British colonists might already have made their way from Gabarus Bay and might be waiting to ambush anyone who passes. But this bay is still ours, and it is only half the distance across the water. You have two sailors to row for you."

"Why aren't you going?" Laz asked.

Morpain's hand returned to rest on his shoulder. "I am needed here. If anything should happen—"

Laz stiffened. "You're saying this could be dangerous?"

"All war is dangerous, Lazare."

"So you're sending me because I'm not important. It won't matter if something happens."

"That isn't true. You are my messenger. You've saved these legs many miles. And I like you, Lazare. Why do you think I searched for you on the battlefield? I consider you a friend." He squeezed Laz's shoulder. "A friend who, at very inconvenient times, fails to recognize the chain of command. The governor has ordered me, and so it goes."

The sting of Morpain's complaint was taken away by that word, *friend*. He was old enough to be Laz's grandfather, but Laz felt the same way. "So this is an order. I understand. But...

why can't the sailors deliver the message?" Friend or not, he didn't want to do this task.

Morpain sighed and kept his voice low. "I cannot completely trust they will do it, though they might say it was done. Given the bad winter, they might even desert. You I absolutely know will see it through."

A sailor hiked up the wooden ramp. "We're ready to leave, Commander." He held a small lantern up to throw light over them.

"Thank you. Berenger is ready to go." Morpain dropped his hand from Laz's shoulder.

"No disrespect, sir, but he's a bit young for such an important mission, isn't he?"

"He's very capable, sailor. So long as you don't put a musket in his hand."

CHAPTER TWENTY-FOUR

The motion of the boat and the quiet slap of oars dipping into water put Laz to sleep in the bow. He woke up, shivering, when the sailors beached the skiff.

A dark, hulking wall loomed to his left, stretching along the shore. Laz was reminded of a beached whale on its side, with the closest of its two towers sticking up like a fin. It was much bigger than it looked from across the bay.

"Hurry up and deliver the message," one sailor whispered. "There might be enemies about. We're staying with the skiff."

Laz hugged the wall and worked his way to the landward side of the battery. He almost fell into a pit. The moonlight showed that some kind of construction work had been going on. He snuck around the site, crouching down. *Just delivering a message*, he kept repeating to himself as he worked his way toward the entrance.

A voice from above just about made him dive for cover. "Who goes there?"

His reply was hoarse. "Morpain's messenger."

"Speak the password."

"No one gave me a password." Laz kept low to hide in the shadows. "Let me in."

"You might be the enemy." Laz thought he heard trembling in the voice.

He replied, "I'm speaking French. How many British colonists speak French? I have an important message for Commander Thierry from the King's Bastion. In writing."

"Then advance, but know there are muskets trained on you."

"Of course there are." Laz sounded more confident than he felt. His real worry was that some of those muskets were behind him in the forest.

The door creaked open only far enough to let him inside. A sweaty soldier led Laz to the left, to a room where over 100 men were gathered around tables. They crowded around and demanded to know what kind of reinforcements Louisbourg was sending.

"I don't know anything. I'm a messenger. Commander Morpain sent me to deliver this letter from the governor." Laz held it out. "Where is Commander Thierry?"

The soldiers parted and a man stepped forward. Laz offered the letter. The man snatched it and used his knife to flick open the seal. He read silently then skewered Laz with a sharp look. "Did they not decide to destroy the battery?"

"I don't know what it says."

A few called out for the commander to tell them what the letter said. The commander held up his hand and the room fell silent except for a crying baby in the corner. Laz craned his neck and saw a cluster of forty or more women and children.

Thierry read, "To the commander of the Grand Battery. You are hereby ordered to spike all the cannons and withdraw to Louisbourg immediately. Signed, Governor Duchambon."

The man's expression shrank into something angry and dangerous. He stuffed the letter in his jacket.

"What does he mean, spike the cannons?" Laz asked.

"Destroy them so our enemies cannot use them."

"But we get to withdraw to the fortress," someone from the back said. Men started murmuring agreement.

"Then let's do it and get out of here," the commander said.

Men rushed toward a stairwell. The commander pointed at Laz. "Come help. We have twenty-eight cannons and spiking is a two-man job."

"But my boat is—"

"Now. We must do this quickly. The men are certain they saw movement in the hills today." His hand latched onto the back of Laz's neck like a vise. Laz tried to squirm free then said, "Shouldn't those women be in Louisbourg? I could take some with me right now in the skiff waiting for me."

"Their men are here. They'll go when we all go."

The commander kept Laz with him, as if he expected him to run. Laz might have if he'd had the chance.

Lanterns hung the length of the battery, lighting a wide hall that stretched in a shallow vee. Men shouted and grabbed tongs, rods, and hammers. One of them delivered a set of the tools to the commander, who handed them to Laz.

At his instruction, Laz used the tongs to hold the end of the rod against the cannon's touchhole. The commander began to drive the rod down into the hole, making the cannon unusable because then the powder couldn't be lit. Every blow vibrated up

Laz's arms. The commander ordered him to hold the rod steady.
The room echoed with a noisy mix of shouts, clashing, clang-
ing, and swearing. There were more than enough men to do
the job, though still the commander insisted that Laz help him.

Once the rod had started sinking, the commander held out
the hammer to Laz. They both turned when two men began
shouting at each other. One grabbed a hammer from the other's
hand, swinging it wildly. It batted a lantern off its hook. The
light flashed toward the back wall and a pile of small barrels.

Something started hissing and sparking and Commander
Thierry shouted, "Down!"

Laz dropped to the floor just as a loud boom thundered,
blasting air and grit everywhere. Smoke rolled through the
room. A man began screaming. Laz stayed down, fear pounding
through him like a frantic drum solo, while Thierry leaped up
and disappeared into the leaden cloud. The sour smell of black
powder made Laz clamp his hand over his nose and mouth, but
he could still taste and smell it. A black-faced soldier pulled
him to his feet and brushed him off with a laugh. "We look like
chimney sweeps."

It took Laz a second to realize the man meant his face was
also soot-covered. "Was someone hurt?" His words quivered.

"A friar who had moved to stop the argument. Commander
Thierry is seeing to him. Let's finish this cannon." The man's
calm helped keep Laz's fear under control.

They each took turns hammering the spike. The blows quivered up Laz's arms like minor earthquakes. During his second
turn he swung the hammer down, and the blowback was so

hard, he lost his grip. The hammer clattered to the floor. The soldier laughed. "The rod hit the bottom of the cannon. No one can drive iron through iron. We are done."

All around, men were finishing, laughing with relief, heading back to the barracks to grab their belongings. Most of the smoke had cleared out. Laz couldn't spot the commander and so assumed he had taken the wounded man downstairs. Now everyone else streamed out of the room, leaving him alone on the cannon deck. He stood at the top of the stairs and listened. The soldiers quickly deserted the Grand Battery, and with a final slam of the door silence rose from below.

They had forgotten about him. Laz retreated to a gun port, opened the shutters, and peered down at the water. The boat that had delivered him was gone. He wasn't surprised. The stillness confirmed that he was alone.

Completely alone in the middle of a war.

CHAPTER TWENTY-FIVE

Laz climbed onto the thick stone ledge of the gun port and pulled his knees to his chest. Below the moonlight danced over waves that sloshed against the stony shore. His thoughts were tidal, rising and falling, as he tried to think what to do.

Maybe he could just wait in the Grand Battery until the colonists discovered him then ask for Captain Hawkins. Again he wondered if he should go instead to Gabarus Bay and search for the captain. But so many days spent with the French made that possibility float farther away, and Louisbourg pulled at him like the full moon pulls on the tides.

Laz lurched off the ledge when a voice startled him. "Hello? Is anyone here?"

"I am," Laz replied. A soldier emerged from a doorway at the far end of the long room.

"We heard faint noise, then nothing. Has something happened?" The soldier advanced rapidly.

Laz was confused. "Where did you come from?"

He motioned back toward the doorway. "From the south tower."

"Wait. There are soldiers in the towers?"

"Yes. Guard duty. There are twelve in the south tower and another twelve in the north."

Laz blinked rapidly. How could the commander have forgotten the soldiers on guard duty? How could everyone have forgotten?

"Who are you?" the soldier asked.

"A messenger from Louisbourg."

"What happened here?" The man pointed to Laz's face.

"We were spiking the cannons and somehow some gunpowder exploded."

"Spiking?" The soldier's voice rose in an alarmed manner.

Behind Laz, footsteps rattled down the stairs like a machine gun volley. More soldiers charged into the room. One pointed out a gun port. "Everyone's leaving!"

"Speak sense, imbecile," the first soldier replied.

"They are! We saw the boats. A dozen *chaloupes* at least."

"What do you know of this, messenger?" the first soldier asked.

"It's true. I brought a letter telling the commander to abandon the Grand Battery."

The man started swearing and marched back toward the south tower. Over his shoulder he ordered everyone to stay right there until he had gotten the other men. When he returned with the rest of the guards they decided to search for another boat. Otherwise they would attempt to walk back to Louisbourg and hope the road wasn't guarded by the colonists.

The men swarmed down the stairs to the main level. Again Laz was left alone. The word *siege* popped into his head. He hadn't heard the word spoken, but it seemed that's what Morpain was preparing for.

If Laz went back into the town, the gates would close and he would be trapped there with everyone else. Unless he left now.

Go with the soldiers or try to leave. His thoughts bounced back and forth like a ping-pong ball.

"Messenger? Are you coming?"

Laz startled and rubbed his face. The soldier from the south tower stepped back into the room. "Come. You are afraid, yes? We are all afraid. I am so relieved to be returning to the fortress, I cannot say. Let's go."

Still Laz couldn't convince his feet to move. As the soldier turned away, he said, "Come on, messenger. You don't want to return to Louisbourg alone. There is safety in numbers when enemies might be hiding in the shadows."

The image of Cooper's contorted features came to mind. He was out there somewhere, looking to take another shot. With a shudder, Laz joined the remaining soldiers for the return to Louisbourg. They found a *chaloupe* in a creek not far from the Grand Battery. Once they were on the water and rowing across the bay, Laz felt only relief. He was going home.

Two days later, in the afternoon, Laz was running yet another message for Morpain, this one to the military blacksmith on the north side of town. He came out of the compound and almost bumped into Isabelle. She had a basket of clothes that looked like military issue, probably for mending. Laz took the basket and walked with her down Rue Royale.

The two-storey wooden building on the right cast its shadow over them. On the left, the military compound's wall stretched for a block to where a gate opened to the architect's garden beside his house. They had almost reached it when a boom sent a shiver through the ground and rattled windows.

Laz dropped the basket, grabbed Isabelle's hand, and pulled her into the garden. They huddled against the fence.

"What was that?" Isabelle whispered.

It took a second for Laz to respond. "Cannon. The colonists have been digging in along the high crest of land beyond the walls. The officers are worried they might find a way to get their cannons across the soft ground."

Another boom was followed by a thud that vibrated the fence. Laz shuddered. A cloud of dust floated upwards. He guessed the outer wall had been hit.

"Apparently they found a way." Laz was surprised how calm he felt. He noticed they were still holding hands and gave a gentle tug. "Let's get you back to the Richards' house. You should be safe there."

Fear stamped onto Isabelle's face. "What's happening?"

"The siege is starting."

CHAPTER TWENTY-SIX

The trick, Laz decided, was to keep moving. Fear couldn't flap through his mind if it couldn't keep up with him. After he took Isabelle to the house, he tracked down Morpain to deliver his next message.

Morpain was a whirlwind, overseeing the defense of the city, not from the safety of a bunker, but from every corner, every bastion, and every street. He encouraged civilians and soldiers alike. Strain lightened on faces when he arrived. He held the town together while the other officers mostly hid, and the governor quivered in obvious fear.

Soon, faces began to light up when Laz arrived with Morpain's messages. The commander's importance rubbed off on him. And he didn't feel in danger so long as he kept moving. The cannonballs weren't aimed at him, not like Cooper's musket had been, and knowing that made him feel safer. Laz got to know from the sound of the cannon where the shot was coming from, and whether he needed to take cover.

Mortars were the worst. They made a deeper *whump*. And they were made to break apart on impact, sending shrapnel flying and tearing apart whatever they hit. Laz always took cover when he heard a mortar.

The bombardment usually came in a wave, then in fits and starts, then another wave. The unpredictability made everyone edgy. It would be quiet for several hours, then—*boom!*—it would start again, sending everyone scurrying for cover. Mostly, Laz just kept running. He'd worked out some shortcuts through yards and over fences, sometimes along fence tops. Hard to hit a moving target, he decided.

A week into the siege, Morpain took Laz up on the wall in the northeast corner, away from the reach of the landward cannons. The blockade ships were close enough to be visible now. They kept their distance because the town's walls were higher than their cannon, so they could be fired on before they could get close enough to fire back. Unfortunately, the surrounding hills were higher than the town's walls, so the colonists could lob cannonballs into Louisbourg, but the town's return fire couldn't reach them.

Dusk was falling as Morpain paced, squinting out to sea, then surveying the town. Some buildings had been hit, and their roofs were jagged, like broken teeth.

Morpain turned toward the bay. "I hate this view most of all. All our ships scuttled. My beloved *Castor*, grounded on a sandbar, a hole in her belly."

"Why did the governor order them sunk?" Laz asked.

"To prevent the enemy from capturing them. Also, the men onboard are now free to defend the city."

"You told me the day I arrived that we were safe. But now the colonists have repaired the cannons in the Grand Battery and are firing across the water on the town, as well as firing from the ridge to the west. Are we really still safe?"

"Ah, the ignominy," Morpain said. "Attacked with our own cannons. I told the governor we should have fought to keep control of that battery." As he often did, he rested his hand on Laz's shoulder. He liked how protective it felt. Morpain continued, "Are we safe? Yes. Our walls are damaged but holding. We will prevail. Have you watched them out on the hills? Buffoons. Undisciplined and slovenly. You can tell it from this distance. Their lack of discipline will result in their failure. They will grow bored and frustrated, and will go home."

Silence seeped up from the ground to wrap them in night. Only the quiet lapping of waves on shore interrupted the hush. Laz felt a moment of unexpected peace. The tang of salt air flared his nostrils and cleared his thoughts. He had the sense that everyone who built this fortress town was standing shoulder to shoulder with him. Laz felt part of something bigger than himself, something that mattered.

Fingers squeezed Laz's shoulder. "What are you thinking, my young friend?"

After a long pause, Laz admitted, "I love this town. I want to protect it."

"As do I, my friend. As do I."

Distant campfires silhouetted the far line of hills. Laz searched the narrow glow for figures or movement. Then, *boom!* A cannon at the Grand Battery fired.

Laz blinked then squinted as he watched a glowing dot arch over the bay and grow into a ball. "What's that?"

"Despicable!" cried Morpain. "They have heated shot."

The glowing ball sailed over the wall, the warehouses, and the inns. It hit a house in a street two blocks past Madame Richard's.

Another distant crack of thunder and another red ball flew toward the town. Against the blackness, the glowing cannonball looked like a bad special effect in a movie. A jolt of unreality rolled over Laz, and he pinched his thigh to make sure he was awake.

In the street that had been hit, shouts rose. Someone was yelling that his house was on fire. Morpain sighed. "We have to get everyone out of their houses and into the storerooms built into the walls in the bastions. We must move quickly, Lazare."

The second cannonball landed. With a nudge from Morpain, Laz bolted into the night.

That night and the next, Laz didn't get any sleep. He helped Morpain direct people fighting a fire. And another. Long lines of men and buckets, from the wells to the flames. He delivered messages to get food and water to the civilians hiding from this new threat.

A few snatches of sleep in the day were interrupted by Morpain sending Laz with yet another message. That second day, Laz was bleary, running at half speed. He was so tired his ears were ringing. His footsteps thudded against the hard-packed dirt as he bolted down Rue Toulouse, toward the yellow gate.

The white wall on his right exploded outward. Tossed Laz against stone.

Threw him into darkness.

CHAPTER TWENTY-SEVEN

"**What some people will do** to get a little sleep." Morpain's voice coaxed Laz awake.

"What happened?" Laz rasped. "I only remember...a wall attacking me."

Morpain touched a stein of spruce beer to Laz's lips. "A mortar shell. You must not have heard it. The surgeon pulled a narrow sliver of wood from your left arm. We are lucky it chose your arm, not your neck or chest."

Laz's head pounded as if a hammer was lodged behind his eyes. "Arm hurts a bit. Not too bad." Morpain gave him another sip of spruce beer.

"Isabelle came. She said the night after the siege started you told her if anyone in the family was injured she should clean the wound with boiled water, then pour alcohol over it." Morpain took a damp cloth and wiped Laz's face. "You do things strangely on Île Saint-Jean. But she insisted. It doesn't seem to have worsened your wound, but it did waste some of my best brandy."

"Thank you," Laz whispered.

"No. Thank Isabelle. She is a good friend."

"Yes. How long was I out?"

"Out? You mean asleep? More than a day."

"Any more houses burn?"

"One." Morpain lifted his head. "Here is your angel, come to watch over you. I will go. Heal quickly, Lazare. No one runs messages as fast as you. I need you." He patted Laz's shoulder and left.

Laz couldn't keep his eyes open. He inhaled slowly and got a nose full of stink. Sweat, blood, dirt, and something fouler, diarrhea maybe. The cool cloth on his forehead coaxed his eyes open.

"You're awake," Isabelle said. "I'm glad."

Beyond his pallet and out of his line of sight, a man coughed and groaned.

"Where am I?" Laz whispered. It was dark, and the single candle on a nearby table didn't throw much light. His head hurt too much to turn and look around.

"Dauphin Bastion barracks. There are two other injured men here."

"I want to go home."

"To Madame Richard's? Commander Morpain doesn't want anyone in their houses at night when the red cannonballs are falling. The men spend all night fighting them to save the houses that are hit."

Red glowing balls, raining destruction at night. It was to scare everyone, Laz realized. They wouldn't be nearly as dramatic in the daylight. His eyes grew heavy.

"Thanks for being a friend. Please don't leave," he whispered. He never heard her answer.

Laz woke up wanting to get outside. Better to be dodging a few cannonballs than suffocating in the smell that filled this barracks.

He found Morpain in the King's Bastion, meeting with the officers, giving orders while the governor slouched in his chair, shoulders up around his ears, and nodded to everything. Laz sat until the meeting ended.

Morpain looked pleased to see Laz but commented that he looked pale. He was sent away with a message and orders to walk, not run, until he was feeling stronger. Laz ran out of gas mid-afternoon and retreated to Madame Richard's empty house and his attic bedroom, doubtful that any bombardment would happen before night because there had been a round at noon. He felt as if he'd been trampled by an angry moose.

Isabelle found him there, asleep. She'd come looking when Morpain had asked her about his whereabouts. On the way back to the barracks, they started talking about what they wanted to do when the siege was over. Laz realized he had stopped thinking about ever getting back to that other time.

For the next five days, Laz tried to find time to at least eat a meal with Isabelle so they could talk. Sometimes their laughter drew irritated looks. Once Laz gave her hand a squeeze and she didn't pull it away. It had felt...really nice, he decided.

On May 31, the guards at King's Bastion sent Laz to the wall nearest the harbor entrance. When he arrived, Morpain handed him the extra spyglass and pointed out to sea. Laz searched the horizon, then closer in.

A French ship was attempting to run the blockade. Word had spread and a group of onlookers had gathered. When the ship got close enough, Morpain announced it was a warship. Everyone cheered. Soon no one needed a spyglass to see what was happening.

The warship was in full sail, racing toward the harbor mouth. But two British men-o-war were on an intercept course. When the biggest British ship got close enough, it turned to run parallel with the French ship. Laz leaned on the parapet, eye glued to the spyglass so he could see better. The cannon covers lifted on the British ship, so he figured the French were preparing to fire too.

Cannons firing made a distant drumroll—*boom, boom, boom, boom*. Smoke billowed around the two ships, hiding the results in a fog. The smoke drifted away on the wind. The British ship launched a second volley. Everyone on the wall gasped.

The battle continued for a while, but it was obvious the British were winning. The second British man-o-war arrived. It came alongside the French ship on its port side. Instead of the French ship opening its hatches to fire cannons, the French flag began to lower.

Everyone around Laz groaned then drifted away. The spyglass showed the French ship being boarded by redcoats. The sight punched Laz in the stomach. He turned his back on it and handed over the spyglass. Tears burned behind his eyes. "We're going to lose, aren't we?"

Morpain laid his arm across Laz's shoulders. "You are not allowed to say such things in public, Lazare. We will fight on. If the walls hold. If the Island Battery holds. If our food lasts. If God favors us, we will prevail."

The New England colonists seemed to get energy from the capture of the French warship. Their land cannons thundered all afternoon. When Laz had to pass by Madame Richard's, he saw that his attic room, along with half the second floor, was a gaping hole.

Black wings flapped through his mind.

CHAPTER TWENTY-EIGHT

$\mathbf{I}$n the following days, most of Laz's message running was to get updates from the Dauphin Battery for Morpain. The colonists had built a new battery close enough to exchange fire with the French battery. Other new batteries had cropped up, closer than the line of hilltops, which gave the cannon and mortar fire more power. More houses received damage. The holes gouged into the outer walls by repeated attacks inched toward being full breaches.

On-and-off thunder rattled the town. Quivering, stinking people crammed into shelters where they only spoke in hushed, fearful whispers. Sentries were uncertain and jumpy. The beer and wine was gone, replaced with flux-inducing water. Rations thinned to the basics: bread, fish, and peas.

Isabelle and Laz often ate without talking, but their shoulders touched, and that seemed to give them strength.

During a lull in the fighting, Laz found Morpain with the other officers on the wall, beside a crater that had taken out a cannon along with a chunk of wall. They were all spying out the newest defenses of the colonists. "Could we overpower them in a frontal assault?" one asked. "This has to end," another said.

Morpain lowered his spyglass. His face looked more drawn

than usual, like a starving wolf instead of one on the hunt. "Yes. We must act soon. Our powder supply is getting dangerously low."

The officers all looked uneasy. One said, "Look. There is activity at the cannons. They are preparing to attack again."

The officers scattered. Morpain glared at the hilltop for a moment, then turned. He spotted Laz, grabbed his elbow, and steered him down the ramp to the parade ground. The long barracks had taken several hits and the bell tower's steeple seemed to be leaning slightly. Laz asked, "Shouldn't the steeple get propped up so it doesn't collapse?"

"It's been like that for a week. No one wants to attempt repair," Morpain said.

A single *boom* announced the start of another bombardment. Laz felt the thud underfoot as the shot hit the outer wall of the neighboring bastion. Morpain's grip tightened and he pointed with his free hand. "Get into one of those shelters. Stay there until this attack stops."

"But—"

"No." He gave Laz a shake. "You must stop taking so many chances. I have seen almost 100 men killed in this siege. I do not want you to be one of them. Go."

"I'll go crazy in a storeroom. You can barely breathe in there."

Morpain's eyes glimmered as he took Laz's chin and fixed him with his stare. "Please, Lazare. Do this for me." His voice rasped with emotion.

Laz nodded, gave Morpain a quick hug, and ran toward the row of six red doors set into the north wall of the bastion.

The storeroom was guarded by thick doors and lined with stone. As safe a place as Louisbourg could offer. Fresh air entered through small barred windows on either side of the door. A scattering of candles, constantly burning, created a thin layer of smoke that clung to the ceiling. Bodies carpeted the floor as people huddled in groups. Whispers quivered with fear. The nuns near the back, with children crowded around, conducted school lessons.

Laz picked his way past a few groups, hoping to see Isabelle. It would be easier to be stuck here with a friend. In the corner, a woman in an expensive but dirty dress watched Laz work his way toward her. Three children clung to her, colorful chicks tucked under the wings of their fancy mother hen. She looked ready to peck his eyes out for daring to look at her.

The daughter in a shimmery blue dress lifted her head, as if she felt her mother tense. She looked for the source of disturbance, and turned toward Laz.

Emeline.

It couldn't be, Laz thought. She fixed dark eyes on him. *Oh God. Was it?* Laz stumbled over people, apologized. The girl's expression grew from curious to uncertain. Laz tripped on a leg and fell to his knees beside her.

He grabbed her hand. "Emeline? Is that you?" He could barely breathe for the weight crushing his chest.

She pulled free and her mother hauled her closer. "Get away from my child."

"Y-your? It looks—" Laz searched the girl's face. She looked so much like Emeline it was like a sword had been run through him. The woman's fury radiated off her with blacksmith furnace intensity. Laz raised both hands. "I'm sorry. She...looks like my sister. I didn't mean—"

Laz bolted for the door, not caring if he stepped on anyone. Cries followed in his wake. Out on the deserted parade ground he turned and turned again, searching the sky, the walls, watching a cannonball fly over the barracks. He could barely breathe. Barely think.

When had he last thought about his family?

Laz dropped onto his hands and knees, and vomited up his small breakfast. Acid taste filled his mouth and he spat. He got up. Arm across his convulsing midsection, he made his way out of the bastion and down the Rue Toulouse to the yellow gate. He heard some cannonballs landing, but the sound was muffled by the roaring in his ears.

He had been gone from his time for over two months. In the last four weeks, he'd barely given his family a thought. More like never.

How selfish am I? Laz thought. *Have I really given up on returning?*

He slumped onto the ground and leaned into the corner, where the low, gray harbor wall met the yellow wooden gate. Laz wanted to cry, but his dry eyes burned. In the next street, a mortar shell hit a house and the exploding debris sent a plume of smoke and dust into the sky. He flinched but otherwise felt nothing.

They were destroying his home. Except it wasn't. He had a home in Boston. With his parents and Emeline.

Laz wondered how he could have forgetten that. *Morpain*, his inner voice whispered. Morpain was a magnet. He loved Louisbourg because Morpain was here. Because he loved Morpain like a friend.

Like a father.

The realization was another punch to the gut. This one drove the truth deep. Morpain believed in him, trusted him. He never criticized, even when Laz deserved it.

He deserved it now. Emeline would never give up on him. But he'd given up on her.

She'd be waiting for him to come home. Expecting it.

For her sake, Laz thought, *I have to try.*

CHAPTER TWENTY-NINE

The problem gnawed at Laz for two days. How to get home. The key was his St. Christopher medal, in Captain Hawkins' possession. To get it back, all Laz had to do was try to sabotage the French.

Isabelle and Laz were silently nibbling lunch when he realized that sabotaging the French would bring the siege to a quicker end, and that was a good thing for the town. They were losing the battle, even if no one would say it. If they lost it faster, Isabelle and Morpain would be safe, so doing what Hawkins wanted would save French lives. It was so obvious.

That night, Morpain dragged Laz from his pallet in their shelter. They raced to the yellow gate, joined by soldiers from every bastion. The men spread out along the low wall in the foggy night, muskets at the ready. The sounds of battle floated across the water from the Island Battery. Shouts and shots and screams. Laz's lungs sucked in air as if he'd run a marathon.

People were dying. If the battle came into the town tonight, he wouldn't be able to save anyone. He'd be lucky to save himself.

The men were silent except for a few who whispered prayers.

Laz whispered, "Could this be a distraction and they're going to attack on the west?"

Morpain clapped his back. "Sentries are still there, but go check."

Laz raced up the main road and into the King's Bastion, calling to the guard as he flew past him. Up the ramp to the top of the wall. The sentries asked what was happening. Laz told them. They all strained to see any movement. The fog hid everything but there were no sounds of men approaching. Laz told the sentries to wake some artillerymen and fire a cannon if they spotted signs of an attack.

Laz stopped on the edge of the parade ground. Mentioning the cannon made him think of black powder. Morpain had said their supplies were running low. And Hawkins had said that wetting powder would make it useless. Wet powder couldn't be lit. If the cannons couldn't fire because they had no powder, then Louisbourg would have to surrender.

All he had to do was wet the powder and escape over the wall, and Hawkins would return his medal. And he could get back home. To Emeline.

The attack on the Island Battery had been repelled, with no major injuries for the French, but the men in the battery had captured 116 men and claimed they had rained death on the enemy. The next day's silence from the colonists' side seemed like proof. A full day with no shots fired.

Everyone came out to enjoy the weak sunlight, hidden behind a gauzy layer of fog. On the pale faces, smiles were more like grimaces. Laz sat on the edge of the wall, feet dangling over the inner compound and watched people from different storeroom shelters hug.

Most soldiers were resting or working on repairing walls. The repair work was never-ending, and generally undone with a few well-placed shots. The soldiers were more exhausted than the civilians. The longer Laz watched, the more he knew he was doing the right thing. He had to help end this, even if everyone hated him for it.

Feet still dangling, he lay back and stretched out his arms. The pale gray sky was remote, uncaring about any suffering. He wished he could be like that. It scared Laz how much he cared.

Isabelle sat on the grassy wall top beside him. She tucked her skirt around her ankles. "What are you doing?"

Laz shrugged. "Thinking."

"About what?"

Laz squinted one eye. "I'd really like a bath. I haven't had one in weeks."

She burst out laughing. A nearby sentry asked to hear the joke. Isabelle replied, "We are nearly starving and all Lazare wants is a bath."

He sneered and made some comment about Morpain's lapdog. *If that's what I am I want to be a clean lapdog*, Laz thought. He stank. Though everyone did, so most of the time he didn't notice. He rubbed at his teeth with his index finger, which had been his only toothbrush since he'd arrived. Ben had showed him how to use saltwater to help with cleaning, and he'd continued finger-brushing in Louisbourg. He paused. He hadn't thought about Ben in weeks. Since he was part of

Captain Hawkins' crew, Laz assumed he was safe. He hoped he got to see him when he made it back to Hawkins.

"Where are you now, Lazare? Not here," Isabelle said.

Laz reached for her hand then stopped himself. "If anything happens...know that I like being your friend."

"On the one day no cannonballs fly, you would talk about dying?" She frowned. "I don't understand you, even if we are friends."

"My thoughts are jumping all over today. I should go. I have a lot of work and probably won't be here at dinner." Some work for Morpain, and a lot for his plan. Laz had come as close as he dared to saying goodbye to Isabelle. If things went the way he hoped, he'd be back on the *Constance* before morning.

The quarter moon and clouds gave Laz good cover of darkness. He had a wooden bucket with a rope tied to it, and a crowbar in case he needed it to open powder kegs.

He picked the easiest bastion first, where they'd watched the French warship get captured. It was lightly guarded. After Laz filled his bucket from the well closest to the bastion, he snuck along the walls to approach the powder magazine. The thudding in his ears was so loud it seemed to block out every sound.

With the spare master key he'd stolen from Morpain's desk, getting into the magazine was easy. But inside was a tomb. He skimmed his hand over the wall near the door and found the alcove shelf with a candle and flint. It took a few tries to light the candle. He set it in a lantern casing attached to the wall and started working. There was only one full keg in the magazine. He pried off the top and poured the whole bucket over the powder.

It took him longer than expected to make two more trips to soak the two partial kegs. Then he headed up to the larger Queen's Bastion, beside King's Bastion. This one was trickier because of the troop barracks inside it, but the well was near the magazine entrance. He entered through an unguarded sidedoor from King's Bastion.

Laz felt more confident now, certain the sentries were focusing their attention beyond the wall, not behind them. The pitch black hid a lot more kegs. He was starting to doubt he could get this one, plus King's Bastion and Dauphine Battery done in one night.

But he couldn't stop. Prying the lid off the first keg made an awful screech. He winced at how loud the sound was inside this stone cavern. The sound didn't carry outside.

The noisy part was getting water from the well. He had to feed the pail slowly down the shaft as it clunked quietly against the well's walls. The pail was heavy as he drew it up, and thunked with a deeper, fuller sound. But the sentries never looked.

He lifted the pail out and returned to the door he'd left open a crack. Each time he went out he had to snuff the candle, so relighting it wasted another minute. The second keg also shrieked as he pried it open. He set the lid aside and reached for the pail.

"What are you doing?" a gruff voice demanded.

Laz dropped the pail and wheeled around. A sergeant he recognized, who was in his nightshirt, stood in the doorway. Without thinking, Laz charged the slight man, bowled him over, and raced toward the bastion's exit.

The sergeant began shouting, "Saboteur!"

CHAPTER THIRTY

Laz crashed into the guard at the gate to Queen's Bastion, knocked him flying, and kept running. Fear's black wings flapped around his head. He'd be safe if he kept moving.

With all the civilians sleeping in the storerooms of the bastions, Laz had the freedom of the town. But the trick was getting out. Behind him, shouts were spreading alarm. He tried to ignore them, to focus on his route, his next move.

Get up high. People don't look up. His dad had told him that once during a game of hide-and-seek. Without meaning to, he arrived at Madame Richard's house. He shot inside and up the stairs, and almost fell into the hole made by the cannonball that had destroyed his room. Pausing to let his eyes adjust, he searched for an escape. Details emerged from the dark. He leaped from the broken stairs to the still-intact side of the attic, and rolled away from the splintered edge.

Then Laz climbed out the back dormer and clung to its roofline until his footing was solid. He edged along the gutter, bent forward so his palms were pressed against the wooden shingles. That house met with its neighbor. He eased down until his shoes tapped the top of the pole fence separating their yards. Shouting was coming from two directions, but he let the sound pass over. He pivoted on the post and eyed the length of uneven fence, visible now that the moon had decided to come out. He took a breath and sprinted along the top.

Laz leaped the four feet to the neighbor's low barn and raced over its gently sloped roof. He dropped off that, bolted across the yard, vaulted the fence, and ducked into the next street.

The route was taking him to the northeast, closer to the bastion he'd already sabotaged, but farther away from the landward walls. Maybe he could swim to the Island Battery and steal a boat. After sprinting through another yard, he hopped onto a fence and pulled himself onto a roof. The houses were lower in this block and their rooftops weren't so steep. He clambered over three roofs that were close enough to jump one to the next, then stepped off the last roof to land in a crouch.

Laz raced toward the fence separating the yard from the roadway and vaulted over.

He landed on the other side. Straightened. A half-circle of bayonets greeted him, their points glinting in lantern light.

A sergeant held the lantern high. "Try to escape, you filthy saboteur. Give us an excuse to lance you."

CHAPTER THIRTY-ONE

Two soldiers grabbed Laz. Two marched behind him with bayonets that poked him if he slowed. He only tried that once. The other six encircled him and the sergeant, who led them down Quay Road toward the yellow Frederic Gate, almost white in the moonlight.

Beside the gate they dragged Laz up onto the platform with the tall post. He remembered sitting on the platform his first day in Louisbourg. Now the two men holding him slammed his back up against the wide pole. Another came up behind him and pushed his head forward, then clamped an iron shackle around his neck. The sergeant locked a padlock on the manacle and slapped Laz. Then he spit on him.

Leaning close, the sergeant breathed foul air over Laz's face. "That will keep you until morning." The man punched Laz in the stomach. He started to double over but the chain reached its full length with a *clank*. He was gasping for air as the sergeant sent messengers with word the saboteur had been caught. He ordered his men to form up, and he marched them back along Quay Road.

Laz tugged at the heavy collar, yanked the padlock, reefed on the chain where it was anchored to the post. Nothing budged.

The chain wasn't long enough for him to sit. It only allowed him a step forward or to either side of the post. The moon sank toward the horizon. Laz stood in the growing darkness and tried to stay calm, but black wings dive-bombed him. He ducked, and the shackle slammed his jaw closed. Teeth aching, he leaned against the post, waiting for dawn.

Unable to keep moving, fear caught up and flapped wildly through his mind.

After sunrise Morpain emerged from the half-dark, a block down Rue Toulouse. He slouched, head down, hands clasped behind his back, like an old man. Without changing his slow pace, he trudged to the punishment platform and stepped onto it. Only then did he lift his head. Georges had followed, and stood a dozen steps away, holding a knife and looking like he wanted to use it.

Morpain's eyes were watery and rimmed red. His cheeks sagged. He kept silent and searched Laz's face. A tear escaped, then another. Laz couldn't speak. His betrayal was branded on Morpain's expression. After long moments, Morpain cupped his hands on Laz's cheeks, bent his head, and kissed him on the forehead.

As Morpain left, Laz broke down. Begged him to come back. His step slowed, but he never turned. Laz started to sink down, but the chain stopped him. He had to grab it to haul himself back up, and kept holding it so his knees didn't buckle. It took a long time before strength returned to his legs.

When the day began quietly, some brave people ventured out. A group of soldiers came by, hurled insults, then stones.

Laz hid behind the pole. Some children pelted him with mud balls. One caught him on the cheek and a stone in it sliced a shallow cut. Two women came by with brooms and laid into him. A soldier with them kept his musket pointed at Laz, so he covered his head and pressed his face against the pole. His back throbbed for an hour after they left.

Around noon, a familiar figure flew down the road, skirt held high. As Isabelle got closer, the horror on her face stung Laz. She stood near the platform and quietly asked, "How could you do this to us?"

"The British are my only way home," Laz said. "They gave me no choice."

"You had a choice!" she yelled. "You could have chosen your friends!" She covered her face with her hands and started sobbing.

He stretched out a hand but couldn't reach her. "I'm sorry, Isabelle. You're right. I'm sorry."

They were both standing, both crying, when the colonial battery beyond the Dauphin Gate barked. Laz froze, dumbstruck, as a cannonball arched over the battery and crashed into the end of the warehouse half a block away. Stones and shingles and bricks sprayed into Quay Road.

"Take cover, Isabelle!" Laz waved his arms.

"I hate you. I hate you." She continued crying.

"Hate me from the King's Bastion, Isabelle. Run!"

"I hate you!"

"Cannons!"

They kept screaming at each other. Another cannonball launched, thumped to the ground thirty feet away and rolled into the low wall overlooking the wharf. It shattered the wall and dropped from sight. Isabelle's eyes grew round. She stood, silenced by shock. Laz's voice was ragged. "Please, take cover. Please." He felt tears tracking down his cheeks again.

Isabelle gaped at Laz for the longest ten seconds of his life. Then she spun and raced up Rue Toulouse, back toward the King's Bastion.

His situation hit him full force. He couldn't move or hide. He yelled at the top of his lungs. "Hello! Anyone! Please let me take cover."

The streets were empty. Dauphin Battery was the closest place with people, and it was over two blocks away. Everyone there was a soldier so they wouldn't help. Laz wondered if they thought it was funny: the person who had tried to help the enemy was now in danger of being blown apart by that same enemy.

Musket fire came from the Dauphin Gate. Puffs of smoke rose into the air. Then it began: the staccato rhythm of multiple cannons firing.

Two balls crashed into the walls, throwing up dust and debris. Three shots catapulted over the walls and through the smoke. Two landed close, destroying pallets and lobster traps and a fence. Laz started pulling at the chain. His heart thundered against his tightening ribs. Panic flailed and beat around his head.

The low, hollow *whump* of a mortar sounded. Fear over-took Laz.

Completely.

CHAPTER THIRTY-TWO

His fear-driven insanity lifted during an afternoon lull. Laz barely knew where he was, what he'd been doing. There was a lot of rubble in the streets.

Pain wreathed his neck. His hands were bloody and his fingernails throbbed. Two of them were torn off. The weight of the shackle around his neck helped him remember. He looked up at the pole and the iron ring anchoring the chain, saw scratch marks in the wood. His legs were shaking and it was all he could do to stay on his feet.

He tasted blood, but his mouth was so dry he couldn't swallow. He hurt. So much. He touched his neck above the shackle, under his jaw, and hissed when he found torn skin.

Laz braced his back against the pole with stiff legs. Someone would come now, he thought. They'd had their fun, had scared the saboteur. No one came. He didn't know how long he waited, maybe an hour, but it felt like three. His legs grew shaky.

The cascade of cannons firing in quick succession made Laz flinch. He gritted he teeth, began repeating: *I won't move, I won't freak out. I won't move, I won't freak out.*

It worked for ten or fifteen minutes. Until one cannonball whistled past him, so close he felt the whoosh of air. Laz began shaking. He grabbed the chain and started pulling. Desperate to get free, he rammed the post then switched back to pulling.

Nearby, half a building blew apart. Mortars. He hated mortars.

He yelled for help. It came out as a croak.

The wings swooped in with the next mortar. Fear flapped and slapped and beat at his mind. He tried to hang on, to not let the darkness win. Under his breath he whispered, "Help me. Help me."

More cannons fired.

Laz was looking up when a cannonball sheared off the top of the pole. He flew through the air.

"It's quite remarkable he's still alive." The voice belonged to the smell, which belonged to the surgeon's office in the King's Bastion. Laz's eyes didn't want to open.

Someone else murmured something. The surgeon's fish breath washed over Laz as the man turned the boy's chin one way, then the other. "If you won't let me treat him as I've been trained, perhaps you should treat him."

Whatever the other person said, he huffed. "Fine. Have it your way. If he likes his wounds cleaned with boiled water, I'll do it. But I don't have any strong spirits—"

Something clunked onto the table near Laz's feet. At least, it seemed like a table by its hardness.

"This is particularly fine brandy," the surgeon said. "You must have been saving it for a special occasion. Seems a waste to use it on a prisoner." A sigh. "Don't look at me like that. I'll do as you wish."

He muttered to himself and set about cleaning Laz's neck. His back arched in reaction to the pain. Laz fought to ignore it and tried to remember what had happened.

Candlelight flickered on Laz's eyelids, so he guessed it was night. He didn't want to open his eyes and see how badly he was hurt. What he felt was bad enough.

A cool cloth covered his forehead. Someone was working with the doctor. He hoped it was Isabelle. The smell of brandy filled his nose. When it dribbled onto his neck, he almost bolted upright, but someone held him down.

Laz opened his eyes then, and stared at the upside-down face of Pierre Morpain. Pain twisted his features. Was he injured, too?

The surgeon lifted Laz's head and poured a cap of brandy down his throat. He coughed but kept it down. "Go back to sleep, boy. We'll get you bandaged up. Our commander is making sure of it."

Laz nodded slightly and slid into a half-awake state where nothing seemed real. But he felt safe, anchored by the hands holding his shoulders down—shoulders that felt as if a sledge-hammer had clobbered them. In pain but safe.

Four soldiers stomping into the room woke Laz up. He was still on the surgeon's table, loosely tied, either so he wouldn't roll off or wouldn't escape. But Laz was in no condition to do that. He was a giant bruise, pulverized in a few places that were covered by bandages: his neck, his fingers.

The four men untied Laz, picked up the corners of the table-cloth under him, and used it like a stretcher to carry him out of the room and onto the parade square. It was early morning and the light was topping the wall to make the red doors of the storage-room shelters glow.

The men carried Laz across the grass, past the six storage rooms to an opening in the wall he'd never noticed. He lifted his head as they maneuvered down a short slope and into a cave of a room. They set the tablecloth down, a blanket actually, and stepped over him as they filed out. The last man slammed a barred gate and padlocked it.

Cold filled the room, along with a sewer smell. The gate didn't quite reach the top of the arched doorway, but only a toddler could crawl through that space. To the left of the gate was an open window with flat iron bars with spiked bits fluting out from the central bar. *Decorative and deadly*, Laz thought. *A nice homey touch.*

He shivered and wrapped the blanket around his shoulders. He tried but couldn't get comfortable. And moving hurt. He settled for a rough edge digging into his thigh.

A gutter cut through the middle of the floor, which sloped down to the outer wall. It was a trough of fitted curved stone probably for rainwater to drain off the parade square and beyond the walls via a miniature arched opening cut into the stone. It was the perfect size for rats.

This couldn't be a prison Morpain would choose, Laz thought. Unless Morpain was angrier than Laz had ever dreamed.

A short time later, a soldier returned with a cup of water and a bowl of thin fish soup. He slid both through the gap below the bottom bar of the gate.

"What's going to happen to me?" Laz asked.

The soldier glared into the dark cell and stalked away. Laz reached for the cup and studied the scum floating on the water. He was thirsty, but knew the scum would give him the flux. He set it aside and tackled the soup, which was cold and greasy.

By mid-afternoon he'd gotten thirsty enough to drink the water, though he tried to use a corner of his waistcoat to soak up the floaters. He slept on and off through the day, trying to heal. The most comfortable spot was tucked into the corner under the window. So he was out of the way when someone came with a bucket of waste and threw the contents into the cell, only half aiming for the rathole exit. The smell made Laz gag. A gift from the soldiers, he guessed.

After suffering cramps during the night, the flux hit Laz the next day. His only toilet was the gutter. The stink clung to him like a second skin.

This continued for five days, along with regular bouts of bombardment by the colonists. Laz could sleep through more distant shelling, but when the closest cannons thundered, he'd wake up yelling, and he'd shake violently until the attack stopped. It always left him feeling weak and wrung out. Helpless.

Sunday came. He knew it was Sunday because the cannons were silent in the morning, and the priest wasn't. Tucking himself against the bars of the gate, he could see the priest standing on the parade ground before a makeshift altar, facing the wall lined with storage rooms. He imagined the red doors propped open and the people facing him from inside their shelters.

The priest's voice swept into Laz's cell like a gentle summer's breeze. The mass was in Latin, so he didn't understand much, but the singsong cadence of the priest's voice rose in defiance of the misery around him. Muffled responses from the storage rooms were a bass undertone. He sang an acapella song, his voice full-bodied and sure. Laz heard hope in the man's voice that promised his people a future.

It choked him up, knowing that if he'd chosen his friends instead of a distant, fading family, he could have stayed part of this community. Instead he'd chosen a memory, and feared he'd soon be one.

Laz realized he had become the traitor the British had accused him of being. So he expected to die a traitor's death.

Everything he'd done was for nothing.

The priest spoke. His flock replied as one. Back and forth. Answer and response. Community. The words were worse than a brutal beating.

CHAPTER THIRTY-THREE

Exhaustion. Nightmares. Hunger. Laz could feel his body caving in on itself. Hollowing out.

Everything still ached. He'd unwound the bandages on his two left fingers to find pulpy messes in place of fingernails. The bandages went back on. He was afraid to take off the bandage around his neck. Touching it still sparked pain and made his eyes water.

He'd lost track of time, and hadn't thought to mark off the days. In the middle of the night, shelling woke him. When the cannons fell silent, he tried sleeping again. Though the thought of sleeping made him shudder for fear of more nightmares.

Something skittered outside his cell. Laz froze mid-exhale, listening. Muffled footsteps moved along the wall, and down the slope to the gate. Breathing.

Then a whisper: "Lazare? Are you in there?"

The whisper was hard to identify.

"Lazare?" Slightly louder. The shock of hearing Morpain's voice again made Laz inhale loudly. Morpain said, "I must speak with you."

His voice came from beside the iron-barred gate. Laz felt along the bumpy wall, ticked his fingers against the bars, then sank down. He leaned with one shoulder tucked between two bars and his head resting against the metal.

It was a few days past the full moon, and out on the parade ground, moonlight and shadow played tag. In this black nook Laz couldn't see Morpain. The man shifted but Laz didn't realize he had also sat until a whisper sounded almost in his ear. "I'm sorry."

Laz squeezed his eyes closed. His voice was rusty. "Nothing is your fault."

Morpain's words came, tight and angry. "I left you exposed during one of the worst bombardments we've had. I knew you'd been captured but I did nothing to move you. When the cannons fired, and Governor Duchambon ordered you left there, I didn't oppose him."

"Why would you?" Laz covered his eyes, refusing to remember that day. After several moments he said, "What did the surgeon mean when he said he was surprised I was alive?"

"By the saints, it stinks here." Morpain coughed. "Do you remember a cannonball striking the top of the pillory post?"

"Sort of. I wasn't thinking straight."

"Few would in that situation." Morpain's fingers bumped against Laz's shoulder, stayed there. "We found you thirty feet from the post. I thought you were dead, that the force of being wrenched through the air had caused the shackle to break your neck. That's what the surgeon meant. But even unconscious, you hung onto the chain so hard we had to peel your fingers off the iron links. I think your arms and shoulders took the force of the blow, and saved your neck."

"That's why my shoulders have been so sore," Laz whispered.

Morpain groaned and became silent. Laz couldn't bring himself to speak either. Outside, the moonlight had won; and it lit the parade ground, reflecting off the few unbroken windows in the barracks. Morpain became a silhouette against a silver backdrop. Laz traced the profile of that face with his eyes, wishing Morpain could still be his boss and friend. Laz had messed up so badly it made the ache in his body was nothing compared to the twisted hurt inside.

The look on Morpain's face when he had kissed Laz's forehead and walked away, played over in Laz's mind. Morpain hadn't been angry. He had been crushed.

Clouds covered the moonlight again, plunging them into deeper shadows.

Morpain moved so his shoulder was touching Laz's, and cleared his throat. He whispered, "I need to understand why you betrayed us, Lazare."

Laz swallowed. He had expected the question, but it still took effort to form the words. "I told myself that if you couldn't fire your cannons, you'd have to surrender and lives would be saved. Louisbourg would be saved from further destruction."

"You thought you were helping us?" Puzzlement wove through the question.

Laz sighed. "Helping both sides."

"Why would you help the British colonists?"

Laz knew he could never explain everything, but Morpain deserved something closer to the truth. A minute passed before he found a way to start. "I'm not from Île Saint-Jean. My father wasn't spying on Canso while I went to warn Port Toulouse."

"But you are Acadian?"

"Yes." Laz couldn't remember where Hawkins had thought he was from so he skipped that. "I was captured by a New England captain who was sailing to Canso. The head of the expedition, Commander Pepperrell, decided I should hang as a spy. Captain Hawkins saved my neck by forcing me to agree to come here and attempt sabotage."

"How could he force that?"

"He kept a family heirloom that is...hugely important to me. Said I would get it back when I'd at least tried..." Laz trailed off.

"You betrayed us for a trinket?"

"No!" Morpain shushed him and Laz repeated a quieter, "No. It's hard to explain, but that medallion is my only hope. I can't...can't go home without it."

"That makes no sense, yet I hear truth in your voice. You believe in whatever power this trinket holds. So the British blackmailed you." Morpain reached through the bars and gripped Laz's arm tight. "Why didn't you tell me? I would have found a way to help you."

Those words, and Morpain's desire to always help people, were sandpaper on exposed wounds. Laz's eyes burned. "*I know.* I wish I had. It's tearing me apart. I feel like I've betrayed my family."

"How so?"

"From the first day you took me under your protection, gave me a job, made me feel...like I belonged." Laz's voice cracked. He cleared his throat. "The whole town welcomed me without question. I've only ever felt I belonged that way on Grandmère's farm."

When Morpain didn't reply, Laz dropped his voice to the quietest of whispers. "If it helps, I'm sorry. More sorry than I've ever been."

Morpain stood. "I don't know if it helps, Lazare. Your betrayal was a knife between my ribs."

He walked away, taking all the air with him.

CHAPTER THIRTY-FOUR

Morpain's visit turned Laz into a caged animal. Unable to sit still, he paced. He stretched. He did exercises. Anything to move, even though it hurt. He'd survived weeks of the siege by keeping moving, so days of not moving felt like it was rotting him from the inside. That feeling was increased by the sewage smell, the horrible conditions, and the half-rotten food.

The guard delivering breakfast arrived, slid the bowl and cup under the bars, and picked up yesterday's empties.

"Can I put my order in for lunch now? I missed it yesterday," Laz said.

The soldier had started to turn away. He came back. "Would you like it served on white linen and china?"

"I wouldn't want you to go to any extra trouble."

"Oh, I won't." He spat onto Laz's breakfast and marched away.

Before his back disappeared, Laz called out, "I'm still waiting for my bath."

He spun around. "How about a good drowning instead?" Laz almost responded again, but thought maybe he'd pushed far enough. This was the first soldier who had answered anything.

The water was scummy as usual, but finding some peas in his fish soup was a nice change. Laz pinched off the mould patches on his bread and ate it. They'd forgotten to give him a spoon, so he picked out the pieces of fish with his fingers, licked them off between bites. The three cubes of fish were rubbery, but were the only flavorful part of the meal.

Again he'd forgotten to save some food for the afternoon. He set the water into the corner where he slept so it wouldn't get splashed if someone threw waste into the room. It seemed to occur to them every three days.

He drifted off and woke to the priest singing, a more welcome way to wake than with skin-crawling terror. With another Sunday here, Laz guessed he'd been in this hole for nearly two weeks. He wondered how the siege was going, and didn't know what to hope for. He spent the day pacing, running questions through his mind in an endlessly replaying loop.

Rain spattered the slope outside his cell and trickled down the gutter, but not enough to clean it. Laz gripped the bars on the gate, stuck his face through, and inhaled the freshness of the damp evening breeze. The clouds split open and dumped truckloads of rain. Water sluiced through the center of the cell, overflowing the gutter. Laz stayed at the gate smelling the rain.

He tried stretching out his empty cup to catch some rain, but the overhang was too deep. So he lay on his stomach and slurped muddy water at the top of the slope, thinking it couldn't be worse than well water.

The rain ended, leaving a wet velvet night. Everything was damp, including Laz and his blanket. He couldn't sleep for shivering, even though no cannons had fired since the rain began. He was desperately tired.

After the noise of the rain, the night silence was heavy. Laz imagined guards huddled in their sentry boxes, warm in their wool cloaks; people in the storeroom shelters huddled together in warm kitten heaps. He'd never realized how much he liked being with people, until it was taken away.

An odd sucking sound glopped through the silence. Footsteps on wet ground. Laz clutched the iron bars, squeezed his face between them, and listened as the slow steps came closer.

Thick cloud cover made the blackness complete. Even when the footsteps eased down the slope to his cell, Laz couldn't see who it was. His hope was confirmed when Morpain whispered, "Lazare?"

"I'm here. At the gate," Laz replied.

Morpain gasped, as if startled by their unexpected nearness. Laz reached through the bars, curled his fingers in Morpain's coat. "Thank you."

"For what?"

"For coming back." Laz's eyes burned. He didn't want to blubber like he had when Morpain had turned his back at the post, but it felt like he might. Laz struggled to calm himself.

"How are you doing?" Morpain laid a hand over Laz's.

"Maybe going crazy. Mostly, I'm so hungry I think my stomach is eating itself."

"Everyone suffers that. We only get two scant meals a day."

Laz blew out his longing in a slow breath. "Two would be great."

A moment of silence. Morpain's grip tightened. "You are only eating once a day?"

Laz replied, "I keep trying to save half for the afternoon, but I'm always so hungry by morning I never do it."

"Those weasels! I ordered them to feed you the same as the townsfolk. I should have overseen this myself."

A shiver went through Laz as he imagined the soldiers turning on Morpain. "No. Your men wouldn't like you taking more interest in the traitor. Worry about the siege."

He snorted quietly. "Are you thirteen, or thirty-nine?"

"Prison ages a man." Was that from a movie? Laz almost burst out laughing, mostly from relief that Morpain was here.

"I know."

"You were in prison?" Laz asked.

"Captured by the British in 1711. I spent nearly a year in captivity. Of course, the British treat officers with respect so my incarceration was not crude like this." Morpain stepped back, forcing Laz to let go of his jacket. "Which is why I came. Where is...? Ah, here it is."

Morpain bumped a bar then pressed something against Laz's chest. "Hold this candle and we'll get it lit."

"Won't someone see?"

"No one is moving tonight. With the cannons silent everyone except the sentries are getting much-needed sleep. This alcove is tucked into the folds of the wall. No sentry will see."

"And they tend to face outward." A smile had sprung up, but it faded when Laz remembered he had noticed that while commiting sabotage.

Morpain positioned Laz's hand and the candle, and began striking the flint. It took almost a dozen flicks to light the wick.

He whispered, "I never thought to bring a candleholder."

"Hang on." Laz knelt slowly to protect the tiny flame, got his bowl, dripped wax onto its licked-clean surface, and stuck the base of the candle to the soft wax. He stood back up.

"Let me look at you." Morpain reached through the bars and touched his chin, directing him to turn it side to side. "You're filthy."

"Are you offering a bath? I could be talked into one," Laz said. Wrinkles fanned out from eyes that glowed almost orange in the light. Laz remembered thinking how wolf-like Morpain looked. Maybe it fit. Wolves were pack animals, loyal to the end.

Morpain chuckled. "Sadly, no. All water is for drinking these days. Let's get this throat bandage off. I want to see your wounds."

Laz stretched out his neck and Morpain worried the knots until they came loose, then he unwound the dirty band. The inner layers were slightly less gray. The final turn only came off with a little tug. Laz winced.

Morpain had him hold the candle to the side and tilted his head to get a good look. "Lots of scabbing. It looks like you survived the hangman's noose. You should leave it open to the air."

"Will it scar?"

"The worst parts maybe, but I don't think you will live your life with a hangman's scar," Morpain replied.

"Considering how short my life will probably be, that won't matter much."

Morpain cleared his throat and gave Laz an irritated look.

Laz said, "You know it's true. The governor is probably

eager to order a firing squad, or hanging, whatever way he likes to kill traitors."

The candlelight quivered. Morpain cupped the bottom of the bowl and steadied Laz's hand. "Lazare, I will not let that happen."

"How can you stop it?" Laz's eyes were burning again. Worse, Morpain stared with concern, drawing his brows together and thinning his mouth. He saw Laz's fear.

Finally, Morpain said, "You need to know you didn't do any harm."

"What do you mean?"

"The men dried the powder you wet. It's hard in this damp climate, but it can be done."

"So I didn't bring this siege even one day closer to ending? Then I'll die for nothing."

Morpain kept one hand on the bowl with Laz's and gripped his shoulder. "Have you considered that if the British defeat us, they will release you as a hero?"

Laz blinked. He hadn't thought beyond having betrayed people he loved.

Morpain smiled. "The foolish look on your face is my answer."

"But wishing that for myself is wishing defeat for you. You've worked so hard. You've held us all together, kept us believing in the town and each other. Everyone loves you." Tears welled up so fast, one escaped before Laz could blink them away.

"Do you love me, Lazare?"

Laz wiped his nose with the back of his free hand. "I wish you were my father."

Morpain cupped his hand over Laz's ear, burying his fingers in tangled hair. "My wife and I never had a family. You have a place in my heart too. I would wish the same."

"But I betrayed you."

"Yes. Do you remember me telling you my parents both died when I was young? I spent so many years wishing they were alive, wanting to be with them. So I can forgive you because you acted in an attempt to return to your family."

"I don't deserve your forgiveness." The stupid tears were leaking steadily now. Laz felt like a fool.

"Nevertheless, you have it."

Laz's hand was shaking so badly, Morpain took the bowl. He blew out the candle and set it down, then pulled Laz to the bars. They stood, foreheads touching, while Laz cried like a child. It took several minutes for the storm to pass.

When Morpain spoke again, his voice was flat, as if he were forcing calmness. "We do have a slight problem."

"What?" Laz's voice cracked. They were still head to head and he had both hands wrapped in Morpain's jacket lapels.

"The governor thinks it might cheer people up to have a public hanging."

Laz sniffed loudly. "Hang the traitor."

"Yes. I have held him off by suggesting the dangers of gathering in the open when the enemy fires their cannons at random times. But the shelling of the city has eased somewhat. The colonists have built a new battery across the mouth of the bay, on the lighthouse point. They are attacking the Island Battery. If it falls, the town will not last long because ships can enter the harbor."

"But we're still being shot at here in the town."

"Yes. Only enough to keep us inside and miserable. I have not mentioned that to the governor, of course."

"What about the other officers? They must have noticed."

"They are pompous idiots with no vision or sense. But I've heard them whispering and I know some of them side with the governor. Time is running out."

"What can I do?" Laz asked.

Morpain patted a pocket then took Laz's right hand and placed some metal sticks in it. He closed Laz's hand and a curved end dug into his palm. "I took these away from one of my crew a year ago. He assured me they can be used to pick any lock with a skeleton key. I don't know how they work, but if you figure it out, perhaps you can escape and find this blackmailing captain of yours."

"Captain Hawkins."

"Yes. I will remember that name, should we chance to meet. I must go."

Cool air filled the gap between them as Morpain stepped back. "Lazare, our time together has been a gift. But if you get back to your family, cherish them. Whatever has passed between you and your father, he's alive. He is *alive*. Be thankful. Being an orphan is a hard path to walk."

Orphan echoed through Laz's mind. As Morpain started to turn away, Laz grabbed his wrist. "Can you do something for me, whatever happens?"

"What?"

"Isabelle is an orphan too. She was my friend. If you could..."

"I will see she is taken care of."

"Thank you."

"Goodbye, my son." Morpain left.

Laz heard him sliding his feet over the ground as if he were mushing up the ground, hiding his footprints. Laz remembered the candle. He plucked it off the bowl and pocketed it, then scraped away every trace of wax.

Energized, Laz spent the whole night working on the lock. He'd seen lock picking in movies and knew it required both tools, one held steady, one wiggling around to somehow shift the innards. It wasn't as easy as Hollywood made it look, and it didn't help that Laz was working backward.

His fingers were cramping and the sun rising when everything clicked into place and the lock opened. He almost shouted. Then he noticed the pale sky shot with pink fingers of cloud.

One more day. That's all I need. Let the cannons thunder so everyone stays inside.

Laz rammed the lock closed.

CHAPTER THIRTY-FIVE

It was a surprise to wake up and realize that half the afternoon was gone. But sleeping so long on his bed of stones made him feel like there were bruises on his bruises.

His cold, watery soup waited beside the gate. It was like eating slime, but he forced it down. He combed his hair with his fingers and retied the leather thong. Most of his hair was now long enough to stay in its ponytail, which was good because he didn't want hair falling into his eyes tonight.

Outside, loud voices caught his attention. He pressed against the bars to see. Two soldiers strode across the parade ground, each carrying a bucket. "Don't spill that crap on me!" one yelled. They both laughed. *Seriously, two buckets?* Laz thought.

The landward cannons boomed. Both men froze, looked at each other. They dropped their pails and bolted. Laz laughed, kept laughing until cannonballs slammed into the outer wall not far away.

He stayed sane by focusing on the lock, which was impossible to pick with shaking hands, but it kept him busy. He convinced himself they were targeting the Queen's Bastion next door, not this one.

Near sunset, the cannons and mortars stopped firing long enough for Laz to steady his hands. It went faster this time, taking an hour for the lock to click open. Laz left it hanging so it looked closed. If anyone came a single push would relock it.

No one came.

Full darkness arrived with another round of cannon fire. Laz appreciated the colonists making everyone duck while he snuck out. He locked his cell behind him, hoping it would buy time if his escape weren't noticed in the morning. Lock-pick tools tucked away, he crept from the cell, past the ramp that led to the top of the wall, to an animal pen in the southeast corner.

Laz slipped through the picket gate just as a cannonball hit close enough to spray dirt over him. He dove against the inside of the fence and covered his head. He repeated to himself that it had hit this bastion by mistake. They weren't aiming at him. Not at him.

Finally Laz found the determination to crawl along the pen's fence of vertical poles, behind the animal shelter, which looked like a miniature fort, along the north side to another gate. He peered over the top. Ten feet away stood the partly destroyed east end of the King's Bastion barracks, where a stable had been. The quarter moon showed a blackened, jumbled ruin, but it had to be safer than walking out a gate.

Inside the stable, Laz had to crawl under timbers, and feel his way along walls like a blind man. The roof was half intact, so blocked the scant moonlight. Laz turtled every time a cannonball hit, shaking the unstable ruin. He reached the far wall and crunched over glass to a window that was now a crisscross of wood. He yanked pieces aside, forcing the frame open with loud creaking.

Laz cut himself on some glass as he squirmed through the window frame and onto a pile of splintered wood and bricks. He crouched by the rubble and sucked the cut as he considered his next step. Cannons hadn't fired in maybe twenty minutes so this bombardment might be over, which meant more patrols.

He wondered how to get out of Louisbourg. The walls were guarded. Probably the easiest part of the fortress to escape from was over the seaward wall, near the harbor's mouth, but that left him on a spit of land with no shelter come daylight and treacherous currents nearly impossible to swim. The landward side was where the colonial militiamen were positioned. If he could get close enough to them, he could switch back to English and maybe cross their lines without being arrested. Wouldn't that be a nice switch?

Though it meant sneaking past a lot of French soldiers, Laz hoped scouting that wall would give him an answer. Happy to be moving, he crawled until he reached the streets. Not seeing movement, he pelted down Rue St. Louis for a block, pausing to stare at Madame Richard's house and the hole that used to be his attic room. He crept into the yard and entered the kitchen. It smelled of cinnamon and mouldy cheese. He located the cheese with his nose and took the wrapped wheel.

Laz prowled toward the far side of town and the Dauphin Battery. At the main street, he squinted toward the tall Frederic Gate. The moonlight showed it was half gone. Laz wondered if that had been their target when he'd been chained to the post ten feet away? Destroying your enemy's gate was undoubtedly important.

Voices drifted from the direction of the King's Bastion. Seeing no one, Laz sprinted across Rue Toulouse and past the architect's house. He slipped into the garden by the side gate, to the corner where he'd held Isabelle's hand when the fist cannonball had fallen. Six weeks ago, maybe. A lifetime.

When he was certain the patrol wasn't coming his way, he left the security of the wall and crossed the garden. Its far corner jutted into the yard belonging to the King's Bakery and blacksmith shop to his left. Above the bakery were soldier barracks.

Laz scanned the area, noticing the end of a warehouse straight ahead. Nearly half a block long, it faced onto Quay Road. The end closest to the Dauphin Gate was damaged. He remembered seeing that explosion when he was chained. He licked dry lips and reminded himself that no one was shooting at him now. The French would never expect him to hide so close to the soldiers in the Dauphin Battery.

He hoisted himself from a bench onto a garden shed's roof, then watched the blacksmith's yard. When he was sure he was alone, he vaulted into the yard, raced to the warehouse, and flattened himself against the end wall. No shouts raised the alarm. He crept over the pile of rubble and into the warehouse.

Laz had delivered messages to the officers inside this military warehouse many times, so knew the L-shaped layout. Normally, soldiers were quartered on the second floor, but they had moved to the safer bastions. Still, Laz rolled his steps to stay quiet, past the remains of the quartermaster's office and into the storage area. Wooden floors turned to packed dirt and he relaxed a bit. This area ran almost the length of the warehouse. A series of rooms ran along the right side, each one with a brick archway. There wasn't enough light trickling in through the windows to see anything except nearby shapes.

The siege had left the town in bad shape. Laz knew he wouldn't find any food here. What he needed was a hiding spot. He edged toward a window overlooking Quay Road. The eastern horizon was dark gray instead of black. It would be light in an hour, maybe less.

At the end of the main room, it took a right turn, opening to another wing. In the cave-like darkness Laz stopped to let his eyes adjust. A few broken barrels were scattered around. He arranged them into a corner so they looked like they'd been tossed there. Then he crawled behind his makeshift barricade and curled into a ball. The cold oozed up from the dirt floor, but after a few weeks of sleeping on stones, it felt like eight-inch memory foam.

As usual, cannons woke him.

CHAPTER THIRTY-SIX

Though cannons startled Laz awake, he didn't scream or yell. After listening for a minute, he realized it was because the bombardment was somewhere out on the bay.

After making sure he was alone in the warehouse, he stood by a window and scanned the water, expecting to see British ships. Smoke drifted from the Island Battery. Morpain had said the colonists built a battery on the lighthouse point so they could attack the island. At Dauphin Gate, infantry started exchanging musket fire with colonial militiamen. Laz had picked a front-row seat.

He unwrapped Madame Richard's small wheel of cheese. The mould was as thick as his thumb. Having no knife, he peeled off the thickest areas then scraped off the rest using the lock pick. The remaining chunk was the size of a hockey puck. Laz ate half of it and stuck the rest in his pocket. He kicked a hole in the dirt and buried the cloth and mouldy bits.

A crowd of soldiers gathered along the low, heavily damaged wall beside Quay Road. One of them only had to turn to notice Laz's face in the window. He retreated and poked around a bit. In the second side room he discovered a leaky window. The rainstorm a few nights past had left a puddle on the floor.

He scooped in two mouthfuls but the third spewed out. He wiped muddy sludge off his mouth and sat.

In his other life he'd often drawn out maps of parkour routes he wanted to try, so he decided a map might help now. He snuck to the broken-up quartermaster's office. Any paper was long gone. He found a broken quill beside the overturned desk and retreated to the puddle room, where he started drawing a map of this corner of the fortress in the dirt.

The outer gate, the bridge over the moat, the inner gate, the guardroom, and looming over it all, the Dauphin Bastion. A demi-bastion because it was a half-circle. Laz stared at it as something tried to surface, a thought, a memory.

Then it hit him, a comment from the sentry at the entrance to the Dauphin Bastion. Laz had asked what was behind a door set into the wall around a corner from the bastion's entrance. "That's our postern gate," he'd replied. Then he'd had to explain. A side door, so the soldiers could get outside the fortress. Mostly they used it to go repair outer walls, but it could be used for a sneak attack.

Laz rubbed the drawing away and leaned against the wall, mind racing.

A side door. An emergency exit.

All he had to do was get to it.

Laz tried to sleep in the afternoon under his barrel scraps. He woke to echoes and loud voices that grew louder with every step. Through a crack in his barricade, he saw the off-white jackets and blue trim of regular soldiers. He couldn't see faces, or muskets, though they always carried them.

"A few broken barrels. There's nothing here," one said.

"The quartermaster said to look," the other replied.

"Waste of time. He could come himself, but God forbid any officers stick their noses out of their holes."

"Yes. Commander Morpain is the only decent one."

"We should have killed them all last winter when we had the chance. Or made them give us safe passage to France instead of asking for better rations and a share of plunder. What good is any of that now? We're rats who can't get off our sinking ship."

"Shut your mouth. Let's report back. This warehouse is swept clean. Not even any crumbs for the mice."

"If he doesn't believe us, the fool can look for himself," the first fellow declared then added, "Maybe we could hunt for mice. Do you think they'd taste good, maybe cooked on a spit in a fireplace?"

"That's disgusting." Laz silently agreed.

After the soldiers' footsteps faded away, Laz didn't move for an hour, until a leg cramp had him groaning in pain. He snaked from under the pile in slow motion, but still caused some clattering. He froze like a trapped rabbit, aware this area was a dead end. *What an awful phrase*, he thought.

He decided to wait for darkness near the collapsed wall. In the quartermaster's office, he sheltered between the overturned desk and the window looking out at the bay.

The bombardment of the Island Battery continued. Though it was far, over one and a half miles, he was surprised the Dauphin

Battery wasn't firing at the lighthouse point. He wondered if they were out of powder. Stores had been low two weeks ago.

He knelt and peered over the sill to watch, and caught sight of Morpain standing in a group of men. As usual, he patted backs, working his way through the group, making sure he spoke to each man. That was why they were loyal to him.

Morpain left them and paced along Quay Road toward the Dauphin Gate. Almost directly across from Laz he stopped again. Hands clasped behind him, his head did its little inner discussion bobblehead dance. Laz touched a finger to the glass, wanting to tap it so Morpain would hear, turn and greet—

Laz whipped his hand down, realizing he could be recaptured if anyone noticed. The low evening sun lit Morpain's face when he turned toward the bastion, offering a side view of his long nose and gaunt cheek. The wolf in profile. He walked slowly, deliberately, a man who refused to scurry in fear or bend under the weight of his burdens.

In his mind, Laz walked beside him and felt the familiar weight of a hand on his shoulder. Warmth spread through his chest. Whatever happened, Morpain had been a father to Laz. "Goodbye, Papa," he whispered, as Morpain strolled out of sight.

Laz had to get out of Louisbourg for his own safety, and rejoin the colonial forces until after the siege ended. But he knew that if he didn't get back to that other time, he *was* home. Here. Now.

CHAPTER THIRTY-SEVEN

Laz spent a big chunk of the night snaking across the grass on his belly, working his way up the slope to the base of the wall beside the Dauphin Bastion. He slithered beside the wall toward the entrance to the bastion, slowly so his movement didn't alert a sentry.

With the attack on the Island Battery continuing through the night, he figured the sentry's attention would be there, not on the wall to his right, or on a shadow by the wall.

At the base of a triangular slab of wall that shored up the slope, Laz peered around the slanted stonework. Directly in front of him was the door to the postern gate. It was set into a wall fifteen feet long. Around that next corner, twenty feet farther away, was the entrance to the Dauphin Bastion. Cloud cover had darkened everything so Laz stayed motionless, waiting for the moonlight to return so he could see before he moved.

Ten minutes later the clouds skudded away. The L-shaped area in front of the bastion entrance was clogged with silent men wrapped in dark cloaks, tricorns pulled low. They were watching the bombing of the Island Battery. One of them was leaning against the wall six feet away from the door to the postern gate.

Laz waited, thankful he hadn't rushed forward. He kept waiting until it was almost too late to retreat. Back down the slope he wriggled. At the fence of the first building's yard, he crept around the corner and rested for several minutes. He'd spent all night on his belly, was cold and starving. He couldn't imagine another day in that warehouse. He checked the road and scurried into the backyard of the Lartigue house. It was situated oddly, between the Dauphin Bastion and the military blacksmith's shop, but was admired by everyone as being one of Louisbourg's finest.

The back door was unlocked. Laz slipped in and stood with his back against the door as his eyes adjusted. The room grew more visible and he realized he had barely beat the dawn. He scavenged for food in the kitchen, finding a pitcher of water, and a bowl of rotten fruit, possibly oranges. When Louisbourg wasn't blockaded, ships from the Caribbean bought exotic spices and fruits, or so he'd been told. Laz left the mould piles. In a box on a counter, he discovered a dried heel of bread, miraculously fuzz-free. He took the pitcher and bread upstairs.

One corner of the roof had been clipped by a cannonball. In the biggest bedroom, Laz found a chest with men's clothes. He stripped out of his muddy, grass-stained clothes and rifled through the chest, finding a shirt, red stockings, brown breeches. No waistcoat or jacket. Laz laid his out to dry. Clean clothes felt like silk compared to the filthy stuff he'd been wearing.

He broke off pieces of dry bread, interspersing them with sips of water. He was still hungry when he was done, but not hungry enough to eat the mouldy contents of that bowl.

When they left, the Lartigue family had taken all their bedding, so Laz dragged one of the smaller mattresses from the other room, flopped it onto the large bed, and crawled between the two. Asleep in seconds.

That night Laz tried again. He didn't have much energy, but he made himself crawl faster, especially after the quarter moon disappeared behind heavy cloud. He reached the triangular slab of wall the same time the rain started. It was almost impossible to see, but he couldn't make out any figures. Who would stand in the rain if they had a choice?

Laz slithered toward his target. When he reached the door, he couldn't open it. He felt the handle, and a rod leading down to a D-ring and a padlock. He pulled out the lock-pick tools, knowing that he'd have forgotten them if Monsieur Lartique had left behind a jacket for him.

With the ongoing bombardment across the water, the quiet clicks and scratches of the tools went unnoticed. It took less than an hour to spring the lock. He was getting better.

Behind the door, a tunnel yawned. Laz closed the door behind him and heard the latch click. This was the darkness of nightmares, so complete that he didn't know if the next step would be into a wall or off a cliff. His hand brushed over the left wall to keep him on track.

He sensed something in front of him, like an absence of air, and extended his right arm slowly. Another door. This one wasn't locked. Laz depressed the latch slowly, taking care to not make noise. There could be someone on the wall directly above him.

When it clicked, Laz wanted to burst outside and run, but knew that was asking to be spotted. And shot.

He stood still until he calmed down, then pushed the door open enough to squeeze out. In front of him, moonlight shimmied over the pond that crowded this side of the wall.

Off to his right a voice whispered, "My watch isn't ended yet. Why are you here?"

CHAPTER THIRTY-EIGHT

The sentry outside the postern gate gaped at Laz in surprise.

Why would there be a sentry? Laz wondered if there was a nighttime repair crew somewhere along the wall.

The sentry stepped forward, musket across his chest. "Aren't you—?"

Laz plowed his fist into the sentry's face, making him stagger back. Laz grabbed the musket from his loosened grip and slammed the butt against his head. He dropped. Laz flung himself against the wall, breath huffing. What had he done? It had been like a movie—*bam, bam*, down. Had he killed the man? His hand ached.

Laz crouched and felt a steady beat on the man's neck. Relieved, he laid the musket beside the soldier.

Then he tried to think. The bridge spanning this pond had received a direct hit. Left was toward King's Bastion, where a repair crew would likely be working. Around the curve of the Dauphin Bastion, this pond narrowed into a moat, and a dam separated the pond from the ocean. There were always several very alert soldiers at the Dauphin Gate.

Laz talked himself into going straight. He waded into the

water, pulling himself along the bridge supports. When he reached the destroyed section, he pushed off and did the side-stroke across the moonlit water. He reached a post and clung to it for several moments, hoping he hadn't been seen. No one shot at him. Exhausted, he splashed water onto his face, rubbed it to return to alertness. He licked his lips.

They tasted salty.

The dam between this pond and the bay had to be damaged. Laz squinted at the bank he was heading to. The bridge ended on a shored-up slope leading up to a wall that was maybe waist-high. It was completely exposed to the Dauphin Bastion. If he went that way and managed to make it over the wall without being shot by the French, he would be on a slope that went down to the nearest colonists' battery, and he'd be completely exposed to them. Target practice.

He'd gone the wrong way. So he worked his way back to the postern gate. The sentry still hadn't moved. He plastered himself against the wall of the Dauphin Bastion and started around its base.

Sentries have no reason to look straight down, he told himself. Keep moving.

He ran out of dry land and had to wade silently through water. Now he was around the curve, out of sight of the postern gate, but he still had a ways to go. He came to a rubble pile from a damaged section of the wall, and eased into deeper water to get around it. His hand slipped. Splashed.

He flattened himself and didn't move. When no one raised the alarm, Laz stayed in the water, deep enough to walk along the bottom with his hands, his legs floating. Like when he was a child at the beach, pretending to be a shark.

His hands started going numb from the cold water. He reached a shallow corner. Above him, fifteen feet ahead, was a stone sentry box jutting out from the wall. Laz stood, pressed against the wall and stared at it, trying to grow X-ray vision. Clouds had been coming and going, covering the moon and exposing it every few minutes. Now the cloudy curtain opened, showing that the sentry box was half missing. Did that mean empty? The cloud curtain closed.

Laz eased forward with careful steps. Under the sentry box, around another corner, he inched closer to the Dauphin Gate. The water was knee-deep against the wall. It tugged at him. He knew that feeling from trips to the beach with Grandmère. The tide was going out.

The moonlight returned to give Laz a glimpse of the gate. It was thirty feet away. The short drawbridge was up. The walls on both sides of the gate, and the gate itself, looked ragged. Men were barricaded behind those damaged areas, watching against a night attack.

It took Laz thirty minutes to go that last thirty feet, pass under the drawbridge, and reach the dam six feet beyond the bridge. He had never been so thankful for video games and learning camoflauge tips from his dad for paintball.

Behind the barricade, French voices whispered, too quiet to make out what they were saying. Then a slightly louder voice spoke. "Did you hear? That little pig escaped from his cell in King's Bastion. Disappeared like a ghost. The padlock was on, still locked."

"When?" Several voices shushed that exclamation.

"Last night or the night before. No one is certain. The guard who delivered breakfast found food from the day before untouched."

"We cannot win against ghosts," a timid voice said.

It was answered with a slap. "Shut up and keep watch. D'aoust, save the gossip for the guardroom."

"Yes, sir."

The smile that had grown during the conversation faded. Laz couldn't make a mistake now, when he was so close. He studied the dam. Fortunately, the damaged section was close, but the water was lowering fast.

Laz sank into the icy water and walked his hands along the side of the dam until he reached the breach. He slowly wriggled through it, trying to ignore the thought that men with muskets were in easy shooting distance.

Keep moving, he told himself.

Laz eased over the last of the rubble and into Louisbourg Harbor. His foot splashed.

CHAPTER THIRTY-NINE

"**D**id you hear that?" a soldier shouted.

A musket fired. Laz was already under water, swimming away, being pulled into deeper water by the tide. He surfaced.

"I see something!"

"A seal, you idiot."

"We could eat seal."

"Are you going to swim out and get it?"

Laz ducked under again, swam with all his might as he tried to stay parallel with the shore. He came up for air. Heard English.

"What are those crazy Frenchies shouting about?"

"How would I know?"

"Stay alert. Maybe they're creating a diversion for an attack."

"They're too lazy to attack at night."

"Night hasn't stopped those Mi'kmaq fighters. They attack and slip away like shadows."

Laz decided that really alert sentries might not be the best people to approach. He kept swimming, angling toward shore, searching for footing. When he found it, he stayed deep so only his head stuck above water. Numbness seeped into his bones, made it hard to move.

The moonlight broke free of clouds again and he spotted the

burned-out ruins of the house that had been closest to the Dauphin Gate. He waded out of the water, stumbled and splashed, too cold for stealth.

Laz collapsed onto the grassy shore, shivering. His bones felt crystallized. He expected pieces of himself to start breaking off.

Two colonial militiamen appeared in the moonlight, muskets trained on Laz. "Who goes there?"

His teeth chattered violently. "L-Laz Berenger." He stressed the English pronounciation. "S-spy for Captain Haw-Hawkins of the *C-Constance*. I've b-been in Louisbourg." His teeth clacked like a machine gun. He curled into a ball to stop from vibrating. It didn't work.

Arms hauled him to his feet. The two militiamen dragged him around the back of the blackened ruin. "Get that fire going again," one of them said to someone. "We need to warm this fellow up."

Stripped of his clothes and wrapped in two wool blankets, Laz kept edging closer to the flames. The men had to reel him back a few times. When he finally started to thaw, a wave of exhaustion crashed over him. He slept until midmorning.

When he finally opened his eyes, a man was sitting near his feet, watching him. Laz didn't recognize him. The man smiled. "We had bets laid on when you'd open your eyes or if you'd give up the ghost."

Laz stared. *Say something. Speak English.*

The man smiled wider. "You won me some coin. Thank ye."

Laz nodded. "What day is it?"

"June 24."

"Time?"

"Ten o'clock I'm guessing. Hungry?"

Laz nodded again.

"We dried your clothes over the fire. You should get dressed. You won't be wanting an officer show up, what with being naked as a newborn babe." He pointed to a rumpled heap beside Laz's head.

One blanket draped over his lap, Laz pulled on his long shirt then his stockings. After he'd tied them in place, he got up and slipped into his breeches. He stood by the fire, doing up the dozen buttons of his waistcoat. It was odd to think what a struggle getting dressed had been three months ago. Laz smoothed the waistcoat, sat cross-legged on the blankets, and draped his blue jacket across his shoulders. The inside of his shoes were still damp so he turned them on their sides toward the fire.

His guard hollered at a man who came over and handed him a wooden bowl heaped with pottage. Laz hadn't seen that much food in weeks. He made himself eat slowly, but it was hard. He wanted to gobble it all down then gnaw on the bowl.

The man watched him with squinted eyes. "So you were in Louisbourg? How long? How'd you get in?"

Laz shot a glance at the bay. "What's with the mortar fire?"

The man curled his lip. "Them Frenchies are dug in and cannons weren't budging them. So Commander Pepperrell ordered our biggest mortar—Big-Mouthed Bess—be set up by the lighthouse. Bess is pounding them Frenchies like my wife pounds down bread."

Laz nodded and tried a heaping spoonful of pottage. A hard

swallow got it down. He waited to see if it would stay down.

"James!" the man called. "Bring this fellow some ale." He leaned forward. "Didn't take us more than a day to realize we couldn't drink the water on this forsaken chunk of land."

"Flux," Laz replied.

"That's right. Plenty of men got it. Then a whole pile more just got outright sick. French Papists must have ice for blood to live in this cold, wet, miserable place. We've got to end this fight. I don't even know if my neighbors got my crops planted like they promised."

Laz remembered what Morpain had told him. "Once the Island Battery is defeated, the town won't last long."

"That's exactly what Commander Pepperrell said." The man stuck out his hand. "Eli Johnson."

"Laz Berenger." They shook hands. The man named James returned with a mug of ale. Laz took a sip, set it down.

"So how are things inside that fortress?"

"Bad."

"How bad?"

"Short of food, short of powder, short of hope."

He laughed. "Now that *is* good news, Laz. Sure is. Let them Papists rot, I say."

Laz scanned the bay. "How can I get to the *Constance*?"

He snorted. "Sure in a hurry." He pointed toward the Grand Battery. "If you walk all the way around this cove and all the way to the lighthouse—" He swung his pointer finger toward the mouth of the bay. "Then if you hike across that spit of land, you'll get to the bay where they landed the cannons. I hear boats are there to run messages to the man-o-war that Commodore Warren captains. The fleet will be readying to enter the harbor as soon as the island is silenced. If the *Constance* is with the fleet, you might be able to talk some sailors into rowing you to her."

"That's a lot of ifs," Laz said.

The man laughed again. "Sure is." He reached over and helped himself to half Laz's ale. "Or you could sit here and listen to sweet Bess's song, and wait for the ships to enter the harbor. You'd get to watch our ships finish off that stubborn papist stronghold, which could be right entertaining."

Laz lowered his head and stirred his pottage. It wasn't very entertaining to be on the receiving end of that kind of attack. He set the bowl down and grabbed his shoes.

"What are you doing?"

"Going for a walk." Laz slid his feet into the mostly dry shoes and stood to shove his arms into his jacket sleeves.

"It's four or five miles around the bay." The man grabbed the ale and lifted it in a toast. "Enjoy your blisters."

Laz smiled. "I won't get any. I've put more miles on these shoes than you can imagine."

He gave Laz a puzzled look then guzzled down the rest of the ale.

Laz started walking.

It took until early afternoon to get all the way around the bay. Laz had to stop to rest more often than he liked. He drank from a brook along the way. Thanks to a French road to the lighthouse, the going was easy. As he got closer, he started to catch glimpses of Louisbourg.

The narrow road curved and the lighthouse stood before him. All the action was on a rise behind it, where the militia-men had build a rough bulwark to shield their cannons, and a large mortar that really did look big-mouthed. Laz flinched as a shell launched skyward and arched over the bay. He watched its flight and winced again when it struck its target less than half a mile off shore. All the men at the battery cheered.

Then Laz spotted Pepperrell and dived for cover. He snuck through the forest at the base of the rise, past scrubby spruce and around low bushes.

Twenty minutes later, Big-Mouthed Bess spit out another mortar. Earned another cheer.

With Pepperrell and his crew out of sight, Laz hiked along the rugged coast, looking for signs of boats. Ships were gathering like Eli Johnson had said, beyond the breakwater. But he needed a way to reach them. He followed grooves cut into the grass by cannon wheels. The fresh salty air blew away memories of being in that dank cell.

Almost half a mile down the coast, Laz came to a landing spot with three boats on shore. He raced down the slope toward them. Some sailors stood around a beach fire. They watched him come. All of them crossed their arms at the same time.

Laz stopped and braced his hands on his knees, panting. Two weeks of near starvation had made him weak. "I have to get out to the *Constance*." They stared. Laz straightened. A comment from his dad popped into his mind: *When I'm in charge of men, I blister their skin with my fiery breath if they don't hop to it.* And Mom's reply: *That's fine for your soldiers, honey, but Lazare is only nine.*

Laz knew he needed dad-sized bluster. He approached the closest man and poked him in the chest. "Are you deaf? I have to get to the *Constance*. Now. Captain Hawkins is expecting my report. Yesterday."

"The *Constance*? Isn't that the one collecting wounded to return to New England?" a man on the other side of the fire said.

"I think you're right," replied the one Laz had poked. "Leaving on the evening tide, is what I heard. I guess you're too late, mister."

Laz gave him a small shove. "Get that boat in the water. Hawkins will delay leaving for me. But if you're the reason he has to, he will keelhaul every one of you."

Uncertainty entered their faces. Now Laz crossed his arms. "Your decision, gentlemen. I've seen Hawkins angry, and believe me, you don't want to." He gave them a grim smile.

Laz returned his glare to the one he'd shoved, surprised he hadn't gotten flattened for that. The man held his gaze for two minutes then swore and tramped toward the nearest boat. "Come on, boys. Let's get this swaggering lackey out to his captain. Maybe we can toss a line into the water on the way back and fry up some fish."

Laz helped them push off, jumped into the boat, and settled in the bow. He half-turned to scan the gathering fleet. There were three, no four, gaff-rigged schooners. Only one had its bowsprit aimed toward open water. Laz pointed it out and hoped he was right.

When they cleared the cove, the Island Battery came into sight. Smoke rose from it in a steady plume. It wouldn't hold out much longer by the looks of it. Then what would Morpain do? Laz squinted at the Louisbourg silhouette, over a mile distant. He still didn't want to leave. With every stroke of the oars he had to bite his tongue to stop from telling the men to turn back. But he had to see Hawkins, had to try to go home like Morpain had urged him.

Laz studied the town until they started rowing between ships and it was lost from sight. Finally, they bumped against a ship's side.

"Here we are, lackey. You knew which ship was your captain's, sure enough. Now get out of this boat before I throw you out."

Laz offered his hand. "Thank you." The man spat on it. Laz lunged for the rope net draped along the ship's side at the same time the one sailor pushed the boat away with his oar. Laz barely managed to grab hold then hung on until his grip was sure. He climbed the rope, much slower than the first time he'd done it in Chebucto Bay as a new prisoner.

After pausing to catch his breath below the gunwale, Laz climbed over the edge and waited. It was Ben who spotted him. He cut across the deck, a coil of rope slung over his shoulder. He'd grown in two months. Laz smiled.

At that, Ben jutted his chin forward and studied Laz. Then he shouted, dropped his rope and sprang forward. He wrapped his hands around Laz's waist, hoisted him up and spun him around, hooting and laughing.

"Put me down. You'll capsize us both." Ben dropped Laz, who gripped both his shoulders. "You've grown."

"You have, too, Lazare. I hardly recognized you." Ben squinted. "Might even be a shadow of fuzz on your chin. Or dirt."

Laz laughed as memories of friendship flooded back. "I missed you, Ben."

The smaller boy gave Laz a hug that nearly squeezed the air out of him.

"Who are you and why are you distracting my crew?" Captain Elijah Hawkins barked.

Laz looked toward the quarterdeck. The captain glared with no sign of recognition. So, as Laz had several times before, he touched two fingers to his forehead in a mock salute. Hawkins shot off the quarterdeck like he'd been fired from a cannon. He grabbed Laz by the chin and narrowed his eyes. *Have I changed that much?* Laz wondered.

"Well. Lazare Berenger." Hawkins said the name with its French inflection. "I'd given up on you. I thought you'd be in that town for a few days at most."

"That's what I thought, too," Laz said. "But then a bunch of unruly, undisciplined colonials decided to lay siege."

Both eyebrows rose. "An interesting assessment. Is it yours, or someone else's?"

"The words of the man I worked with while I was inside the walls."

"And who would that be?"

"Commander Pierre Morpain."

Thunderclouds settled over the captain's features. His voice tightened. "Don't lie to try to impress me." He backhanded Laz and sent him flying into Ben's pile of rope.

CHAPTER FORTY

Laz wiped blood off his mouth and peered at Captain Hawkins. He stood, hands on hips, with fury rippling across his features. He pointed. "Get into my cabin. Right now."

Laz rolled off the coil of rope. Poor Ben was the picture of shock. Laz patted him on the shoulder as he walked past him to the captain's quarters. With a tug, Laz reefed the door so it crashed against the wall, then he crossed to the table and sat without being invited.

Hawkins slammed the door. He pushed aside the chair across from Laz then rested his fists on the table and leaned over it. "Why would you lie to me?"

"Lie about what?"

"Pierre Morpain. French pirate. Terror of the New England coast. Known to most as *Morepang*, because he brings such misery."

Laz stood and matched his pose. "Pierre Morpain. Privateer commissioned by King Louis, retired. Now Commander of the Port. And thanks to a lack of leadership by Governor Duchambon and most of his officers, the actual leader of the defense of Louisbourg."

Hawkins fell back into his chair and steepled his fingers. Laz held his stare. Hawkins folded his hands across his stomach. "You aren't lying."

"No." Laz closed his eyes, opened them. "No, I am not lying."

"So you fought against us."

"I ran messages."

"That's fighting against us."

"You told me to get into the town. Blend in. Try to sow uncertainty. I did that. Do you want to know what they thought when I said there were hundreds of colonial ships at Canso, preparing an attack on Louisbourg? The French officers all laughed. They said you were incompetent. And they kicked me out. Pierre Morpain followed me outside, listened, believed I might be telling the truth, but didn't think there was reason to worry because of how well defended the harbor was. Then he took me on as his messenger." Laz straightened. "Should I have refused him? Refused the chance to learn everything about Louisbourg's defenses."

"Stop saying that town's name like a Frenchman."

"I am a Frenchman. Acadian. Remember?" Laz said. "And now I want my St. Christopher medal back."

"No. First we are going to report to Commodore Warren and you will allow yourself to be questioned. You will not use the belligerent tone you are using now. And you will pronounce your words like a proper Englishman. Understood?"

Laz narrowed his eyes. "*D'accord.*"

Hawkins slammed his fist on the table. "Enough." He stood and brushed off his jacket. Probably needing to wipe off spittle,

Laz thought. Hawkins motioned toward the door. "After you, Master Berenger." He said it in the flat English way.

Commodore Peter Warren was middle-aged and softening around the waist, but not nearly as much as Pepperrell, who had reminded Laz of an evil Santa Claus.

Warren rained down questions, and Laz answered each one honestly. The siege was almost over, so his hope again was that his information might help bring it to an end. The man fed Laz while he interrogated him, which won Laz's admiration.

The surprise on Hawkins' face when Laz explained trying to wet the powder and getting caught was hugely satisfying. Laz said he escaped from the prison cell, but avoided details.

Laz confirmed, and reconfirmed two more times, the horrible conditions inside the fortress. Warren seemed particularly interested in that. And pleased.

He said, "Stay a few more days before weighing anchor, Captain Hawkins."

"Yes, sir. May I ask why?" Hawkins said.

"As soon as the Island Battery is taken, we are sailing into that harbor. And we will give them what I'm sure will be a final pounding. You might have more wounded to transport, though if the French truly are almost out of powder they won't be able to mount much of a defense." He turned to Laz. "Do you know how many cannons are still operational?"

"Not at all the bastions. One of the last reports I carried to Morpain was from the Dauphin Bastion." Both men looked blank. Laz explained, "The demi-bastion on the northeast, by the main land-ward gate. Two weeks ago it only had three cannons still working."

"Just three?"

Laz nodded.

"Very good." Warren looked at Hawkins. "Dismissed."

Hawkins saluted and ushered Laz out. Back on the *Constance* Laz asked if he could raid the kitchen. Even a hardtack biscuit would do. After he scored some stew, he asked permission to go aloft.

Laz was a little shaky climbing up the shrouds, and ended up using the lubber's hole to get onto the platform. The view from the top of the forward mast was worth the climb. He stayed up high, watching the Island Battery attack and studying Louisbourg. Laz's fear he'd never enter the town again hurt worse than torn-off fingernails.

How could a person fall in love with a place and time? It wasn't just Morpain, or Isabelle, or the town and its residents. All three had conspired to hook him, and it was a barbed hook that had sunk deep under his skin.

Laz slept in a hammock that night, and woke up feeling slightly seasick.

That day Laz paced, climbed the foremast to stare at Louisbourg, returned to the deck to find something to eat. He repeated the cycle until Hawkins put him to work, mending sails. The Island Battery had been silenced.

On June twenty-sixth, the *Constance* got word that the French had sent a messenger under a flag of truce. Laz felt like he couldn't breathe as he waited for truce to be agreed upon. On the twenty-eighth, the *Constance* was the fourteenth ship into Louisbourg Harbor. Peter Warren's sixty-gun man-o-war led the fleet. When the ships were moored, they gave a broadside salute, all firing their cannons. Then all the sailors and soldiers gave three cheers. Laz blinked rapidly as emotions battered him.

Hawkins called him onto the quarterdeck and dangled the medal and chain from his index finger. "Yours, I believe, Master Berenger."

Laz scooped it into his palm, studied it, then tucked it into his jacket's inside pocket. "Thank you, Captain Hawkins."

The captain pointed at Warren's man-o-war. "They're signaling us. It looks like Commodore Warren is requesting our presence."

"Why ours?"

"The flags don't tell me that much. I'm assuming he wants your presence. He might want your ability to translate, or your connection with Morepang. If I'm wrong, a boat will bring you back to the *Constance*."

"Don't call him that."

Hawkins eyed Laz curiously. "If you insist."

"I do. He's an honorable man. He should be treated with respect."

"Oh, not to worry, Master Berenger. We New Englanders have always respected Pierre Morpain, though many wish we could hold him in much less respect."

Commodore Warren sent Hawkins and Laz to be his eyes and ears inside the town for the official handing-over ceremony.

Laz convinced Hawkins that he should take Ben along, a messenger if he needed one. So the three of them joined the New England soldiers, including Commander Pepperell in his bright red suit, and they marched around the town walls to the Queen's Gate—the same one Laz had followed Morpain out of when they'd tried to repel the first landing.

Any colonial militiamen who had instruments played them as they marched onto the parade ground where the French soldiers waited. Drums, along with pipes and trumpets and violins, made for an odd, discordant victory tune.

As the official ceremony unfolded Laz struggled to look unbothered, but inside he felt hollowed out by seeing the French soldiers, their filthy uniforms and sad expressions. Some of them were almost crying.

At the far end of the front line of soldiers, Morpain stepped up to join the officers then scanned the victorious colonials. His gaze stopped at Laz. He gave a slight nod and turned to another officer to answer a question.

Relief filled Laz and he gripped Ben's shoulder. He wriggled free and whispered, "Why are you smiling?"

"I'm glad it's over, Ben. Very, very glad."

"Were you really in the town when cannonballs were flying?"

Laz nodded.

"Did you have any close calls?"

Laz lifted one eyebrow. "One shot nearly gave me a shave."

Under his breath, Hawkins said, "Stand back if you're going to chatter."

They fell silent as the French marched out of the fortress with flags unfurled. Hawkins explained in a whisper this was called the "honors of war," a formal retreat by soldiers who had fought valiantly.

As soon as they'd marched out of the Queen's Gate, Hawkins sent Laz running to bring Morpain back inside. Hawkins asked the French commander to accompany them in a walk through the town back to the harbor, and to explain the damage so Hawkins could report to Commodore Warren. To Laz's surprise, Morpain agreed in clear English. Then he remembered Morpain saying he'd been a prisoner of the English for a year. Not needed for translating, Laz and Ben followed a few steps behind. Townspeople huddled in their homes and only colonial soldiers were on the streets. Some of them were carrying household goods. Laz halted as one man staggered by with a large mirror. They were almost to the broken gate by the harbor when a man walked by lugging a wooden crate with a familiar-looking set of dishes.

"Hey," Laz yelled, "Those are Madame Richard's dishes. The orders were no looting. You can't take those."

The man spat at his feet and kept walking.

A shout spun Laz and Ben around. Cooper strode toward them, musket bouncing loosely in one hand. He halted ten feet away. "If it isn't the French scab."

"Still as ugly as ever, I see, Cooper." Laz gave him a tight smile.

"You slimy misbegotten snake. You fought against us."

Ben stepped in front of Laz. "He was spying for Captain Hawkins. Laz is a hero."

Cooper tilted his musket in their direction. "He fought against us in the field, boy. Don't protect the scum."

Around them, colonial militiamen had shifted their attention to what Cooper was saying, but no one moved to intervene. Ben shouted, "He'd never fight against us!"

"I saw him in the field with my own eyes. On the day we landed he was in the force that tried to repel us. He carried a pistol. I missed with my musket, but followed up with my bayonet." He sneered. "That pirate, Morepang, saved him from my blade. But nothing will save him today."

Dazed by his hatred, Laz shook his head to clear it. The man was dead serious. He said, "Go back to your celebrating, Cooper. You're drunk."

With a bellow, Cooper dropped his musket and charged. He flung Ben aside and tackled Laz.

The first hit almost knocked him out.

CHAPTER FORTY-ONE

Laz got his arms up to deflect the blows pelting him like hail. All around them was shouting in English and French, and above it all, Ben's high-pitched cries to stop. Cooper didn't stop, not until two burly militiamen dragged him off his victim.

When two other men helped Laz to his feet, a small circle had formed. Ben stood to his right, Hawkins to his left, and Morpain faced them with militiamen on either side of him, their muskets aimed and ready. Laz tried to walk and his legs gave out. The two men held him up.

Behind Hawkins, Cooper continued to seethe and swear, until ordered into silence.

In English, Morpain said, "Are you okay, son?"

Laz wasn't sure, but he nodded.

Morpain faced Hawkins, "My good captain, Lazare spoke of you as an honorable man. I would ask that you keep this boy safe."

"I will do my best, but he will likely face treason charges. I can only do so much."

"He did your bidding in Louisbourg," Morpain said. "He committed sabotage."

Hawkins narrowed his eyes. "Then he betrayed you. Why would you defend him?"

"He is very young, forced by you into a situation he could not understand. You and your Commander Pepperrell should be ashamed of how you took advantage of him." For a few seconds Morpain looked like the proud victor, and Hawkins like the defeated man.

"Nothing innocent about that deceitful froggie," Cooper yelled.

Hawkins silenced him then moved closer to Morpain. They spoke quietly for a few minutes. Laz strained to hear. Hawkins stepped back. "I will do my best. With any luck, I will have sailed before Pepperrell remembers our young friend."

Morpain thanked him then approached Laz. In French he said, "I love you, my son." He kissed Laz's forehead. Tears stained his cheeks.

"No. No, Papa. Let me stay with you. Please," Laz begged in French.

"I cannot. I am a prisoner. I will be returned to France. Come to Rochefort, and find me when you're free." He wiped at his cheeks and whispered, "Goodbye."

Laz squeezed his eyes shut so he didn't have to watch Morpain walk away.

Everything moved quickly. Hawkins received permission from Commodore Warren to leave immediately, so he didn't have to seek Pepperrell's permission. The only hitch was Cooper, who had followed them and insisted he was personally going to guard Laz and make sure he stood trial; and if Hawkins stopped that, then he'd report the underhanded affair to Pepperrell.

Laz guessed Cooper really wanted the chance to kill him. He tried to stay as close to Hawkins as possible, even sneaking onto the quarterdeck after they were in full sail. He sat on ropes, facing the receding town behind them and rubbing the pocket that held his medallion.

"Get off my quarterdeck, Berenger," Hawkins told him.

"Cooper's going to kill me."

"Then he will stand trial for murder."

The captain's voice was so flat that Laz hastily retreated. Though his head and arms were throbbing from the beating Cooper had laid on him, Laz climbed to the top platform where he could watch everything. He hated that he had to use the lubber's hole. He sat with his legs dangling over the edge and alternated between watching the ocean and ship below. Cooper stayed in sight but didn't climb up after him.

Laz felt a trap squeezing in around him. However far they were going, it was going to take days, possibly weeks. He couldn't protect himself from Cooper for that long.

He took his medallion out and cupped it in his hand. He hadn't put it on in Louisbourg because he had wanted to stay. But he knew life as Morpain's son was out of his reach now. How could he find a way to get to France when he likely wouldn't survive this voyage?

The medallion, though, would take him home. That far-distant home where Emeline waited for her brother. Laz swallowed. He wanted to see her, but he wanted to stay. He felt someone watching him and saw it was Cooper. He could feel the man's hate, a pure deadly thing.

"I have to go back," Laz whispered.

His hands trembled as he lifted the chain over his head. He squeezed his eyes closed and let the metal disc slip under his shirt. He waited for the sliding sensation, the dark twisting slip through time.

"Ho, Lazare, what are you doing?" Ben's voice forced Laz's eyes open.

He squinted against the piercing rays of the sinking sun. "I..." He sighed. He'd been so sure that putting the medallion back on was the secret. "Nothing. I'm doing nothing."

"Nothing? That sounds dull." Ben swung off the futtock shrouds and onto the platform. "I'm to fetch you for the meal. Though the cap'n might stop feeding you if you ain't working."

Laz snorted. "You're probably right. But this seems the safest place to be."

"You fear the cap'n?"

"Cooper. He's watching me with death in his eyes."

Ben looked worried. "Did you really do what he said? Did you really fight against us?"

"I somehow ended up on the field, yes, as Morpain's messenger, but it wasn't like he said. I've never fired a musket in my life."

Ben looked confused, as if trying to figure out a puzzle. His eyes cleared and he smiled. "I know you have reasons, good reasons, for everything you did. You're still a hero, no matter what Cooper thinks."

"I wish." Laz shook his head. "But thanks, Ben."

His friend popped to his feet. "Now, Mr. Berenger, my stomach is complaining about your tardy ways."

Laz laughed then said, "You know my full name, but I've never even known yours. You must be more than just Ben."

The boy flushed red. "Ben is what I like to be called. My father insists on calling me Ebenezer. I'm Ebenezer Wright. Please don't call me that."

"Fathers can be cruel. I never used to like my name, either, but I don't mind it now." Laz followed Ben down the shrouds, wondering why that name sounded familiar.

CHAPTER FORTY-TWO

The days passed and Laz sensed his time was running out. Ben helped him keep an eye on Cooper, and so did the red-trousered Turner, though when asked, the man refused to stand guard over Laz's hammock at night.

The two places Cooper didn't follow were the top platform and the hold where the injured colonial soldiers were quartered. Laz found himself helping the surgeon to escape Cooper's beady gaze. And he discovered that a surgeon was a medic. A doctor who cut people open was called a physician, and one was needed on the ship if the smell of rotting flesh was any indication.

Several days out from Louisbourg, Hawkins called him onto the quarterdeck. "I hear you are attending the wounded. Thank you for that."

"You're welcome," Laz replied. "I like feeling useful."

"Cooper keeps insisting you should be in fetters."

"The better to gut me when I can't put up a fight."

Hawkins huffed. "Cooper is behaving in an exemplary manner. Stop making base accusations."

"But you don't stop him from accusing me." Laz pressed his lips together.

"You started as a traitor. You have further to go to earn

my confidence." Hawkins called out a string of orders, then said, "You need to understand that you will face trial. Though I promised your Morpain I'd do my best to defend you."

"New Englanders hate Morpain. If you bring up his name I'm as good as dead."

"That is a concern. You can be assured someone will mention your connection to him."

"So you're telling me I'm dead anyway, whether it's Cooper or your judge who kills me." Laz started to step away. "Is that all?"

Hawkins looked angry. He squinted at the western shore they were running parallel to. "What would you have me do, young Berenger? Let you go? Just row you to shore and turn my back?"

"Would you?"

"Even if I wanted to, I could not."

Laz knew Hawkins was too honorable a man to so openly disobey Pepperrell's orders. He squinted at the shore too. A thought struck him. "Are we close to where you picked me up? The big bay. Chebucto."

"I can't let you off as if you were a passenger." When Laz said nothing, Hawkins added, "We're not far. I'd say tomorrow, late afternoon, is when we'll pass by the bay's mouth. What are you planning, young Berenger?"

"Only hoping you'll discover some mercy between now and then, Captain."

"I'm a merciful man, but a just one. Return to your nursemaid duties. I simply wanted to make sure you understood our situation."

"Thanks. I'll write up my will. Do you want your kit back? Morpain gave me a few items, so it's not what you originally gave me." That earned him a narrow glare. Laz left the deck and climbed to the top platform to think.

By noon the next day he knew what he had to do. The medallion hadn't been the way back, so he only had one play left.

He was eating lunch with Ben when he recalled why Ben's name was familiar. Ebenezer Wright had been his mother's ancestor, a New Englander who had gone to Halifax as part of the first force to guard the then brand-new Citadel. Laz laughed, but it came out as more of a gasp.

"What's wrong?" Ben asked.

"Wrong? Nothing. Why?"

"You gasped. Now you're looking at me like you've never seen me before."

Laz shook his head. "I'm only looking at a foolish molly, who's so daft he doesn't know he shouldn't be my friend."

"I'm no molly. And you're the daft one. Sometimes I think maybe you're tetched in the head." Ben stole Laz's biscuit. "And you've no appreciation of fine food." He knocked out the weevils and dipped the biscuit in his tea.

Laz laughed again, but this time it rang clear. "I'm going to miss you, Ben."

"Where are you going?"

"They're going to kill me, don't you know?"

"Then I'll be the one missing you, not the other way around." Ben bit into his hardtack and grinned. It was obvious he wasn't taking Laz seriously.

"True." Laz indicated the door. "Let's go to the forecastle. I want the breeze to blow my stink away."

They went up top and stood on the starboard side of the forecastle deck, facing land. Laz noticed the captain was sailing the ship closer to land than usual. It only looked two miles away at most.

Ben scanned the horizon. "I wonder if the cap'n is expecting a storm to blow in."

Laz considered the clear sky. He hoped the captain wanted to rid himself of a problem. A glance showed Cooper at the top of the forecastle stairs, watching them with crossed arms and an angry scowl.

They remained silent for a long time, watching the waves, the shore, and the birds wheeling above. Ben pointed ahead. "Ahoy. That's looks like the mouth of the bay where we captured you, Lazare."

The captain had been dead on with his reckoning. Laz didn't have much time. He turned to Ben. "I want to give you something." He lifted his medallion and chain from around his neck, grabbed Ben's wrist, then lowered it into Ben's open palm.

"What is it?" Ben asked.

"A St. Christopher medal. He's the patron saint of travelers." Laz pointed to Ben's neck. "I want you to have it."

"But it's papist."

"Yes. A papist trinket. But it's all I have. Put it in a box, somewhere safe. You don't have to wear it. Just keep it and remember me."

"I can't. Your family should have this." Ben started to hand it back.

Laz stopped him. "That's the great part. They will. Trust me."

"I…" Ben swallowed. "You're right uncouth, Lazare. But I'll keep it. I just don't understand. Why give it to me now? Why not wait until we reach Portsmouth?"

Cooper had moved closer. He looked suspicious. Laz shrugged. "I don't want to forget."

"You fought the cap'n so hard to get this back. It makes no sense you'd give it away."

"Other than Morpain, you're the closest I've had to family on this voyage, Ben." *Closer than he would ever know*, Laz thought.

Ben put on the medallion and tucked it out of sight. Laz gave him a small smile.

The ship was only a mile from shore now. Laz was certain Hawkins had figured out what he planned to do, and was helping. They were almost to Chebucto's wide mouth. Laz gripped the rail, wondering when he should jump.

A hand swung him around. He staggered away from the railing and faced Cooper. The man snarled, "You'll not escape on my watch, filthy French rat."

Laz held out both hands. "What are you talking about? I'm not going anywhere."

"You're right." Cooper drew a sword.

Laz backed up. He didn't have much time. He had to jump before the captain ordered the ship away from shore. Cooper lunged and Laz leaped to the side. Ben started yelling for the captain.

No! Laz wanted to cry. He backpedaled and tore off his jacket. "You're crazy, Cooper."

The man approached slowly, his blade making a lazy circle.

"No one gives away his most precious possession unless he's going away."

"Yes. I am. To trial and death. What do I need with a trinket?"

"Let's skip the trial." Cooper attacked.

Laz got the mast between them lunging one way, then the other. Finally he faked left and raced right. He threw his jacket at Cooper's face.

He was almost to the side when pain slashed down his leg. He stumbled. Dived. Went tumbling over the ship's edge with Ben yelling like a banshee.

Laz hit the water hard, on his side. He surfaced with blood swirling around him. He rolled onto his other side and began a slow sidestroke. His upper leg was bleeding.

On the ship, Cooper raced toward the ship's stern, yelling to turn the ship around or launch a skiff. He thundered onto the quarterdeck with a musket in his hands. Laz could only watch and swim and hope he was far enough away.

Cooper took aim. Fired.

Pain exploded in Laz's chest.

Laz sputtered and struggled, the water red and churning. He didn't know what had happened. He was sure the musket ball had hit him, but other than hurting so bad he thought ribs were broken, he seemed intact. He continued a slow stroke, that was getting slower.

The *Constance* didn't turn and didn't launch a boat. It angled toward open water.

After a long, slow swim, Laz made it to shore and pulled off his stockings to bandage the slice on his thigh. He had lost one shoe, so he alternated wearing the remaining one on one foot then the other. He walked for two hours, and by the end he could barely stand. His leg was doing badly. He was getting weak.

Now Laz stood on the shore, staring across the narrow channel of water to where he guessed the Citadel stood in modern times. It was the highest hill in the area. Farther inland, the water opened into Chebucto Bay.

Laz rested by a log then dragged it into the water and floated across the Narrows, paddling with one hand. He rested again.

He guessed he was a third of the way up the hill when his leg gave out. He crawled. And then he passed out.

Voices brought Laz back to awareness. He was shaking. He listened, wondering if Hawkins had come back for him after all. As the voices came closer and became clearer, he heard a vaguely familiar language. It was Mi'kmaq.

He called for help in French. A voice called back, asking where he was. While he was trying to describe his surroundings, three Mi'kmaq men stepped into the clearing where he lay.

They squatted beside him and talked among themselves for a minute. One spoke in French. "Who are you?"

"Lazare Berenger. Please, I need your help."

"You are past help. You die soon."

Laz felt his eyes widen. "Can you...take me up the hill?"

"To die?"

Laz tried to shrug. "There is a cave, in tree roots. I can sleep there. And live or die."

The man spoke Mi'kmaq with his friends. They all nodded. The same fellow spoke again in French. "We take you, but then we leave."

Laz whispered, "Thank you."

They left him beside the edge of the tree root cave and walked down the hill without looking back. Laz wondered if Ben would find his bones when he returned to be a soldier in the Citadel.

An odd smell teased him. It seemed to give him a burst of energy. He pushed himself backward and fell into the darkness.

CHAPTER FORTY-THREE

Something stank. Laz didn't think it was him. The smell burned the inside of his nostrils. It took a minute to convince his eyelids to crack open. The light was so bright he slammed them back closed.

Soft steps padded closer. Something rustled. The steps padded away. There were so many noises: buzzing, humming, voices. Other tinny voices. Laz wanted to block it all out.

He remembered the smell. Hospital cleaner. He was in a hospital, which meant he was back. A tear leaked out of his closed eye. He ached with wanting to be with Morpain and Isabelle, or with Ben. He wanted to be on a sailing ship feeling the wind. Another tear escaped. Morpain, Isabelle, and Ben had all been dead for over 200 years.

Firmer footsteps. "Hello, young man. The nurse said you're awake."

"Who are you?" Laz whispered.

"Open your eyes and see." The voice belonged to a man.

"The light's too bright. And it's too noisy."

More footsteps and the sounds muffled. "The door is closed now. That should help." A chair scraped. The voice sank closer to Laz's level. "I'm Doctor Malik, your surgeon."

"I need a physician. Surgeons only do small stuff."

There was a long pause. "Exactly what year do you think it is?"

The question surprised him. Laz opened his eyes to let in a sliver of light. He waited until the doctor came into focus. The man's brown face was calm and serious. He looked prepared to wait until Laz gave him an answer. "It's 2017."

"It is. What year were you in yesterday?"

Laz blinked. "What kind of uncouth question is that?"

Doctor Malik rested his forearm on the raised metal railing. "I was not the one brought to the hospital wearing hand sewn clothes that looked to belong in the 1700s."

The invisible clamp squeezed Laz's chest. "What are you talking about?" His voice came out in a whisper.

The doctor held up his finger for silence. "And, most interesting of all, you came to the hospital with a souvenir." He held up a plastic pill bottle and rattled it. "A musket ball. I couldn't resist saving it for you. It was imbedded in one of the buttons of your long vest."

"Waistcoat," Laz whispered.

"Waistcoat." Doctor Malik set the bottle on the bedside table. "Your sternum has the smallest of cracks. I sutured a gash on your leg that was so clean-edged one might think a knife, or perhaps a sword, made it. So, mystery boy, I'll ask again. What year did you come from?"

Laz still couldn't bring himself to answer. The doctor dropped his voice and said, "You aren't the only one, you know. I've tracked these unusual appearances for a decade. It's quite fascinating, the idea we might be able to step through time."

"Slide," Laz whispered. "It was more like sliding."

The doctor puckered his lips in a way that said he conceded the point. "Sliding, then. You don't seem very shocked by your surroundings. That is unusual. Other patients have ended up in the psych ward. Over there, they know to alert me when people in odd clothing who are acting psychotic show up. They think I'm simply fascinated by people in a dissociative state who believe they're from another time. Did you meet someone from this time who prepared you?"

Laz said, "If it's the beginning of July now, there was a woman three months ago, right?"

"Why yes. How did you know?"

"I saw her. The day I disappeared."

The doctor looked astonished. "You mean to say that *you* traveled back to the 1700s—"

"To 1745," Laz corrected.

"Okay. To 1745. And then you found a way to *return* to the present?"

"Returning seemed like a good idea. The alternative was dying." Laz's chest ached, as did his leg, but in a different way from before. The heat was gone. But movement made pain explode like fireworks.

"You almost did die. A tourist found you in the tunnel under the outer wall of the Citadel."

Laz groaned. "Same place I disappeared. I think it was a wormhole. Timehole? Aren't they anchored at both ends? That's why I thought going to the same spot would return me. That woman must have come through a different timehole, from later. Halifax wasn't there in 1745. Maybe this whole city is a... timehole port. Lots of gates. Lots of destinations."

Doctor Malik chuckled.

"If you're recording this, I'll never get out of the nuthouse."

"We don't call them that anymore.... And what should I call you?"

Laz stared, suddenly uneasy.

"The police will be here after I report to them that you're awake. The nurse may already have made the call. Will they find a missing persons report on you?"

"Yes. I'm Lazare Berenger. Thirteen now. Twelve when I disappeared. My family lives in Boston, if they're still there. Grandmère lives near Moncton."

"You seem much older, but I'm sure you've been through a lot. So, Lazare, what should we tell the police?" The doctor only looked curious.

Laz shrugged. "I ran away?"

"Did you have cause?"

"Dad and I were arguing a lot. I didn't like that he had moved us to Boston."

"I'll keep your belongings out of sight." The doctor stood. "I'm not sure 'ran away' will satisfy the police. Keep it simple, and as close to the truth as you dare. I'd like to talk some more with you, if I may."

Laz agreed. "It'll be nice to have one person who believes me." He held up his hand before the doctor could reply. "I know. I can't tell anyone."

Doctor Malik nodded. "Rest until they get here."

The police weren't happy with the story of hitching a ride on a private yacht with a guy nicknamed Hawk, full name unknown. Laz claimed to have gotten off in Louisbourg where he'd stayed, working odd jobs.

The story would fall apart once they contacted Louisbourg, but Doctor Malik was impressed they'd left so quickly. He expected them to return. Laz didn't mind; he had learned how to bluster.

They had a long talk about the past and different travelers the doctor met. That's what he called them: travelers. They couldn't decide if the St. Christopher medal had opened the timehole, or if it randomly opened and closed, or if something else had triggered it. A phase of the moon, maybe.

Laz blurted, "I want to go back."

That startled the doctor. "What for? It was primitive compared to modern society."

"I have friends there. Good friends. I felt like I belonged there. I haven't felt that much here. Maybe staying in this time is a mistake."

"That could be true, Lazare. Before you decide, though, I would ask that you stay until you talk to your family. You're stuck here for a few more days anyway."

"My family?" Laz felt the warmth drain from his face.

"Yes. The police contacted them. They will be here tomorrow."

"My family."

"You need to see them, Lazare, whatever you decide. If you stay, I would enjoy more conversations. I would caution you that thirteen is far too young to be alone in the world, even if you do seem much older."

"My family."

"That is the third time you've said it. Yes. Your family."

Laz knew things would be different with his parents, because he was different. He could stand up to his father, or anyone, without losing his cool now. So he would explain his plan to recover at Grandmère's, where he would relearn how to live in this modern world. And he would say goodbye in his own way to his long-gone friends. Maybe he could talk Grandmère into that trip to Louisbourg she had always wanted to take. He'd like to see how the historical park was different from the fortress he had known.

Laz touched the spot where his medallion used to hang. Would he ever see it again or was it caught forever in some weird time loop? It didn't matter. He would never forget Ben, or anything that had happened.

A clatter sounded in the corridor. He peered at the open door, a little nervous, but mostly calm. Then he heard a voice, loud and excited. It was Emeline.

She sounded like...home.

A grin widened as Laz whispered, "I did it, Morpain. I made it back to my family."

The first Siege of Louisbourg in 1745 was a significant event in the creation of a nation. It was the first time that American colonists planned and fought a battle as an independent military force. It helped to convince the colonists, just a few decades later, that complete independence could be achieved.

I strove to depict the siege as accurately as possible. In my research, some calendar variances of the time and human error conspired to have the dates of some events vary by a day or two in different records. Where that happened I went by the dates I found in more than one place.

The only incident I knowingly changed was the stage at which the colonists started using heated shot, having it happen a few weeks before it actually did. That was strictly for dramatic purposes.

Six characters in the story were real people. Here is what happened to them:

COMMANDER WILLIAM PEPPERELL was made a baronet for his leadership in the siege, the first American to be so honored.

He raised regiments for the "French and Indian War," went on to be an acting governor of Massachusetts and was made a lieutenant general. But he died in 1759 before he could take up the command.

SIR PETER WARREN, British naval officer, became the governor of Cape Breton (Île Royale) after the siege, a post he didn't want. He entered politics in America and then in England. He died suddenly in 1752, in Dublin, Ireland, of a "most Violent Fever."

GOVERNOR LOUIS DU PONT DUCHAMBON returned to France shortly after the Siege of Louisbourg ended. After a trial concerning a mutiny at the fortress the winter before the siege, he retired and lived off a small pension and income from his property.

ANTOINE LE POUPET DE LA BOULARDERIE was captured by the colonists when he and Morpain tried to repel them off the beaches. He spent the siege in Boston as a prisoner, then returned to France. Like many aristocrats of the time, he lost all his money. He died as a pauper in Paris in 1771.

COMMANDER PIERRE MORPAIN'S tireless courage was feted in victory lore of the New Englanders. He returned to France and was offered his old post in Louisbourg when Île Royale was restored to the French. He died in 1749 before he could return.